# SINGAPORE
# FIRE

Also by Murray Bailey

Singapore 52
Singapore Girl
Singapore Boxer
Singapore Ghost
Singapore Killer
Cyprus Kiss

Map of the Dead
Sign of the Dead*

The Lost Pharaoh

Black Creek White Lies

I Dare You
Dare You Twice


* previously entitled Secrets of the Dead

# SINGAPORE FIRE

Murray Bailey

Heritage Books

First published in Great Britain in 2021 by
Heritage Books

167976120

ISBN 978-0-9955108-4-5

Heritage Books, Truro, Cornwall

For David Leighton Bailey
(1934 – 2020)

If the measure of a man
be the amount he was loved
by his children and grandchildren
then you were a giant indeed.

.

# PART ONE

# ONE

*Tuesday 9th February 1954*

Pale light washed through painted windows of the old factory. Two men entered a room that had once been an office. It was spotless—except for the splatter of blood on the floor and walls.

The first man had an air of superiority. Because he was superior. He was recognized as a wealthy business leader and philanthropist, but he was also the head of a Chinese secret society.

Although sixty-four, Andrew Yipp moved like a much younger man. Only his thin hair and neck normally betrayed his age, but today he also looked tired. And he knew it.

"Have the police been?" Yipp asked.

"Yes, and they found nothing."

The second man was Wang, a lieutenant in Yipp's empire despite appearing on no official organization chart or payroll. He and his team were Yipp's muscle.

Yipp said, "They weren't suspicious, then?"

"They only found what we wanted them to find."

The operation was coming to an end and Su Ling had come up with a cunning plan. Su Ling—Yipp's assistant, his confidant, his mistress—what was she really up to?

The blood came from a naked man, chained to a chair in the middle of the room with two of Wang's men standing over him.

"What's he told us?" Yipp asked, lifting the man's head and studying the severe damage to his face.

"Not much."

Yipp looked at Wang with hard eyes.

Wang said, "He told us that Su Ling visited Christian Chen two days ago."

Christian Chen, the head of the second-largest secret society. Yipp's biggest rival.

"A second time? That's something."

"But they discussed an arrangement, nothing more—as far as this man knows."

"The arrangement or *an* arrangement?"

"That's the word he used."

"So was there something else?"

Wang shook his head. "He doesn't know anything. If there was another deal then Chen could be helping her."

Yipp turned away in case his lieutenant could read his thoughts. Su Ling didn't trust Wang and they hadn't told him the precise plan about the money. But why did she visit Chen again? Why hadn't he known about it?

"I don't want an open war with Chen," Yipp said, "but I will if I have to."

Wang looked like he expected his boss to say more, but Yipp didn't. He just kept hold of the prisoner's hair and looked into his face again.

Wang said, "What shall we do with this man?"

Yipp pulled out a long knife and slit the naked man's throat. The move was so lightning fast that the two henchmen were covered by the scarlet spray before they could react.

Yipp walked out of the room, Wang a pace behind.

"I may be old, but I'm still strong," Yipp said.

"You are."

"I demand loyalty. I can't abide betrayal."

"Of course not, Mr Yipp," Wang said after a beat.

"Find Su Ling and bring her back—alive."

"Yes, sir."

"And if you find out that Captain Carter has anything to do with her disappearance, deal with him."

"Deal with him?"

Yipp looked at his lieutenant and knew what the man wanted: a clear instruction because he'd enjoy it.

"You kill him," Yipp said. "You kill Ash Carter."

# TWO

*Saturday 30th January, ten days earlier*

My office was on the edge of the government sector in the best city in the world—Singapore. Although a stone's throw from the sea, the view from my office window was of another building. But I didn't mind. The morning sun canted through the windows and I knew it would be another glorious day.

Six months ago I'd set myself up as a private investigator, having been in the Special Investigations Branch of the British military police. When I arrived on the island two years ago, the Secretary for Internal Security had coerced me to work for the government. Whether he knew why I'd left the SIB in a hurry, I'll never know, because he died of a heart attack last year. Since then I'd had a good relationship with his replacement, Philip Norris. I also continued to provide support to 200 Provost, the military police based at Gillman Barracks.

Establishing myself as a serious private investigator hadn't been easy. Initially, I attracted local girls made pregnant by soldiers and looking for compensation. I also provided a distraction for lonely army housewives, it seemed. My break had come from putting an end to the extortion of a small group of merchants. It had been one of my easiest jobs, but I guess that's how life works. The greatest recognition can come from the smallest of things.

Word had spread, and now I could pick and choose the jobs I took.

The Chinese New Year was rapidly approaching and life was good.

At least, that was what I tried to convince myself.

"You're in a bad mood," Madam Chau said, looking at me across the room. She was my receptionist—refusing the title of secretary for some reason known only to her—and extremely unattractive, with a flat face that was permanently fixed with a sour expression. With so many beautiful girls on the island, I'd deliberately chosen one who wouldn't appeal to me.

"Uh eh," I said noncommittally, focusing harder on the letter in my hands. It was a complaint about the government. A family had been evicted from the house they'd lived in for almost twenty years. "Planning and Development re-appropriation" was the explanation provided.

Madam Chau carried on a conversation we weren't having: "For the past few days you've been happy," she said. "Today you are sad."

"Am I?" I suspected happiness was an alien concept for Madam Chau since I'd never seen her smile or heard her laugh. Neither had she ever commented on my demeanour before.

There was a long silence and I thought she'd got the message. I didn't want to talk about it. I'd worked out hard in the boxing gym that morning then followed it with a run along the coast. However, she was right, and the exercise hadn't shaken the underlying melancholy.

I casually glanced up and met her scrutinizing gaze.

"You were in the Middle East before and then resigned from the military police," she said.

"That's right." I turned my attention back to the letter, hoping to end the personal conversation. Madam Chau would never discuss her personal life with me—not that I was interested—and yet she found it perfectly acceptable to quiz me about mine.

Undeterred, she continued: "You came here looking for a friend who'd disappeared."

"Right."

"He'd been killed in a car crash. It's the second anniversary? Is that why you are sad?"

"Yes," I lied, and then changed the subject. "I've another complaint about this re-appropriation programme. Please would you make an appointment for me with the head of the department?"

She waited a beat before picking up the telephone and asking the operator for Government House. From there she asked to be put through to the Housing Planning and Development department.

Most people worked on Saturday, even government staff, so I expected Madam Chau would be successful.

"Two o'clock today," she informed me, "with someone called Major Tam."

"Chinese?" I asked. Of course, I knew that a small number of parliamentarians weren't of British heritage. In 1948, the first elections had been held, appointing six members to the Legislative Council. However, it had been an appeasement. In 1952 a second Legislative Council election allowed a further three elected seats, but they still had cosmetic influence. After all, Singapore was a Crown Colony run by a governor. Members of parliament had no real power, and I was astounded to hear that a Chinese man might have been promoted to head a department.

"They didn't say. He sounds Chinese, but a major? Perhaps he's mixed-race." She paused. "Perhaps he's Eurasian."

I sensed something more in her tone, but if she was baiting me, I didn't rise to it.

An hour passed and she made tea for us both before returning to her probing questions.

"You like living here?"

"Of course."

"The weather? The girls?"

I looked up. "All right, what's this about?"

"Why won't you tell me the truth?"

"The truth?"

Madam Chau's eyes held mine. "You were happy before because of a girl."

I tore my gaze away. "It's not your—"

"But it's not just any girl, is it, Master Carter?"

I said nothing and lowered my head, pretending to read.

She continued: "It's not just any girl. I know you have had several girlfriends, but no one special. None of them made you happy like you have been this week."

I faked a laugh. "Am I that shallow?"

"Yes. You have been seeing a special girl."

I didn't respond.

She shrugged. "I'm only saying because I care about you."

"Fine, yes, there's a special girl." I looked up and expected her to say something like "I knew it!" But she didn't. She gave a little nod and busied herself with papers on her desk.

Eventually, I could take no more of the enforced silence.

"What?"

She looked up, all serious. "It's *that* girl, isn't it?"

I knew she was referring to Su Ling, the translator I'd met on the first job. And she was right. I'd been dating the stunning Eurasian young lady and she occupied my mind.

Even now, I imagined her lithe body against mine, the touch of her smooth skin, the smell of her exotic scent.

"Why do you say that?" I asked, trying to sound like she'd got it wrong.

"Because you mention her more than necessary. And every time you hear her name, you go *chi lian*."

"What does that mean?"

"You English would probably say: gooey- or soppy-eyed?"

I shook my head.

Madam Chau's eyes drilled into me. "You know she's dangerous."

Dangerous? I guess that was one word for it. Su Ling was the niece of a man called Andrew Yipp, the head of the biggest secret society in Singapore, probably in Malaya as well.

In other countries they called such gangs Triads because they had three leaders, but not in Singapore. And, of course, Chinese secret societies were illegal. The previous Secretary for Internal Security had wanted me to find the proof that Yipp was a crook. He used me because of my history and his lack of trust in the police. Senior officers were undoubtedly on Yipp's payroll.

However, it had worked both ways. I'd entered into a relationship with Su Ling only to find that she was playing me—or more accurately, Yipp was using her to get information from me.

Back then, our relationship had been fiery but brief. It could never work. Different sides of the track, plus I didn't trust her motives.

So what had changed?

Now, I was sure Yipp didn't know about us. Su Ling had kept our relationship secret. Furthermore, over the last two years, I hadn't got her out of my mind. And whenever we'd met, I'd sensed she felt the same.

Neither of us could admit it, until a week ago when I received a cryptic message. Four passionate nights of love-making had followed, but then last night had been different. She hadn't turned up nor had she messaged.

Was it over as quickly as it had rekindled? Would it be another two years before she flung herself into my arms again?

I got up. "I'm going for a walk. I'll get lunch and then go to that meeting with Major Tam."

From the corner of my eye, I saw her tracking my movement. When I reached the door, she finally spoke.

"Whatever it is, Master Carter—"

I hesitated, the door half-open.

"—with that girl, you should know that you are playing with fire."

# THREE

Major Tam turned out to be Major Rupert Lamb. I wondered whether Madam Chau had made an honest mistake or had simply used the opportunity to say "Eurasian" and watch my reaction. Su Ling's mother had been Chinese, her father an officer in the British Army. The result: Eurasian. Golden silky skin, lustrous long black hair, almond eyes that could shift between alluring green and deep brown, and legs that were impossibly long.

I shook the image from my mind and introduced myself to Major Lamb's personal assistant.

"Ah the famous Captain Ash Carter," Lamb announced as I entered his office. For someone I judged to be in his fifties, he rose quickly from his chair and pumped my hand. "You're ex-Special Investigations Branch and have a famous father."

"You have me at a disadvantage," I said.

"I was 6th Gurkha Rifles, first war. Sat out the second war. A bit old and more use in the diplomatic service. After India, I spent a lot of time in Siam—or should I say Thailand these days?" He laughed, although I didn't get the humour. Then he indicated that we should take the comfortable chairs. "Thought about retirement but love the country and took up this little post. Mary likes it out here as well. Which is a good thing, if you know what I mean?"

Lamb was almost as tall as my six-two. He had an easy smile but my eyes were drawn to his bulbous nose above an English moustache—thin with a gap in the middle. The nose looked out of place on his otherwise film-star good looks.

He kept talking: "Now then, so I understand, you've set yourself up as the Philip Marlowe of Singapore."

"I prefer to be compared with James Bond," I said. When Lamb frowned at the name, I added, "Casino Royale?"

"Has it been on at the cinema?"

"It's a book by a chap called Ian Fleming. Came out last year. Bond has more class than Marlowe—and is British. Although I confess he's a government agent rather than a private detective. Anyway, it's a good read."

"I'll take your word for it."

I nodded and glanced around the room. The furniture was made of walnut wood: a wide desk and a couple of tables. He had paintings and certificates on the walls and a large array of photographs in silver frames on the tables.

My eyes alighted upon a large portrait of a handsome grey-haired woman; formal, in a dark velvet gown with a twin row of pearls.

"My wife, Mary," he said.

I smiled, looked back at my host.

"So what can I do for you, Mr Bond?" There was a hint of laughter in his tone.

"All sorts of cases come across my desk. Missing people, thefts, murders—"

"I can imagine."

"They come to me because they can't trust the police or they're unhappy with police progress."

"Yes, I understand you help with police liaison, working for Secretary Norris."

"And supporting the provost at Gillman Barracks. It's my independence that's important."

He raised his eyebrows, waiting for me to get to the point.

I said, "I've now had a handful of complaints about your department."

"Really?" He sounded genuinely shocked.

"Re-appropriation."

"Ah," he said, nodding. "Of course! People don't like being turfed out of their homes. Individuals don't understand the bigger picture. You see, city planning is a difficult task. We have parts of the city that are crumbling and—quite frankly—unsanitary. We have a long-term programme of renewal, and unfortunately some people have to be rehoused. Old buildings need to be knocked down and facilities modernized, housing improved. I do my best, but the Planning and Development Committee makes the decisions and it's my job to oversee the execution."

"I understand, but—"

"But you'd like me to look into some cases?"

"If you wouldn't mind?" I pulled a piece of paper from my pocket and fortunately glanced at it before handing it over.

"Wrong note?" Lamb asked.

Instead of the names and addresses of the five complainants I intended to deliver, the piece of paper had a single address and "midnight" written underneath.

I stuck the paper back in my pocket and withdrew the correct one.

Lamb glanced at it, placed the note on his desk and stood. Then he shook my hand and promised to investigate.

★

At midnight I was upstairs at the property on Hock Lam Street—the address on the slip of paper. Many shophouses had two storeys, but the buildings here had an extra room at the top. Rattle and chatter carried up from the street like it was the middle of the day.

Being cautious, I hadn't approached from the road. I'd come the back way, climbed steps to the top floor and found a door key under a plant outside.

I removed the Beretta that I carried in an ankle holster and eased open the door. There was a single lamp beside a bed casting an orange glow. A similar light bled through closed curtains. After moving the bedside lamp to the door, I sat on the bed in the shadows, my gun at the ready.

At ten past twelve the handle turned, the door opened and a woman wearing a coat and hood stepped inside. She locked the door behind her, took off the coat and stood for a moment, illuminated by the lamp.

She wore a dark blue silk cheongsam, tight with a long slit to the top of her thigh. Her hair was tied up, a couple of needles holding it together.

"How did you get the note in my jacket pocket?" I asked.

"I paid someone. It was easy to guess where you'd have lunch."

I raised the gun.

"Are you going to shoot me?" she asked in mock seriousness.

"I'm considering it."

Su Ling dropped the coat and walked slowly towards the bed, her smooth movement reminding me that she'd once been a dancer.

"Do it," she said, nodding at the gun, "before it's too late."

"It's already too late."

She stopped just out of reach and looked down at me. I felt that same frisson of electricity that I'd sensed the second time I'd met her. The first time had been in a warehouse when she intervened and stopped a fight between me and some of Andrew Yipp's thugs. On the second occasion, she'd walked into a gentleman's club offering her services as a translator. She'd looked sensational, and I couldn't take my eyes off her.

I went to lay the gun aside.

"Don't."

She raised her arm and pulled the needles from her hair and let them fall. Then her other hand went behind her back and I heard a zip.

She eased the silk dress from her shoulders and gave a subtle wriggle. The dress began to slide down, revealing her delicious naked body. When the garment reached the floor, she stepped over it, towards me.

★

The desperation of our love-making made me wonder if this might be the last time.

Afterwards, we lay naked, her head on my chest and a leg between mine.

Eventually, I found my breath. "I was worried."

She ran a hand lightly over my thigh but said nothing.

"I was worried we were over."

She raised her head and looked deep into my eyes.

"I'm sorry," she said.

"You should have warned me about last night. I waited for you."

"I couldn't make it." She looked away and stroked my thigh again.

I said, "Is it because of Andrew Yipp?"

"Yes. He wouldn't approve. That's why he stopped me being your liaison. He guessed that I had real feelings for you."

Last year I'd been introduced to a young man as the intermediary between me and Yipp. I'd hoped it was his decision rather than Su Ling's and now she had confirmed it.

"All the secrecy," I said. "You don't want Yipp to know about us."

"No. He would be angry."

"So, why?"

"Why see you?" Her eyes looked moist in the soft light. "Because I have no choice—and I know you feel the same. I have tried to forget you, but I can't. I believe in fate, Ash Carter, and I think you and I were meant to be."

I touched her face, drawing a line over her cheekbone and down around her mouth to her chin.

"I love you," I said, and I was surprised that the phrase came so easily. And so honestly.

She raised her head again, and this time I thought there were tears in her eyes.

"Su Ling, I didn't mean to—"

"I love you too," she said, making my heart leap. "But it's impossible." Her head lowered to my chest and I felt the wetness of her tears.

I waited for her to explain and eventually prompted her. "What is?"

"Getting away from him."

Previously, she'd asked me to help her escape, and I had found a friend with a boat who could smuggle her away. But she'd never given me the signal.

"What was wrong with my plan?" I asked.

"Andrew would find out. He would track me down."

"Why?"

"Because he is a proud man. He could never let me leave him."

"I don't understand."

She pushed herself up and looked at me. "Don't make me say it."

"Where were you last night?"

She shook her head slightly and said nothing.

I took a breath, finding this harder to discuss than I'd imagined. She slid off me and we both sat up.

"Were you with him?" I asked. "Were you with Andrew Yipp last night?"

She swallowed, didn't look at me. "I had duties to perform."

"He isn't just your guardian, is he?" I knew it; at least I'd been told. He was a married man but he'd taken this young woman as his concubine. I just found it hard to envisage the old man on top of the beautiful girl who'd stolen my heart.

Su Ling cried openly now and I put my arms around her and let her sob into me.

Eventually, I said, "I love you."

"But—"

"But nothing. You are mine and we will be together."

She looked away and I wondered if she was struggling with something.

"Tell me," I prompted.

A smile flickered on her lips, but she still held back. When she did speak, she said, "We can't keep sneaking around like this. I only have a few rooms we can use. It won't be long, he will discover the truth."

"So we get you away."

"I already explained…"

"We make a better plan," I said. "One that involves both of us escaping."

# FOUR

*Sunday 31st January*

In his office, Su Ling sat opposite Andrew Yipp and looked out across the city.

"You seem distracted," he said.

She was. She'd cried last night with Ash Carter. It had been the third time in her life—that she could remember. Only this time her tears had been different. Also, she hadn't been totally honest with him. She'd told him she had other duties, and he'd assumed she'd been with Yipp. She loved Ash, had feelings she hadn't believed in. So why couldn't she tell him the truth?

Her reflection didn't answer.

"The numbers?" Yipp said, interrupting her thoughts.

She read the latest figures from his various business interests—revenues were down again.

"May I suggest you stop the charitable donations?" she said.

"It has just been a bad month. January is always the worst month."

"Why don't we follow the Hong Kong model?"

"Three heads of the society?" He looked at her like she'd lost her mind. "You're suggesting I promote two of my men to help run the business. Not only would I be watering down my control, but I fail to see how that improves my finances."

"I was thinking about the Chens. If the two societies merged…"

Christian Chen was the head of the second most powerful gang in Singapore. He'd taken over when his father died last year. Su Ling assessed him as educated and intelligent and ambitious.

Yipp grumbled his disapproval.

She said, "It would be—"

"—a capitulation! My organization is much bigger and more successful. Why would I share with the enemy?"

"To stop the war." Despite calling it a war, she knew there were only a few deaths per week as a result of their rivalries. Boundaries had to be tested and maintained. It was tit for tat and hadn't escalated in years.

Again he scoffed.

She read out the numbers for their morphine operation. It was the sector that had taken the biggest hit since Yipp had legitimized it.

He said, "I had to strike a deal with the British Army on drug production or be investigated. We had to do it."

"And Chen has moved into the market we vacated. He's bringing it in rather than manufacturing."

"I know this."

"Then why don't we let him smuggle it in and then we distribute. That way we both win."

"That's the weak way. You disappoint me."

"I'm sorry, Uncle."

"Come to dinner tonight."

"Will the old goat be there?"

"Don't say that in public, Little Flower." He raised a finger admonishing her for referring to his wife as the old goat, but his eyes betrayed humour.

She smiled but her insides knotted. "Sunday," she said, "like always. Unfortunately, I have dinner plans tonight."

He raised his eyes. "Who with?"

She gave him the name of two girlfriends and he nodded.

"Sunday then."

Later, Su Ling was in her room above the bar where many people played mah-jong all night. She lay on her bed and, listening to click-clack of tiles and low chatter of voices, she thought about the first time she'd cried.

February 15th 1942 had been a Sunday. The start of the Japanese occupation of Singapore. But that wasn't why she was crying.

Andrew Yipp's wife was called Chenguang, a severe lady who may once have been beautiful but had traded her looks for good food and alcohol. Every Wednesday and Sunday she had her friends round to play mah-jong. They were in the back room now and Su Ling could hear the click-clack of tiles and the constant chatter of semi-inebriated women.

They played on, despite the brief war, despite the change in rulers. And today, Chenguang Yipp had been crueller to her than ever.

"Your mother's not coming back," she'd said.
Su Ling knew her mother had been gone for months. Mrs Yipp hadn't explained her statement, nor had Su Ling understood the smile in the older woman's voice.

Su Ling's mother had been Andrew Yipp's assistant and mistress. Many years later, Su Ling guessed at their relationship, but for now she lay on her bed crying because her mother had abandoned her. All she had was her adoptive uncle, Mr Yipp, and his bitter wife.

Mr Yipp came into her room that night and stroked her head and told her everything would be all right.

"How can you be sure, Uncle?" Su Ling asked when the tears stopped.

"Because I know in my heart that she will return."

"But what of the Japanese? People are saying they are ruthless."

"I am prepared and I know how to behave. The British ruling class thought that they were the masters, but they merely set the rules. The Japanese will set new rules and we will play along. The Japanese need commerce as much as the British did, and you are safe. But do not worry your head about them, Little Flower. Go to sleep and know that I will protect you."

He stroked her head again and spoke soft words that drifted through her mind until she fell asleep.

She had just turned twelve and the abuse wouldn't start until much later.

# FIVE

*Monday 1st February*

The Singapore Club occupied the upper floors of the Fullerton Building. Downstairs was the grandiose General Post Office as well as the Chamber of Commerce and Marine Offices. However, it was the exclusive club that I'd come to visit. More specifically, Arthur Pope, a wealthy businessman who dealt in Japanese goods and artefacts.

I followed a young Malay bellboy wearing a green and gold uniform across the Tampines marble floor, and past windows overlooking the South China Seas, until we reached the smoke-filled reading room.

Pope looked up from his *Times* newspaper and raised his pipe in greeting.

"Captain Carter, my dear chap, how good of you to come and visit me," Pope said effusively as he always did when we met. He switched his pipe to his other hand and his palm was soft and plump in mine. He spent a lot of time in the club, away from the sun, and I noticed his skin looked even more tissue paper-like than ever.

"Now, are you hungry?" he asked, and signalled for a waiter before I could answer.

"Yes, *Tuan*?" a boy said after scurrying over to us.

"Sandwiches and a couple of large stengahs," Pope said, and moments later we were served with a plate of neat white sandwiches without crusts accompanied by crystal tumblers containing whisky and soda.

Pope raised his glass and I mimicked the expression. Despite my habit of avoiding alcohol, I politely took a small sip before setting the glass aside.

"May I enquire as to the health of Amelia and Mrs Pope?" I said, the former being his teenage daughter and the reason for our first encounter. She'd tried to protect a market stallholder from a bunch of squaddies. I'd just arrived on the island and my intervention had saved her, but it got me arrested in return.

Pope took a large mouthful of the drink, savoured it and swallowed. "They are in fine health and desperate for more of your stories. You've been pretty remiss with your updates since the one about the headless man on the causeway."

So I spent the next fifteen minutes telling him about running into Chinese communists in North Malaya, where I'd been lucky to only escape with bullet holes in my Land Rover. I also told him about the supposed hauntings at the barracks in Penang and being buried alive in a cave.

"All very good tales," he said when I finished, "but nothing truly ghastly. You know the ladies like the gruesome stories. Singapore can be so tame sometimes—not that *I* mind of course."

Previously I'd assumed Pope just wanted these stories for his girls. Now I saw that he liked the titillation as much as they did.

He ordered himself another stengah then tried to fix me with his eyes. However, I thought he needed lessons from Madam Chau in how to pin someone down with a hard look.

"There's a big story you aren't telling me," he said. "I heard a rumour…"

"A rumour?"

He smiled. "You know how people like to talk."

"Which story?" I said, knowing all too well what he was referring to."

"I heard you were investigating scalpings."

"I was, but there's not much to—"

"And a man who'd had his face cut off."

I took a proper sip of the watered-down whisky. He was referring to my case last year. Four months had passed and yet dreadful images still haunted my dreams. I certainly couldn't tell him everything, partly because there was still an ongoing SIB investigation and partly because it had been too disturbing.

So I told him a sanitized version, starting with a helicopter crash, a murder and burnt bodies. I gave him some details about the faceless man before he interrupted me.

"I heard he was a British Army officer."

"I couldn't comment," I said.

"I heard he was handling communist gold."

"Did you?" I said, genuinely interested in how he knew this. "Who told you?"

"One of my employees heard something. I wasn't sure it was the same story."

"Does your employee know anything else? Do they know who the army man dealt with?" It was an outstanding issue with the investigation. A major called Chris Broom was believed to be working for someone else, based on the belief that he didn't have contacts with gold buyers. He was a middle man. There was also someone higher up in the food chain. This person was believed to be a more senior officer. As far as I was aware, the investigation hadn't uncovered who it was.

Pope shook his head. "Sorry, dear chap, I didn't ask, but I will. However, I want to hear more, because I know you were up in the north-east and had the army up there for support."

Again, I told a version that omitted the worst parts. I just said there had been a commune-cum-prison run by an evil man. He'd called it Shangri-La but Hell would have been a better name. I gave my host some of the horrific details and he seemed satisfied. If he guessed I was holding back on some, he didn't say. However, what I told him was juicy enough.

By the time I'd finished, his eyes glistened and he dabbed at beads of perspiration on his forehead.

"Wonderful!" he said. "Mrs Pope will be delighted, although I will have to embellish and edit, you understand?"

I smiled and nodded.

He said, "However, you didn't come here to regale me with your derring-dos."

"A while ago I asked for a favour."

"Transportation," he said. "You wanted to secrete someone off the island."

I nodded.

"You said it would be quick, but it's been a year and a half, hasn't it?"

"Not quick. Short notice."

"Are you giving me notice now? Do you need to get her away tonight?"

I was speechless.

He shrugged. "You're surprised that I know it's a woman?"

"Yes."

"I'd go even further," he said. "I could guess who the young lady is."

Again I must have looked surprised.

He leaned forward and dropped his voice. "I'm sure you're not smuggling just any young lady off the island, Captain. I am very aware of your—shall we say—dangerous liaison? I can only think of one person you would need to help in this way."

"Is it so obvious?"

"You took her for a date on my beautiful boat"—he was referring to his *sengoku-bune,* a Japanese junk—"but fear not, I've not shared my knowledge with anyone else."

He ordered another drink and I took a sip of mine.

"There's a difference this time," I said.

"Previously, you didn't have a preferred destination. Hong Kong, Shanghai or Japan?"

"I prefer Hong Kong," I said.

"*You* prefer?" He raised his eyebrows.

I took a breath. "There's been a change of plans. Now you'll be taking two passengers."

We went on to discuss the detail. His business had a warehouse on Alkaff Quay, where I would find boxes.

"Two of them will be marked with an X. Don't get in the wrong ones." He pulled a face. "They'll feel like coffins but more comfortable. The marked ones will have padding and breathing holes for you."

★

That night in the room above Hock Lam Street, I told Su Ling the revised arrangements.

"I'm scared," she said, and I felt her body tremble as she half lay on top of me.

"We'll be fine. We slip in during the night and will be picked up before dawn. They'll carry us along with other cargo to the Japanese junk that'll be at Empire Dock. We'll be out at sea before the sun rises—before anyone knows we've gone."

"When?"

"Tomorrow night."

She breathed in and out. "You're sure we can trust this man?"

"Absolutely!"

"Arthur Pope, you say?"

"Su Ling, we can trust him."

"All right." She looked up at me and forced a smile. "Where will we go?"

"First we'll go to Hong Kong, then—"

"Hong Kong? We daren't go there."

"Why?"

"Because Andrew has many friends there. Shanghai as well. When I run, he will try and find me. He will use his extensive network and track us down."

I felt her body tremble again.

"Then we'll move on quickly," I said.

"No. We must find another plan."

"How about Japan?"

"Still risky. Andrew knows people there as well."

# SIX

*May 1943*

The house had once been a British officer's, but the Japanese colonel had made the interior typical of his home with panels and screens with prints of cherry blossom trees and snow-capped mountains and exotic birds.

"I need you to do something for me," Andrew Yipp had said to her. "It's a duty."

"Yes, Uncle?"

Su Ling was thirteen now, almost as tall as Mr Yipp but still very much a girl. She had grace and poise from her ballet classes but she still didn't understand the world like her adoptive uncle. She attended lessons and spoke four languages. She knew he was proud of her progress despite her struggle to appreciate the teachings of Sun Tzu. War was horrible. The Japanese soldiers were horrible.

Which made it harder to accept that Mr Yipp wanted her to entertain a Japanese man.

"He won't touch you, Little Flower," Yipp had said. "He just misses his daughter, and we have an arrangement."

She was told to refer to the colonel as Engu San, which she thought was an ugly name that befitted the ugly man with white skin and nasty eyes.

After being introduced, her uncle told her to wait. She heard them talking in Japanese but caught only a few words. It was clear that Andrew Yipp was being firm, and she was impressed that he dared be so bold with a senior member of the Imperial Army.

She heard the words "respect" and "daughter" but the rest was lost in the walls.

Her adoptive uncle reappeared, smiling, kissed her on the forehead and left.

Engu San indicated that she should follow him through the house and she found herself in a conservatory set for tea. There were two cushions beside a low table and he told her to sit and make the tea. He left her for a few minutes, and when he returned, he'd changed from a suit into a kimono.

After he took a cushion, he indicated for her to pour. Then, as he drank, he told her about his day and asked her questions. Her uncle had said that she was playing a role, so she made up silly stories about what she and her friends had done. It wasn't interesting, but he seemed absorbed by her anecdotes and asked questions, encouraging her.

"Your Japanese is excellent," he said after a lull. "Although your accent occasionally slips into that of a peasant."

"I apologize, Engu San."

He asked her to say some words and then adjusted her pronunciation. "There," he said with a slight smile. "Now you talk like a lady. Like my daughter."

"Thank you, Engu San."

"Please, I would like you to read." He gave her a book and she read Japanese poetry while he drank tea.

Afterwards, he said, "You dance, I understand. Will you dance for me?"

She got up and he instructed her to put on a gramophone record. It played the traditional Japanese music that was everywhere in the city these days. No more Western music since the occupation. But it had beauty and refinement and she had danced to the same music at her ballet school.

"Stop," he said after a short while. "You are wearing the wrong clothes. Normally you wear a tutu, no?"

"And ballet shoes."

"Those clothes are too restrictive. You should dance in your underwear. Yes, that would be better."

She hesitated, but then decided it made sense—after all, her uncle had told her to please this high-ranking officer. He wasn't so bad. He was polite and charming despite his unfortunate face.

She danced again and felt his appreciative gaze.

"You'd feel more comfortable without your slip," he said, and she removed it.

He was right. She often danced naked in her room, and her small breasts felt free. She felt free, like a nymph in a meadow.

The music ended and he told her to put the record on again and keep dancing. Although starting to feel dizzy and tired, she played the music for a third time.

She was enjoying the creativity, flowing as one with the melody, when she realized he was now standing. His kimono had parted. She stopped mid-step and stared.

She knew men had penises, of course she did, she'd seen horses and bulls with erections, but this was unexpected. It jutted out, a little white stick like a mast with no flag. And it had a funny pink end. Suddenly the great Japanese soldier looked comical, and she must have smirked because when she looked at his face it was flushed with rage.

"You insult me!" he screamed at her. "Get on your knees and beg forgiveness!"

She didn't need the instruction. The power of his voice made her knees collapse and her head went down. Even as she hit the ground, he was grabbing her. The teapot went flying as he pulled her over the table, pushing her head down, her bottom in the air. Her knickers were torn away and then she felt the first sting of his baton against her buttocks.

She cried out and he struck again and again until the stinging was so intense that she could no longer tell whether the beating continued or had stopped. His other hand was still on the small of her back, pinning her down. A turn of her head showed his reflection, dark in the window glass. He was still over her, striking with the stick, but then he stopped and his hand moved beneath the kimono.

The music finished and the needle started clicking at the end of the record. A moment later, he grunted, and for a long time there was just the stinging, the pressure of his hand and the click of the record. Then the hand came off and he stroked her bottom, which made it sting more than ever.

He was sitting in a chair when she got up from the uncomfortable table. A glance down showed a ridge just beneath her breasts where the edge had dug in. Engu San had his elbows on his knees, his hands clenched in front of his mouth, watching, considering.

As she carefully pulled on her torn knickers, he said, "You should not have laughed."

His voice was full of contrition and vulnerability, and if she hadn't already been beaten, she may have smirked again. There was a lesson here, she told herself. Even the most powerful men are weak.

Much later, a driver returned Su Ling to her uncle's home. The Japanese colonel had fed her and let her bathe. He'd given her cream for her sore skin, but she was still in pain when Mr Yipp met her. Without hesitation, she told him what the man had done to her, and Yipp flew into a rage, bellowing like a water buffalo.

Then he put his arm around her and apologized for his mistake. "The man will suffer," he said. "He insulted you and he insulted me, and I will make sure this does not go unpunished."

A week later, the Japanese colonel died when his home burned down. There were repercussions. Local men were rounded up before being publicly and summarily executed.

No one questioned her or Andrew Yipp and he just smiled when she asked if he'd arranged it.

It was a Sunday and Mrs Yipp was playing mah-jong.

"How is your bottom?" he asked.

"I'm better now."

He circled his finger, indicating that she should roll onto her tummy. Then he lifted her nightdress and she felt his light touch.

"No scars," he said, letting his fingers follow the contours. And then quietly: "You are perfect."

"Uncle?"

"Go to sleep, Little Flower. You never have anything to worry about." He stroked her hair like he often did and she fell into a deep sleep.

# SEVEN

*Tuesday 2nd February 1954*

I found Arthur Pope at his offices, the Kelly and Pope Building in Commercial Square.

"I need somewhere else," I explained. "Is it possible?"

He smiled expansively. "Of course! I can arrange for my boat to make a little detour. There's Sumatra, Borneo, Brunei, the Philippines—"

"The Philippines?"

He nodded.

"Can we still go tonight?"

He took a ledger from his desk, opened it and ran his finger down a page. "Give me five days to organize it."

"Five?" I said, disappointed and concerned for Su Ling's anxiety.

He waited a second then pointed to a calendar on the wall behind him. "My dear chap, what happens in five days—the seventh of February?"

"Sunday... The fifth day of the Chinese New Year... the parade."

"Exactly, the carnival and parade. It'll be a good distraction. We'll set sail on Monday, in the early hours, with Japan as the official destination and a stopover for emergency repairs in Manila."

"Five days," I said out loud, thinking it would seem like an eternity. I would need to act like nothing had changed, continue as though I had long-term plans in Singapore.

Which gave me an idea.

"Yesterday you mentioned that one of your employees heard gossip about the communist gold trade. Would you mind if I interviewed them?"

"Of course not!" He beckoned his assistant, who sat at a desk outside. When the man came in, Pope said, "Fetch young Jihan."

While we waited, Pope lit his pipe and I gave a subtle cough hoping to deter him. However, he continued, and blue smoke rapidly filled the room.

The assistant returned with a man barely out of his teens. As he was ushered in, I was about to suggest that I interview the man alone—preferably in a room without the smoke—but Pope pointed to the corner.

"Stand there, Jihan, and tell this man what you know."

Jihan's eyes widened, before he blinked, presumably due to the eye-watering fumes. "Sir?"

"About the communist gold."

The man swallowed. "Erm... All I heard was that it was being handled by someone in the British Army."

I wondered whether this was Major Broom or someone else. "Do you know who it was?"

"No, sir."

"What do you know—exactly?"

"That's all, sir. I heard that the communists were getting paid for their gold and that someone in the army was helping them."

Pope asked a question that didn't help then I asked where Jihan had heard the gossip.

"My cousin, sir."

"And where did he hear it?"

"I do not know, sir."

"For goodness sake, who is he, man?" Pope interjected.

"My cousin, sir?"

"Yes, what's his name, please?" I asked.

Jihan wiped a hand across his eyes. "I don't want to get him into any trouble, sir."

"He won't be in trouble."

"Peter Jihan, sir. His name's Peter."

"And where will I find Peter?"

The young man looked from me to Arthur Pope and back. "He's a police constable, sir."

"OK, he won't be in trouble," I said again. "Will I find him at the Hill Street Station?"

"Bukit Timah Road. He's based in the Bukit Timah Road station, sir."

Jihan was dismissed and Pope grinned. "There you go, plenty for you to investigate, and in the meantime, I will arrange everything for the day after the parade."

★

My jeep was parked outside my apartment on Beach Road. I jumped in and headed for Orchard Circus. From there I went up Orchard Road and then cut through to pick up Stevens Road. Tanglin and the Botanic Gardens were over to my left and the city was rapidly petering out.

The police station was where Stevens Road met Bukit Timah Road. It looked as uninviting as a concentration camp, with a high fence with barbed wire on top. I think it was a hangover from the war and was probably due for demolition.

There were wide wire gates, beyond which I saw a single-storey building with discoloured red-brown tiles. I suspected the taller grey block behind the station held prisoners.

I stopped outside the gates and showed the duty policeman my credentials. I'd been given government warrant documents from the time when I worked for Internal Security, and they'd been retained based on my occasional work for the department.

Without questioning me, the policeman pushed the gate so that I could pass through.

After a short flight of steps, I opened a door and went inside.

"Captain Carter for Constable Peter Jihan," I announced to the desk sergeant, who immediately jumped up and hurried away. A couple of minutes later he returned with an inquisitive-looking man. I could see a resemblance to his cousin at Pope's office, although this Jihan was a few years older.

I flashed the warrant card again and his expression changed to one of alarm. When his mouth tensed, I suspected he wasn't about to talk to me. Not in front of the sergeant anyway. So I inclined my head towards the entrance.

"Let's go for a walk."

Peter Jihan hesitated before complying. A few seconds later we were on the street by my jeep. I leaned against it, acting casual.

"Smoke?" I asked.

"Yes."

"Go ahead. This isn't formal. I just want to ask some questions."

The young man took a packet of Players from his breast pocket and lit up. Two puffs later he visibly relaxed.

"Good," I said. "I've just come from the Kelly and Pope Building in Commercial Square. Your cousin spoke to me."

He nodded, part nervous, part intrigued.

"I was involved in the Chinese gold operation—"

His eyes flared with panic.

"Sorry!" I laughed. "Investigating the Chinese gold operation."

"Ah!"

"I was working with the military police, Special Investigations Branch."

He nodded and said nothing.

"It wasn't concluded," I explained. "I'm still interested because it came to a dead end."

"The man with no face," Peter Jihan said.

"That's right. He must have been working with someone else."

Jihan gave a single slow nod like he'd thought the same.

"So," I said, raising my hands, "I'm hoping you can help. Anything you know, whether it's big or small, might lead somewhere. And before you say anything, don't worry, I'm not suspicious that you were involved."

He let out a long stream of smoke. "No, sir, I just know about a few murders."

"Yes."

"Mostly soldiers..."

"Go on."

"There was one found hanged at Takafuji Cliff. Another found with his throat slit at Batu Caves. One found disembowelled and floating in Semenyih Lake. And the worst of all... the corporal found with his heart cut out."

I nodded. He'd got some of the detail wrong, but including the faceless man, these were four of the seven I knew about. The others had been further away from the capital. Which told me something.

Other deaths had been investigated, but they weren't considered connected to the serial killer case.

"You said mostly soldiers," I prompted. "Who else?"

"There was a KL police constable who was shot... and killed, I mean."

A policeman? One of the other cases, I thought but nodded as though it was useful information.

"Do you know his name?"

He shook his head.

"Anything you can tell me might be useful."

He shook his head again.

"That's everything you know?"

"There is nothing more, I swear."

"Then tell me how you know these things."

His mouth clenched shut.

I said, "You learned all this from someone in the KL police?"

"How did you know that?"

"Because all the ones you know about were in the Kuala Lumpur region—except for the faceless man."

Jihan nodded.

"I'd like to know their name."

Jihan's eyes flared wide like before. He'd finished his first cigarette and lit another.

"As I said, Peter, you aren't in trouble. Your friend won't be in trouble either."

His hands went to his lips like he was praying, although the cigarette made the gesture less convincing.

"I promise," I said. "There will be no repercussions. This is not about blame. I just want to find out if there's anything we missed. A good policeman considers everything. Am I right?"

He inclined his head slightly.

"And you are a good policeman."

"Yes, sir."

"Then give me a name and I will just ask him questions like I've asked you."

"No trickery?"

I put my hand on my heart. "None. I promise."

"I heard it from my close friend."

"And he's in the KL police?"

"No, his wife is a typist with the police."

Peter Jihan gave me her name—Mrs Anu Srivats—and I thanked him before jumping in the jeep and heading back to my office.

# EIGHT

*September 1943*

A few months after the death of the Japanese colonel, Su Ling's uncle came into her room.

"Can't sleep?" He moved beside the bed. "Lie on your front."

She rolled over and he helped her remove her nightdress then gently rubbed her shoulders and head.

She said, "I keep thinking about him."

"So do I, Little Flower, but he's gone now and you have nothing to fear. I will always protect you."

"You promise?"

"I promise."

It was Wednesday, and she could hear the old women downstairs, but the click-clack sound faded and she drifted into a wonderful sleep.

Then on Sunday he came again to check on her, but she'd been asleep. She woke up to feel his hands, light on her scalp.

"Shall I roll over?"

"No, you are already sleepy," he said softly.

She was naked under the sheet, and when his hand touched her shoulder and ran across her collarbone to the other side, she tensed.

"Relax and sleep, Little Flower," he said, and she found the gentle touch on her chest even more comforting than across her back.

The next time, she did not flinch when his hand moved to her chest. Twice he touched her nipples, but she hardly noticed, lost as she was in the wonderful sensation, like she was weightless. She loved to dance, and it felt like she was twirling happily through the air.

It went on like this for weeks, each Wednesday and Sunday, to the background sound of foolish old women and their games. Always the touch was light, and each time, if he grazed her breast, she told herself it was just her chest. He was trying to relax her, being kind, nothing more.

He spent time on her stomach, going round and round, sometimes moving back up and other times going down her legs.

When his hand went up her inner thigh, though, she sat up, alarmed.

He bowed his head. "I'm sorry if I…"

She lay back down and relaxed again as he rubbed her shoulders.

She forgot about it, but then the next time, his hand quickly moved to her thigh and brushed the young hair that had grown between her legs.

Her body went rigid.

"Did you like that?" he whispered.

"No."

"You are becoming a woman."

"Yes… but…"

"Relax, Little Flower."

He resumed the previous movement, the flow from neck to thigh and circling just above the pubis, but not between her legs. Gradually, she relaxed again and wasn't worried the next time he visited her.

But she should have been. He soon stroked her and did a tiny swirling motion between her legs.

He stopped. "You're shaking," he whispered into her ear.

"I can't help it."

"It's our special secret," he said. "Enjoy it."

She couldn't relax after that, but he didn't seem to notice. And the next Wednesday when he came to her, she was already afraid before the touching began.

What could she do?

Each time he would whisper, "Our special secret."

And she found herself responding, "Yes, Uncle," despite the fear and disgust. Despite the dread she felt every Wednesday and Sunday, and the background sound of mah-jong tiles and foolish old women.

★

Her fourteenth birthday fell on a Wednesday. Mrs Yipp and her cronies were creating the usual background chatter and noise. She had lain, tense, watching shadows, fearing his approach.

But her uncle did not visit.

Not until much later, when she'd finally fallen asleep.

And then she was awake, his hands lightly gliding over her thighs. He raised her legs, the way he recently did before touching her. This was happening faster than usual, but she'd been asleep. Perhaps he'd been here a while. Her heart quickened, wanting to stop his touch, wanting to scream. But who would come? Who could stop him?

That night he had done something different. He climbed onto her bed, between her legs.

She could smell alcohol on his breath.

Then his hand went over her mouth.

"Shush, Little Flower," he whispered.

Her uncle's weight was on her, and then excruciating pain. She tried to move away from the pain, but he was too heavy.

"Stop!" she cried out, and her sound was smothered by his hand. Her mind screamed panic but she froze. His body pressed down and she couldn't breathe, her small chest crushed beneath him.

It may have lasted for minutes but it seemed an eternity.

When he got off, she could still sense him there, his weight, his smell. For a long time, she couldn't move. Eventually, she curled into the foetal position and cried for the second time in her life. The world was indeed a sad place.

Love was not real. There was only sex. Love was just a cruel trick, a way of satisfying a man's needs.

# NINE

*Tuesday 2nd February 1954*

I have a great contact in the Kuala Lumpur police: Chief Inspector George McNaughton. I'd first met him sixteen months ago when he was posted in Johor Bahru. He'd been a captain back then but had been promoted, thanks he said, to me and my case. If I needed anything from the police in or around the capital, McNaughton would get it for me.

When I returned to my office, Madam Chau grumbled that she hadn't known where I'd been or when I'd return.

"Secretary Norris called for you. He'd like an urgent meeting."

"Before I do that," I said, "I'd like to speak to Chief Inspector McNaughton at the KL police headquarters."

"You're sure? Secretary Norris sounded very impatient."

I forced a smile. "I'm sure he did. But please call the KL police."

Four minutes later I was on the phone with McNaughton.

"How is the indefatigable Captain Carter?" McNaughton boomed through the earpiece.

We chatted about inconsequential things and I saw Madam Chau glaring at me, urging me to get on with it.

"Remember when we last met?" I asked.

"We had dinner at the Jockey Club." The Jockey Club was Kuala Lumpur's equivalent of the Singapore Club, although not as opulent, but with a good view over the polo field, their *Padang*.

"I was just getting involved in that awful investigation," I said.

"All those murders."

"And many of them in your neck of the woods."

"The killer was called something like Blackhand, wasn't he?"

"BlackJack—" I stopped abruptly, as images flashed into my mind.

There was silence for a few seconds and he waited for me to say more. Then he prompted: "Ash?"

"It's not so much BlackJack as the Chinese gold," I said after dispelling the dark thoughts. "The main investigation was into the murders, but it overlapped with the illegal trade, taking communist gold ore and selling it as legitimate."

"I thought that was concluded."

"No. It was a dead end. An SIB officer believed someone high up in the army was involved. Someone with connections."

McNaughton blew out air. "Gracious! And you're working that case?"

"Just following a new lead."

McNaughton didn't say anything for a moment and I figured he was processing the news. Then, "Is there something I can help with?"

"Apparently there's a typist in your HQ by the name of Mrs Anu Srivats. I don't expect you know her."

"No."

"I'd just like to interview her—informally."

"That won't be a problem. You think she knows something?"

"It's possible. You know how it is—follow every lead, just in case."

"And you found her name how?"

"From gossip. A chain of people that led me to a constable at the Bukit Timah Road police station who knew more than he should have. He gave me Mrs Srivats as the source."

"Excellent," McNaughton said. "When will you be here?"

"I could come tomorrow. Will she be at work tomorrow?"

"I don't know, but I'll check." He ended the call and ten minutes later called me back.

"Yes, Mrs Srivats is working tomorrow."

"Great. I'll get there before midday and then you can buy me lunch."

I ended the call and met Madam Chau's sour expression.

"I know," I said. "I'm going now."

"He's in the Attorney General's Chambers."

Less than five minutes later, I was waiting outside an office in the government building as Secretary Norris finished a meeting.

When he was free, I greeted him. "How can I help?"

Norris removed his glasses and rubbed his eyes. "Take a seat, Carter. Can I get you a drink?"

"Water, please."

Norris winced at my request but ordered his assistant to fetch him a whisky and a glass of water for me. Previously we'd met in his private rooms, and I wondered whether this location was significant.

I looked out at the perpetually congested Singapore River and waited for Norris to tell me why I'd been summoned.

He didn't start speaking until after the drinks arrived and he'd taken a large mouthful of his whisky. "Trouble is coming," he said in a half-whisper.

"Trouble? The communists?" I said, knowing that his predecessor had been in constant fear of terrorism on the island.

"Political," he said, before coughing as he probably realized his mistake. The communists were seen as bandits rather than a political body. "I think the governor has made a misstep."

I sipped my water and waited.

"You'll be aware that Sir John set up the Constitutional Committee to make proposals on the future governing of the colony."

I nodded.

"Nine men, including five members of the Legislative Council." He raised his eyebrows. We both knew these local members of parliament were toothless. They had no real power because it was a British colony run on behalf of Her Majesty Queen Elizabeth II by the governor with his team of administrators. Elections were a smokescreen to appease the public. There had been riots in 1950, the first sign of unrest, and they'd been met by strong leadership—which meant a strengthening of the police but also concessions to the public demand for influence.

"The recommendation is for popular elections—the majority of seats in the Legislative Council."

"Is that a problem?"

He shook his head at me. "Dear chap, don't you understand politics? This is like turkey's voting for Christmas. We publish this recommendation and Pandora's Box is open. There'll be no going back."

"Then don't publish," I suggested.

"Impossible. We should never have had the non-Brits on the committee. If we don't publish the recommendations, if we don't follow up with elections, imagine the outcome. This won't be an invasion of communists, it'll be an implosion. We'll have riots like no country has ever seen." He removed his glasses and rubbed his eyes once more.

I looked out at the river swarming with tongkangs and bumboats, crewed on the whole by Chinese immigrants. And the Chinese worked the quays as well. I didn't know the exact mix of races in Singapore, but I guessed seventy or eighty per cent were Chinese. They made up the majority of workers, and the government was British, white upper-class privileged men who—on the whole—hadn't a clue about real work, about strife.

Norris sighed. "So that's all we can talk about. Crisis meetings about how to handle this damnable report. Damned if we do and damned if we don't. Scylla and Charybdis with an impossible channel between."

I waited as he finished his whisky.

"And I can help how?"

"You can help us find that channel."

I said nothing.

"You were in the army. What's the best way of defeating the enemy?"

"Strategy and resources?"

He shook his head.

I shrugged. "So, you mean, kill the general?"

Norris nodded.

I wondered if he was alluding to Sir Pendall, the chairman of the Constitutional Committee. Surely not.

"Who's the enemy?"

"Anyone against our great island. More specifically, anyone in favour of the eradication of colonization."

"The communists?"

"They are undoubtedly a threat. The Malayan Communist Party is efficient and organized. Through their clever propaganda they are more popular than ever. We are losing the war, Carter. Not on the battlefield. Not in the jungles. We are losing in the hearts and minds. This isn't just me talking. This is the governor too."

I'd never heard anyone in the government speak so openly before. Towards the end of his life, I thought Norris's predecessor, Coates, was depressed. Now I sensed a similar malaise over the whole administration.

Norris continued: "So our strategy is to go along with the recommendations and make sure that we maintain influence over the assembly."

"You make sure you win the election."

"Precisely. But first of all, we need to understand the enemy."

"If not the communists, then who?"

"There's a new group. They're academics. Young and educated in England, for Christ's sake! They are proposing the immediate independence of Singapore and union with Malaya. They're underground at the moment, but my sources tell me they will launch soon as the People's Action Party. Not communist but not anti-communist either."

"How do they differ from the Singapore Progressive Party?" I knew this group had been the dominant force in the previous elections.

Norris shook his head and smiled wryly. "The Progressive Party comprises a bunch of conservative lawyers. They're no threat because they're as much the establishment as the rest of us—just a different skin colour."

"But you said this new group were academics. Are academics more of a threat than lawyers?"

"Marx, Lenin and Trotsky were academics, but the Soviet Union wouldn't be the power it is today if not for Stalin. He was the muscle and a major source of funds."

This didn't sound like the Joseph Stalin I'd read about. "So you're saying Stalin was wealthy?"

"He was born into poverty. No, Stalin wasn't wealthy per se. He raised money for the Bolshevik revolution through nefarious activities. He and his gang gained money through robberies, kidnappings, and protection rackets."

That made more sense. I nodded and waited for Norris to continue.

"The People's Action Party will cause a revolution. Not like Russia's—I pray to God—but a people's revolution nonetheless that will lead to the eradication of British rule in Singapore. We stop them and we have a chance of navigating that thin channel."

"So, who is funding this group?" I asked. "Who's this general?"

"Andrew Yipp." Secretary Norris's nose flared and his eyes became ice. "That's why you have to kill Andrew Yipp."

# TEN

*February 1944*

Su Ling didn't cry the second time that Andrew Yipp raped her. Of course, she wanted to tell him to stop, but she didn't dare. She closed her eyes and let him do the deed.

The second time, he whispered sweet words, but she wasn't listening. Her mind was blank. On the third occasion, he rolled her over, raised her buttocks and did it like an animal. When she yelped at how deep he went, he pushed her face down so that she screamed into the pillow.

Afterwards, he lay by her side and stroked her head and shoulders as he'd done in the early days.

"You are so beautiful," he said. "I'm sorry if I hurt you. I can't help myself."

"It feels wrong," she said, having planned the words over many days, hoping he'd come to his senses.

"Oh dear child, I decide what is right and what is wrong."

"What about your wife?"

"The old goat doesn't understand love, but let me explain right and wrong. One animal eats another animal. It's the natural order. It's about survival. That is the meaning of life. When a cat toys with a mouse until it dies, it's doing it for fun. Is that cruel and evil? Of course not. When baby spiders eat their mother, what are they thinking? Should I do this? Is it right to eat my mother? Of course not."

"But they aren't humans. How could they understand right and wrong?" she asked, feeling braver at the conversation.

He continued to rub her shoulders. "If you steal a loaf of bread, is that wrong? What if you are starving? Would you steal it then?"

"To survive, you mean? Yes, of course."

"As I said, it is about survival. You have a justification. It is just. Which means there is no absolute good and evil, right and wrong."

"What about God?" She turned to look at him smiling kindly back at her.

"God does not intervene," he said, shaking his head. "And if he does not get involved, how can he define what is good. And, my child, don't heed the Church. The Church is like the government. It sets rules that it thinks fit. It claims these rules come from God, but how can they be?"

"But we have to obey the Japanese—or whoever our masters are."

He scoffed. "Little Flower, I am your master. You learned that I dealt with the colonel who abused you." He paused before continuing. "Think of it like this: laws of the land are like the walls of a house. They provide structure and stability. However, we must *live* within the house. We must move. We come in and go out. We are not walls. We are not static furniture."

"I think I understand," she said, which he must have thought she meant based on his argument, but she'd hoped he'd stop forcing himself on her and she knew now that nothing was going to change.

"Show me that you understand," he said, getting up and tightening his gown. "I want you to write a dissertation on good versus evil. I want two thousand words, written in English by the end of the week. Use my library for reading."

And so began her education: each time, after sex, he would pose her another challenge, from philosophy to strategy, from business to poetry. However, there was one subject that wasn't covered by his library. He told her she was to have a French teacher, although she thought there was little use for the language. But it had been a pun on French letter, because her teacher was a high-class pleasure girl called Chichi. She was there to teach Su Ling about sex.

"Do you enjoy it?" Chichi asked during their first meeting. "It's all right to say you do."

"No."

"Then how do you cope with it?"

"I try and ignore him."

Chichi nodded. "You lie rigid and stare at the ceiling?"

"Or close my eyes. I try to make my mind go blank."

"That's the opposite of what you should do. Who is the sexiest film star you can think of?"

"Gary Cooper."

"Imagine Gary Cooper is making love to you."

A week later Chichi wanted to know whether things had improved.

"I can't imagine he's Gary Cooper."

"But then don't think of nothing, think of a happy place. You like dancing, so close your eyes and imagine you are on stage or dancing naked along the beach."

Chichi taught her the techniques and the sounds that men liked to hear. She taught her how to take control: the Singapore Grip, legs around his hips, setting the timing, controlling the depth. It was how to be in charge without insulting their pride.

Chichi said, "You pull the strings they don't even know they have."

She also taught Su Ling massage and to recite poems from Shi Jing because men liked to be calmed after sex. "And if he is still tense, then stick a cigarette in his mouth and massage his ego."

"His ego?"

"Tell him he is incredible in bed. The best. Tell him he has a big cock," she said, and they both giggled.

# ELEVEN

*Tuesday 2nd February 1954*

Secretary Norris's predecessor had used me to get Yipp because he thought Yipp was a communist threat. I had never believed this of the business leader. However, I did know two things: Yipp's activities bore all the hallmarks of Joseph Stalin, and he was anti-establishment. If Norris was right about this new political force, then I could imagine Yipp in control behind the scenes.

"I won't kill Andrew Yipp," I said.

"Why not?"

"Cut off the serpent's head…" I said, using a Chinese expression to mean that someone else would take his place. Yipp was the head of the biggest Chinese secret society and would either be replaced or another gang would take over.

Norris smiled. "I wasn't being serious. You're right. Killing him could and probably would make matters worse. At college, I remember the debate about what would have happened to Christianity if Pontius Pilate had imprisoned Jesus rather than make a martyr of him."

I looked beyond Norris and out of the window and focused on a thin line of smoke across the river.

Finally, Norris spoke again. "So what's your plan?" he asked.

"My plan?"

"How do we take Yipp down? You know the man and he trusts you."

"There's mutual respect, but I'm not sure he trusts anyone."

"That's close enough."

I switched my attention from the smoke to Norris. In six nights I would be away from here. I could agree to anything, I decided, and non-delivery wouldn't matter.

"Coates wanted me to identify Yipp as the head of a secret society," I said.

"A secret society would be illegal."

"And despite the certainty, it's difficult to prove."

"In the old days, Yipp would have just been arrested, with hearsay as proof enough." He chuckled. "At least it feels like that. When the Attorney General drafted the law against Chinese secret societies, he should have made it more general. It's gangs and criminality that we are against."

"Which is also difficult to pin on Yipp," I said. "From my experience, he has a complex organization. Find an illegal activity and it'll be nigh impossible to trace it back to Yipp himself."

"What about drugs? Yipp is undoubtedly involved with the opium trade."

I was watching the smoke again, which had thickened, turning from grey to black. If I could get Yipp before we left the country, would that make it easier for us to get away? I feared that I might poke the hornets' nest. What if I investigated Yipp and he wasn't arrested?

I turned my attention back to Norris, who was waiting with narrow, scheming eyes.

"Drugs will be difficult," I said. "He's become legitimate, producing morphine for army medical supplies."

"You need to find a way," Norris said. "Prostitution, extortion, gun-running…"

"Gun-running?"

"If he's helping the communists—"

"But you said you thought he was financing the PAP rather than the terrorists."

Norris banged his hand on the table. "Whatever it takes, Carter!"

"All right."

"My apologies, I shouldn't have lost my temper. I'm just a little tense, you understand."

I nodded.

He reached out and shook my hand. "Good man. You solve our little problem and I'll treble your money."

★

As I left the Attorney General's Chambers deep in thought, it took a moment to realize the excitement outside. More people than usual were milling around. Others were running towards the quays, and I could hear sirens.

"What's going on?" I asked a cluster of chatting ladies.

"Fire," one said. "There's a big fire on the quay."

I looked west. "Which one?"

"Alkaff, I think."

I started running along High Street until the junction with Hill Street and rounded the corner by the imposing police HQ. The shortest route would have been to go down to the quays, but I could see a mass of people that way so I turned and ran along River Valley Road as far as Ord Road. This would take me down to the end of Clarke Quay and the start of Robertson.

The whole time I was thinking about Arthur Pope's warehouse. If Pope's warehouse burned down then our escape plan was in ruins. Whether or not I managed to satisfy Secretary Norris, if there were no crates, we weren't stowing away on Pope's boat.

However, when I burst out by Ord Bridge, I could see where the fire raged. Robertson Quay stretched around a sharp bend, and on the other side of the river was the short stretch of Alkaff Quay. A glance made the fire appear to be on the quay, but I could now see that it was beyond.

Walking, I crossed Clemenceau Bridge onto Pulau Saigon, the small island in the river. On the far side was Havelock Road where many of the dockworkers lived, and it was from here that I saw flames as well as the billowing smoke. It looked like over fifty yards of buildings were on fire.

While relieved that it hadn't been Pope's warehouse, I knew that this was a huge disaster. Major Lamb from Housing Planning and Development had talked about the condition of some Singapore housing. Overcrowding was an issue, and none more so than on parts of Havelock Road. I'd seen how these people lived. Most buildings were split into blocks of rooms no bigger than two double beds. A family of between seven and ten people would be living in each. Separating the rooms was a narrow corridor where the children played, friends met and families cooked.

Fires happened all the time, but this was much bigger than usual. After my initial relief, my legs kicked into action and I started running again. Some people ran the other way, but most, like me, were heading towards the fire.

When I got close, I could see fire engines and men pumping spouts of water into the black and crumbling building. I also saw hundreds of men, maybe a thousand, in lines, passing buckets and pans—anything that would hold water—from hand to hand: human chains, from the river to the flames.

I found the shortest line and joined it, doing what I could to stop the spread of the fire.

★

Eighteen people, mostly women and children, died that day, and over a hundred were injured. From the extent of the damage, it could have been many more, and I gained a degree of comfort from knowing that I'd helped in some small way. And the people of Singapore had once again shown how they worked together at a time of crisis— irrespective of colour or creed.

# TWELVE

That night, despite two showers, Su Ling could still smell the smoke on me.

"I'm not complaining," she said after we made love. "You did a good thing today. Perhaps you should look for a career as a fireman after we leave."

"Why? Because you like the smell?"

"The danger," she said and laughed. However, I could tell she forced it. As soon as she'd come into the apartment on Hock Lam Street, I told her the plan. We'd be going to the Philippines in five days.

"Five more days?" she said, and I heard nerves in her voice.

"The New Year's parade and pageant will be a good distraction."

"Yes."

I said, "And the extra days give me time to arrange where we go next. We shouldn't stay in the Philippines. I have contacts. We'll get a US military flight out of there as soon as possible."

"And then where?"

I'd already given this a lot of thought, but asked, "Where would you like to go?"

"Anywhere, so long as we're together." Then she said, "I've been thinking. Maybe it doesn't make sense to disappear at the same time. If you do it will be more obvious that we've left together?"

"Yes, but he won't know where."

"He might work it out. I wondered if you could follow me. Perhaps leave it a day or two and I'll wait for you."

I liked the idea. I could carry on with my investigations as though nothing had happened. Maybe we would even have time to capture Yipp, satisfying Norris, tripling my money, and removing Yipp from the equation. He couldn't come after us if he was locked up.

"I'll make sure you get on board all right."

She nodded, looked grateful. "If I arrive before you, I'll put an extra X on the box," she said, "so you'll know I'm inside."

"All right."

"And," she said, "we should still use both crates so that no one else knows our change of plan."

★

Later, lying naked on the bed, we talked about various destinations. Neither of us fancied England because Yipp might assume we'd go there. I'd been based in Cyprus for a while and parts were beautiful but trouble was brewing there. Australia was an attractive, unknown country to me and the Perth climate appealed. However, I had relatives from my mother's side in Germany and had thought it was a possible destination. Su Ling knew little of Europe except for an idealized view of Paris, so I told her about the many and varied countries.

"That's it!" she said while I was describing Vienna.

"What?" I said.

"That's our answer."

"Austria?"

"All countries. We travel. We tour the beautiful cities, starting with Europe, and settle only when we've found the perfect place."

It was a romantic plan, and I was loath to spoil it by mentioning money. I had some in the bank, but not enough for two people to live off while leisurely travelling the world.

"Secretary Norris wants me to help him lock Yipp away for a long time."

She said nothing, just looked at me waiting for more, I thought.

"He'll pay well," I said. "And it would solve our problem. He won't be after us if he's behind bars."

"You can't be serious," she said.

"It's an option."

She shook her head firmly. "No, it's not! On what charges?"

"Because he's head of an illegal society. He's a gangster."

"You'll have to prove it."

"You could help."

She took a breath and pulled away from me.

"Su Ling, you know it makes sense."

"It doesn't. You've asked for help before, and I thought I'd explained. It's not something we do. It's about respect and face. I cannot betray Andrew no matter what. And don't forget, he's my uncle—virtually my father."

My jaw tensed. He'd helped raise her and then made her his mistress. If that wasn't a betrayal then I don't know what was. However, I said nothing.

We sat in silence, just looking at one another. Then she reached for me and I held her. Gradually our tension melted away and passion took its place.

★

In the early hours before dawn, she got up and left me with a kiss. After a reasonable period, I slipped out and snuck along back streets with a hood covering my face. A circuitous route took me home, and I left a short time later for a session at the boxing gym.

The Cathay Building with its cinema downstairs and Andrew Yipp's offices at the top stood on Dhoby Ghaut and looked down Bras Basah Road where I trained in the gym. I'd never been so conscious of its proximity.

Jack, the coach, stood behind me as I pummelled the bag. He was a short man but built as square as a brick and with a yell that could make bigger men quake in their boots.

"Take it easy, lad," he barked. "You'll break my bag if you keep that up."

I grunted an acknowledgement and backed away, wiping sweat from my eyes. Images of Yipp with Su Ling together were in my head. They were imagined, of course, but I hated that I was so powerless.

Five more days, I told myself. Just five more days and she'd be free.

# THIRTEEN

*Wednesday 3rd February*

I drove up through the northern jungle to Woodlands Crossing. As usual, a long queue of vehicles and carts waited patiently for the causeway to open. The dawn sky was brightening quickly with sunrise about fifteen minutes away.

I skirted around the queue and was waved forward by the military police. As I approached the checkpoint they raised the boom so that I could pass through without stopping. The benefit of having an ex-military police Land Rover—and being recognized by the men of 200 Provost Company.

Out of Johor Bahru, the southernmost town in Malaya, I went north up Route One. The houses petered out and there was elephant grass before jungle took its place.

I'd driven this road many times. With the roof off the Land Rover and the wind in my hair, I sank into my seat and enjoyed what might be my last journey this way.

I passed the occasional kampong with attap huts and bashas where children waved, dogs barked and chickens ran free. The road did a long, slow loop avoiding the hills and eventually I left the state of Johor and travelled through Negri Sembilan where the jungle closed in and I was forced to stop and clip the roof on during a cloudburst.

Five hours of driving and I finally crossed the river on the outskirts of Kuala Lumpur. The city changed dramatically as I drove to the centre, from shantytown to British colonial, from congested streets to wide avenues.

The police headquarters was in the centre, a squat cream building with a pyramidal roof and a proud sign that read: Malayan Union Police Force.

Inside, I asked the desk sergeant for Chief Inspector McNaughton. He wasn't there. It transpired that the officers were all based at the government building.

The Royal Selangor Club looked like a Malayan *istana*—a palace—but had been designed and built by the British, and as you'd expect from the name, it felt more like a gentlemen's club than the centre of the country's administration.

McNaughton had a modest office with no special view, but then he wasn't in the highest echelons. However, he seemed proud of his position and greeted me warmly.

"How was the journey? You did take the train?"

"I drove and enjoyed it."

"Too much jungle," he said. "I know there's been no trouble for a while, but I still worry about bandit attacks."

He checked his watch. "You haven't eaten?"

"If you don't mind, I'd like to see the typist first."

He led me into the corridor. "She's over at the HQ. It's a short distance."

"I've just been there."

He missed a step, looked confused. "What, you've seen her already?"

"No, no! I was looking for you. I just assumed your office would be at the police station."

He laughed. "Right, let's go and interview this typist of yours."

He jumped into the jeep beside me and I drove back to the police headquarters. Once there, we went into the staff entrance and my friend asked for the typists' room.

"Never been there," he said, chuckling. "I have something to type, I hand it to my assistant who reappears with the work magically completed. Of course, I know it's been done by someone in the typing pool…"

We opened a door to a room crammed with about twenty ladies all typing furiously. However, the clicking of keys and ping of carriages sounded more like a hundred typists.

One closest to us had large in- and out-trays and she stood up as we entered.

"How can I help you, sirs?"

"We'd like to speak to…" McNaughton looked at me.

"Mrs Anu Srivats," I said.

"Ah." The woman's face dropped and she pointed to an empty chair. "I'm so sorry, sir. Mrs Srivats hasn't shown up for work today."

"Time off?" I asked.

"No, sir. Mrs Srivats just hasn't come to work today."

"Sickness," McNaughton said. "It's more of a problem here than back in JB. Overcrowding leads to less than sanitary conditions. There's no problem in the centre, but get too far out… well, the sewerage situation needs sorting."

The lady looked at me then McNaughton. "Is that all, sir?"

"Thank you," McNaughton said. "Please be sure to notify me as soon as she returns."

★

We ate lunch at the Jockey Club and McNaughton apologized for not confirming the typist was at work before I'd travelled all that way.

"You weren't to know," I said. "You checked yesterday."

He nodded. "You don't seem too upset by the wasted visit. Will you stay over and see if she's at work tomorrow?"

He was right, I wasn't upset. I had time to kill and Mrs Srivats was more of a distraction than a serious investigation.

McNaughton said, "I'm not sure what you'd have learned from a typist anyway."

"Who knows?" I said, distracted as a beautiful Eurasian woman walked past and reminded me of Su Ling. After today it would be four days to her freedom. Then my career as an investigator would soon be over. The Chinese gold operation wasn't my problem anyway.

McNaughton was looking at me, his eyes full of curiosity.

"This doesn't sound like the Ash Carter I know. There's something you aren't telling me."

Yes, there is, I thought, but I'm not going to talk about escaping from Singapore. As an appeasement, I said, "Could other deaths be related to the Chinese gold case?"

"Other deaths?"

I tried to sound serious. "My source said that Mrs Srivats mentioned a policeman."

"What about a policeman?"

"A murdered one."

"Ah. Do you have a name?"

"That's all I know," I said.

He shook his head. "There have been some deaths because of the Emergency of course."

"I got the impression it was one of the civil police."

"Really? I'll ask around. How long ago?"

"Within the past six months if it's connected to the case."

"You think it's connected? I thought BlackJack only killed soldiers."

"That's right." Now it was my turn to shake my head. "It's probably not connected."

We were interrupted by one of the Bengali bellboys who handed McNaughton a card

My friend raised his eyebrows. "Lucky we'd finished eating."

"Oh?"

"The commissioner wants me. I'll have to leave you I'm afraid. There's a car waiting for me outside."

The government offices were a short walk across the polo and cricket fields, further by road. Despite this, a black sedan was waiting outside the club with a chauffeur standing by the rear door.

"Will I see you later?" McNaughton asked as he stepped towards the car.

I shook my head. "I'll get back. Let me know about the murdered policeman—if you find one, that is."

My jeep was still outside the police station. I hadn't commented, but I guessed it wouldn't have been seemly for a chief inspector to arrive at the Jockey Club by jeep. So I strolled back to where I'd parked my car and got in. Then I thought and got out again. Since I was here…

No one questioned my authority as I walked through the staff entrance and down to the typing pool. When I got there, the lady in charge jumped up again.

"Sir?"

"Where does Mrs Srivats live?"

"Sir?"

"I'd like to take her some flowers."

The woman gave me an address and directions to the Brickfields area.

"Sir," she said as I was about to leave, "I have to say that the sanitation isn't that bad."

"I'm sure you're right."

"I just didn't want you to have the wrong impression."

I gave her my business card. "I come from Singapore. I'm sure we have much worse places." I almost said "slums" but stopped myself just in time. However, when I got to the address, a shophouse in Brickfields, I found a respectable, clean street and no smell from the sewers.

The shopkeeper greeted me when I walked in.

"I'm looking for Mrs Anu Srivats," I said.

He bowed. "I'm Karthik Srivats—Anu's husband. How can I help you, sir?"

"I hear she's unwell."

He blinked surprise. "No, sir."

"Then, please could I speak to her?"

"Oh, no, sir. You see she's at work. A typist for the police."

"Yes," I said, "I've just come from the HQ. She's not there. She didn't arrive at work this morning."

"Oh my goodness," he said and steadied himself against a counter, where he took deep, shuddering breaths.

"What's the matter?"

"It's happened," he said, his voice quavering. "She said it would happen and it has."

# FOURTEEN

*February 1947*

When she was seventeen, Andrew Yipp moved Su Ling into a private apartment—the one above the mah-jong bar. He also formally appointed her as his assistant, once her mother's job, although Su Ling was by far the youngest person to have held such a position.

The sex continued, as did her education, and one day he let her negotiate a business transaction.

Beforehand, he said, "All negotiations should start from a position of strength. View it like a battle. You cannot win by starting from weakness. Only negotiate if you have to and never go beyond what you find acceptable."

She talked through the deal, what she would start with and what she would accept, explaining how she justified the numbers. When she finished, she could see she'd done well.

"Good," he said, continuing as he always did once he'd begun a lesson. "It is the same with all human relationships. Start from strength or fear. Respect must be earned. Without this approach, any respect will be false. The underling who does not fear his master will wait until he can overthrow his leader."

"Who would dare try and overthrow you?"

"Zedong."

"Mao Zedong, the man who is likely to become the first head of the People's Republic of China?"

He smiled. "I'm impressed with your political knowledge, Little Flower, but I'm referring to Hua Zedong, my chief lieutenant."

"Then you must deal with him." As she said it she realized her mistake. She'd spoken too frankly, and Yipp was immediately cross by her tone.

She apologized, but she couldn't help smile when Zedong was shot and killed in a clash with a rival gang later that month. A coincidence? Of course not.

She didn't mention it but the subject remained on her mind, and she broached it after sex one night as she massaged his back.

"Tell me again why you married the old goat?"

"Because of her father. The marriage extended my business, not least the control over who could work on the merchant quays."

"Who will take over the business when you have gone?" she asked him.

"That is no concern of yours."

Of course not, she thought. I am a woman, and despite knowing everything there is to know about the multiple operations, Andrew would never consider me as an heir.

"And anyway, I'll live forever," he said. "Or perhaps I'll have a son."

In her training, Su Ling had learned the ancient remedy for preventing pregnancy. She had ensured that her uncle would not give her a child. Now she wondered if that had been a mistake. He was almost fifty years older than her.

"I want to be your wife," she said.

He stared at her for a moment then nodded. "Chenguang will not be my wife forever."

However, three years later, Chenguang's father was still alive, and so was she. And Yipp's attitude towards Su Ling changed. He was visiting her less and she assumed he was seeing other girls. She knew who they were and wasn't concerned, because they were all pleasure girls, and not one of them was special.

He started to ask her to accompany other men for strategic benefit.

"Please don't turn me into a prostitute," she said.

"Of course not! I don't want you to sleep with them, I want you to use your charm and wit for our advantage."

"I am still yours?"

"Only mine."

However, it wasn't long before he asked her to use her womanly wiles to find out information. The men expected sex, and she managed to lead them only so far before letting them down gently with the promise of a future liaison that would never happen.

And then her boss told her to sleep with an American officer.

"Make it good," he said. "I want his balls to ache so much that his mind is jelly."

She took a long breath and forced a smile. "I can do that with a long tease."

"This man will give us access to an American tobacco deal. No, Su Ling, you will have sex with him. It is your duty. And if his mind is not blown, then I will be most displeased."

Being asked to perform these other duties didn't arise often, and she redoubled her efforts within the business to prove her value as an associate rather than a prostitute.

And then Captain Ash Carter appeared on the scene.

Yipp had told her to seduce him. Carter had connections and access to the most senior military personnel and the government. He would become a spy.

But she'd fallen for him. From their second meeting, she'd felt a flutter in her heart that she'd never experienced before. He was intelligent and charming, fit and good-looking. Better than Gary Cooper—or Cary Grant, the latest film star she pictured as she had sex.

Yipp had noticed her feelings for Carter. He knew her too well and had intervened. He'd stopped their relationship before it really got going. And his punishment was to make her date an old man, a recent member of the government, a man called Major Lamb, who'd recently taken charge of Planning and Development.

Yipp said that the man was strategically important, but she knew he wasn't that important. Not so important as to require her services anyway.

She learned that Major Lamb was married but that his wife was sick and was rarely seen in public. So he liked to show off that he could have dinner with the most attractive young women on the island. What other people thought, she didn't know, but it seemed odd since he wasn't especially handsome nor was he particularly rich.

However, she was relieved to discover that he had a secret. "I like other men to be jealous," he said with a wink. "I like them to think I'm bedding beautiful girls like you."

She said nothing, just smiled demurely.

"Don't worry, my dear, it's all for show. Your chastity is safe with me."

★

After Lamb, there had just been one other: Sir Graham Pendall.

"A committee has been established," Andrew Yipp said, "and you will entertain the chairman."

"A committee for what?" she asked.

"A new order is coming."

"New masters, you mean. The British are leaving?"

"In a sense," he said. "There will be an end to colonialism. We'll have a new government—one that truly represents the people."

"Then we are finished."

"Of course not! What they call the underworld will always exist. There is the law and there is the way business works. But first of all, we must influence the new order."

After dinner, Pendall had pawed at her and his climax had been thankfully quick. She hadn't bothered to play *the game* with him and he seemed happy with their brief union.

It'd just happened the one time, and afterwards, Yipp appeared to favour her once more. There had been no mention of it until today, sixteen months later.

"It hurts me when you have to attend to other men," he said.

She could have screamed at him "It hurts *you?* You son of a bitch!" However, she just bit her lip and kept walking.

*Stay calm. It'll soon be over.*

They were in the old factory on Selegie Road. He'd been distant, deep in thought all afternoon. Now she knew why: he was thinking about the times he forced her to sleep with other men.

She found herself daydreaming about Ash. She'd cried for the third time in her life, only this time it had been because of love. True love. Of course, the sex was good, but they had an undeniable bond.

"What?" he said, interrupting the images playing in her head.

"I think it's clean," she said, referring to the factory.

"It's acceptable."

"It cost us good money to move everything." They'd discussed finances again. The final figures for January confirmed a downward trend.

"It was necessary. I told you that."

"Because you think Secretary Norris would have found it?"

"Because I think your Captain Carter would have found it. My sources say that pressure has been applied."

At last, what was on his mind. Su Ling shook her head and spoke calmly. "He's not *my* Captain Carter."

"Really?"

"Honestly," she lied and felt confident he couldn't read her. She'd learned long ago to mask her feelings even from him.

"You aren't seeing Carter?"

"Against your wishes? Of course not."

He placed an arm on hers. "Tonight."

She knew the implication. Wednesday night and his wife would be occupied with her friends. Mrs Yipp knew about them and yet he continued to pretend Su Ling wasn't his mistress.

Su Ling took a breath. "It is my red moon, Uncle."

The expression on his face suggested he was trying to work out the timing.

"If you are lying to me…"

"Of course not! Now about this other thing. You've moved the operation and cleaned the factory, but I have a cunning plan." And so she told him something that made him salivate like a dog.

# FIFTEEN

*Wednesday 3rd February 1954*

The shopkeeper sat on a chair and looked at me like I'd sucker-punched him.

"What do you mean, 'It's happened'?"

"Where is she?" he asked quietly.

I placed a hand on his shoulder and he blinked at me. "Could you tell me what you know, please, Karthik?"

"She left for work this morning at the usual time—seven forty. It was just like any other day."

"Perhaps it is just any other day," I said, trying to reassure him. "Perhaps this *thing* she was afraid of hasn't happened."

Again he blinked at me, and desperation turned to hope in his eyes.

I said, "Tell me what she was afraid of."

"She was afraid something might happen to her... Someone might..." He lost his voice and sucked at his lips.

"Karthik?"

He took a shuddering breath and then blew out the air. "Kill her."

"Someone might kill her?"

"Yes." He shook his head. "No one has killed her, have they, sir?"

"Why would someone want to kill her?"

"Erm… Because of what she knew."

"What did she know?"

Again he blew out air. "She wouldn't tell me everything. When she realized it was dangerous she stopped gossiping."

I nodded. "You told your friend in Singapore, Peter Jihan."

"Yes."

"About the deaths around KL. About the killer."

"Yes. And the policeman."

I shook my head. "The killer didn't murder a policeman."

"No, but Anu wouldn't tell me anything else. She was worried and said we shouldn't talk about it, but by then I had already told my friends."

"Tell me about the policeman," I said.

"I think he was investigating one of the murders, that's all I know."

I waited for him to say more, but he didn't, so I prompted: "Your wife thought the policeman was murdered because he investigated the other murder. He discovered something?"

"I do not know, sir."

"And she was afraid that she knew that same thing?"

Mr Srivats said nothing. Blank eyes looked back at me.

Thinking out loud, I continued: "She was worried someone would find out what she knew."

Still the blank eyes.

I realized I'd learn nothing more from this man and eased him to his feet.

"Come on, it could be a mistake. Perhaps something innocent happened on the way to work this morning. Perhaps she's been waylaid." It didn't sound convincing to me, but he accepted my words.

He said, "She might have gone to visit her sister, or"—he shook his head—"Goodness! What if she's had an accident?"

"You should check with family and then check the hospitals," I said. "If she's not there then report that she's missing to the police."

"But what if... the police?"

"You're worried about the police? All right, *I'll* report her missing."

He bowed and shook my hand. "Thank you, sir."

I left him with a business card and drove back to the police headquarters. Without reference to her concerns, I told the desk sergeant about Mrs Srivats's disappearance. Then I drove round to the government building, hoping to give McNaughton an update, but he wasn't available. His assistant had no idea how long my friend would be busy, so I left a message about Mrs Srivats and set off for Singapore.

★

The first hour of the drive went by before I started feeling tired. Spending nights with Su Ling meant that I wasn't getting enough sleep. I must have been running on adrenaline for days, and now the monotony of the journey made me regret the long drive.

I kept myself focused by trying to remember the kampongs along the route. I guessed the distance and counted as I drove. The distraction worked until I was about halfway and had to stop.

I found a village where they sold me a cup of tea with sugar. Ten minutes later, the sugar did its work and I started to perk up. After buying a pair of chickens—which they insisted I choose before they were strangled—I set off again.

When the clouds burst, I kept the roof down and let the rain pound my face. Once the clouds passed and the sun appeared, steam rose throughout the jungle and my clothes soon dried out.

The light was fading as I hit the causeway and again jumped the queue. Once past Woodlands, I drove hard all the way down the island into the city.

I'd previously tried to insist that Madam Chau finish before 7 pm each day, but whenever I went away, she contended that she needed to be there. "In case you need me," she said, and, "To make sure everything is all right." If I ever stayed away, she waited until I reported in.

I drove back to the office and arrived shortly before eight. The office lights were on. Madam Chau was waiting for me.

As I came through the front door she cleared her throat as though warning me she was still there.

"I brought you chickens," I said, flopping the dead birds on her desk.

"Thank you," she said, without expression in her tone. "You're later than you said you'd be."

I had told her I'd expected to return by the end of the day, but I didn't bother arguing.

"Well thank you for being here."

She raised her eyebrows.

"What's wrong, Madam Chau?"

"Secretary Norris has been on the warpath. He wanted to get hold of you."

"You explained I was in KL?"

"Yes, and I tried calling you there. Chief Inspector McNaughton wasn't available either."

"What did Secretary Norris want?"

"I don't know, but he made me promise that you'd see him first thing. I made an appointment for you at eight am in his private office. Tell me you'll be there."

"I'll be there."

"Good," she said, standing. "And thank you for the chickens."

This time I detected real appreciation in her voice and I think she almost gave me a smile. Then again, perhaps that was my imagination.

★

Before midnight, I was in Su Ling's secret apartment on Hock Lam Street. While I waited, I lay on the bed and closed my eyes as waves of tiredness washed over me.

How long I'd been asleep, I had no idea, but I jolted awake as I realized someone was leaning over me.

Su Ling kissed me again and I relaxed into the warmth of her lips.

"What time is it?" I asked when our embrace ended.

"Half past twelve."

No wonder I felt groggy. Just a few minutes of deep sleep.

She kissed me again and I started to unzip her dress, but then her hand stopped me.

"What is it?"

She pulled away. "I'm really sorry. I can't stay."

"You can't…?"

She nodded, and I thought she was about to cry.

"What is it, Su Ling?"

"Andrew is suspicious," she said, sitting up. "I'm sure he thinks I'm seeing someone."

"You are." As soon as the words left my lips I regretted them.

"It's too dangerous, Ash. We are so close to getting away."

"Four more nights…"

We went over the plan again and agreed to meet in Pope's warehouse on Alkaff Quay no later than 4 am, the morning after the celebrations. I would fly to Manila two days later, she would meet me at the airport and we would get the next flight out, and then keep moving.

After she'd left, I lay on the bed staring up, trying not to think about Su Ling with Yipp—but thinking of nothing else. Lights from the activity outside played hypnotically on the ceiling, and I must have fallen asleep because when I woke up the sun already warmed the roofs.

I snuck down the back staircase and out onto the street, conscious of the daylight and my conspicuous presence. However, it was a short road and I was soon in the government sector and jogging back to my apartment on Beach Road.

After a shower and change of suit, I headed back to the government sector and the white Georgian building where Secretary Norris had his office.

The same old Malay butler answered when I used the silver knocker. He bowed curtly and led me down a corridor, and parquet flooring clicked under my shoes. The large oil paintings and expensive-looking ornaments hadn't changed with the change of secretary, but the office had. When Coates had been here, the room felt like a cosy private library with the smell of leather and cigar smoke and polish.

Norris had a large teak desk with a leather inlay and bankers lamp. He'd changed the wall paintings from the landscapes Coates had preferred to African animals, a giant elephant having pride of place over the mantelpiece.

Coates had wingback chairs whereas Norris had two Chesterfield sofas. Normally the new secretary would point to one and we'd sit opposite one another.

Today he just glowered at me as I entered.

"Where have you been, Carter?"

He stood up from his desk chair and made no further move.

I glanced at the elephant, which had its ears out: a warning rather than a real threat. Ears out made them look larger, intimidating. If they were about to charge, they flattened their ears.

The secretary's ears were back. His ears didn't stick out but today they appeared flatter than usual.

"I believe my receptionist informed you of my visit to KL," I said calmly. For whatever reason, he was trying to intimidate me, and it wouldn't work.

He leaned forward, placing his hands on the leather inlay, and glared at me.

"I asked you to do a job."

"You did, and I will do it. I will investigate Yipp. I had other plans yesterday."

"What were you doing in KL?"

"Investigating the Chinese gold case."

He continued to glare, and I swear that his moustache twitched.

"I asked Colonel Ambrose at Gillman. He said you weren't working for him yesterday. You weren't officially investigating."

I shrugged. "I'm a free agent."

He shook his head. "That's not the deal, Carter. You investigate Yipp and you get him."

"I said I—"

He cut me off. "What you say and what you do are two different things. I'm paying you treble."

"You said you'd pay treble if I solved your problem, sir." I kept my voice calm despite the tension I felt radiating towards me.

He took his hands from the desk and straightened, then surprised me by smiling. Was he playing a game with me?

"There's an added incentive," he said.

I waited, expecting him to offer a larger fee.

"You get Yipp and then I won't arrest his assistant."

"Pardon?"

"The pretty girl. What's her name—Su Ling Yong?"

I forced my surprise into an expression of confusion. "What's she got to do with it?"

"Motivation," Norris said.

"I don't understand."

"Additional motivation for you, Carter. You want to get your little lady on a boat. You get Yipp, and I won't get her."

# SIXTEEN

*Thursday 4th February*

I couldn't believe it. How the hell did Norris know about my plans?

"Who told you?"

Secretary Norris smiled and shook his head. "That's not the point, Carter. The point is this: you'd better get working on Yipp's case."

I tried to act nonchalant and calmed my breathing. He was still smiling, but my mind was working now. "So you'll arrest Su Ling for what?" I asked. "If you can't arrest Yipp, what will you charge his assistant with?"

He leaned forward again and his smile turned into a smirk. "Anything. Everything. It doesn't matter. Fair is foul and foul is fair"—he quoted from Macbeth—"and what matters is that arresting her will thwart your plans. I need you motivated, Carter, and if this doesn't work then nothing will."

I took a long breath, stepped back and turned away from the rogue elephant.

"You've got a week, Carter," he said as I headed for the door. "Get me results and all will be well. Otherwise…"

If he said anything else, it was lost behind the closed office door.

There was only one person who could have told Secretary Norris about my plans, and that was Arthur Pope.

I charged over to the Singapore Club and found him eating a hearty breakfast.

"Do join me," he said, waving me over as I marched to his regular table by the window. Security scuttled behind me, but Pope shooed them away.

"How could you?" I said, feeling rage well up in my chest.

"My dear chap, please calm down and explain." He indicated the chair opposite but I remained standing.

"You told Secretary Norris."

"I beg your pardon!"

I lowered my voice. "Someone told Norris about my plan to get away with my girl. He knows, and I discussed it with no one but you."

He blinked surprise. "No, no, no! I assure you that I would do no such thing."

"Then how did he know?"

Pope shook his head. "Please sit."

"I thought you were a friend, someone I could trust," I hissed through my teeth. "Now I realize you're nothing but an old gossip."

I spun on my heels and marched out of the club.

It took me a good thirty minutes in the boxing gym before the red mist cleared and I thought things through. Firstly, Arthur Pope had seemed genuinely surprised. I doubt he was a good actor and I had believed he'd keep my confidence.

What had Secretary Norris said? "You want to get your little lady on a boat." He knew about Su Ling, but then my previous liaison with her hadn't been a secret. I did not doubt that Norris's predecessor had maintained a file on me. Norris would have known about my interest in the girl and the tensions between me and Yipp.

Madam Chau had suspected I was seeing her, maybe Norris did as well. Or it could have been a wild punt.

*Get her on a boat.* I interpreted that as getting her on Pope's Japanese junk—and escaping. But he hadn't provided any detail.

He'd been deliberately vague, and my reactions had told him everything he needed to know.

And then there was the other thing.

Norris had given me a week to get Yipp. A week. If he'd known my plans he wouldn't have given me more than three days.

I felt wretched, and after showering, I returned to the Singapore Club.

The security men barred my entry this time and I figured my previous visit had made me persona non grata.

"Please take a message to Mr Arthur Pope," I begged. "Tell him I was mistaken. Tell him I'm sorry."

The message was carefully written onto a card before a bellboy disappeared with it into the lounge. Two minutes later the boy returned and nodded to the guards. They stepped aside and I was led through the lounge towards the smoking room. Unlike before, I glanced around and noted most faces watching me. At least two members deliberately avoided eye contact.

As I approached, Pope folded a newspaper, put it down, looked up and scowled.

"Forgive me," I began, "I've been a fool."

His eyes were like hot coals. "Yes, you have."

"You wouldn't betray me."

"Of course not!"

"May I take a seat?"

"Only if you have a drink." Pope signalled for the waiter to bring two stengahs, and I perched on the chair beside him. Then, whispering, I explained what had happened and why I assumed Norris had been told.

"How did he guess?" Pope whispered back when I finished.

"I must have given it away. When he mentioned Su Ling I panicked. And the most obvious thing—"

His eyes narrowed, not understanding.

"Members here."

"But I didn't tell anyone!"

"You didn't need to. When I walked through the lounge most members looked at me. It's natural to at least glance at someone walking by. Those who didn't—well, I think there was a good reason."

"I don't follow."

"Members of the government."

"Ah!"

"They saw me visit you here and then told Norris. I think Norris put two and two together. He guessed I'd called on you for a reason—and then I confirmed his suspicions."

Pope took a casual drink and used the moment to look around. I'd been doing the same as we spoke and was certain we were being watched. With our voices low, however, they wouldn't hear our conversation.

I said, "We stick with the plan, but with one variation."

Pope waited.

I dropped my voice even lower. "You just take the girl. The morning after the carnival, you take her. I'll keep working and Norris won't suspect she's gone."

Pope nodded and we spoke some more until I was about to leave. A little louder, hoping to be overheard, I said, "One week."

I apologized once more for my error and rudeness and Pope shook my hand.

"Not a problem, dear chap. However, you owe me at least one juicy story as a result."

★

After visiting my office so that Madam Chau knew where I'd be, I went to the government building and ostentatiously pulled all the files on Yipp and anyone vaguely connected.

Secretary Norris walked past the room where I had papers strewn over a desk and a map of Singapore city pinned to the wall. He did a double-take like he hadn't expected to see me in there, but I was certain it was an act. Someone will have told him what I was doing. And I'd wanted them to.

"Working hard, Carter?"

"Yes," I said flatly. "Trying to link crimes to his known associates and employees."

Norris nodded.

"And after this, I'll review the police records too," I added.

Norris pulled a smile that looked so smug I felt like introducing it to my fist. However, I just smiled back.

"We'll get him."

"I'm sure you will. I'm sure you will," he said and strode away—no doubt with that look still plastered on his smug face.

An hour later, I tidied the desk and made it clear that I would be returning. Then, with the map under my arm and a pile of notes, I walked over to the police headquarters on Hill Street.

My liaison there was a man called Inspector Ishaan Singh, a friendly chap with a ready smile and a pocket full of boiled sweets. His round face split into a grin as we met.

"Captain Carter, oh Captain Carter!" he exclaimed like I was the very person he was looking for. "What a pleasure."

"I'm here on business," I said. "Working for the charming Secretary Norris."

Singh frowned, probably just mimicking my sour expression at the mention of the politician's name.

"How can I be of service?" he said with a bob of the head.

"Yipp," I said. "I need you to arrest Andrew Yipp."

# SEVENTEEN

Inspector Singh's nerves showed as sweat broke out on his forehead.

"It won't be easy," he said, after gauging that I was being serious.

"No, it won't."

"What do you want me to do?"

"Good old-fashioned policing," I said. "We go through the records and we catch him out."

"Drugs?"

"Unlikely we'll get him for that, especially now he's legitimately supplying the British Army."

"Racketeering, then."

I nodded and waited for him to act. Finally, he took a breath and solemnly led me to the records room. We signed in and took the ledgers of recorded crimes dating back to the end of the occupation.

The subterranean room had a dim light and no air. We turned pages and read entries and names, then pulled files and read the details of the crime.

After two hours, Singh wiped his forehead on a handkerchief and moaned, "I'm sweating more than a tart in a church. Can we stop for the day and carry on tomorrow?"

I opened up the map and drew the areas of Yipp's implied control. Two sectors stood out, small areas that appeared to be islands surrounded by Yipp's influence. I'd discovered this when I investigated Yipp's activities more than sixteen months ago. It wasn't where he operated, it was about where he didn't operate—or didn't appear to.

However, I kept my thoughts to myself for the time being. I left the map with the inspector and said we'd resume again in the morning.

I spent another uncomfortable night without Su Ling and couldn't help wondering where she was and what she was doing. Was she with Yipp? Of course, I had no answers but spent most of the night with negative thoughts and fears spinning around in my mind.

In the morning, I trained and then popped into my office. After quickly reviewing messages and yesterday's letters with Madam Chau, I called into the government office and spent a couple of hours shuffling papers and making sure people noticed me working, before going to Hill Street Station.

Singh hadn't started without me, and again I sensed his reluctance. However, we spent the rest of the morning in the sweltering dungeon, during which he devoured a packet of boiled sweets that smelled of strawberries.

"When are you going to tell me about the map?" he asked as we ate lunch.

"Now. I marked the areas where I think Yipp has most influence."

He nodded, his mouth full of noodles.

I said, "We should walk around and visit crime scenes."

He swallowed his mouthful with exaggeration. "Or we could do more research here. What are we looking for?"

"I don't know, but good old-fashioned policing means pounding the beat."

He didn't say anything for a while, and behind his small eyes, I saw him calculating. "You want to be seen," he finally said.

"Of course."

"Are you sure that's sensible?"

"Yes."

"You play poker," he said. "It feels like you're showing your hand too early."

If I had been serious about uncovering crimes, Singh would have been right. But I wasn't. I wanted to be seen doing the job. I figured Norris would like me out on the streets.

We started walking towards the docks and then up and down the streets through Chinatown. A lion dance troupe entertained crowds on Chin Chew Street and we watched their antics for a while.

This wasn't the location I wanted to explore, but with so many people around, we certainly got noticed. Singh, in his uniform, received a few aggressive stares, but on the whole, the mood was good, with people getting ready for New Year festivities.

The *Padang* was almost covered with tents, stalls and displays, and we caught a trishaw and travelled past the fair to the east of town. The two areas I was most interested in were north of the Cathay Building where Yipp had his office and a wedge east of Princep Street and below Selegie Road.

We began at Princep Street and were soon walking through slums where washing was strung window to window across roads that left dust on our boots.

Here I saw faces slack with exhaustion or drugs, and yet the streets were filled with children running and chasing hoops or kicking cans.

It felt like we had returned to civilization when we appeared on Albert Street. Immediately, a black Austin 7 shot past, squealed to a halt and came back to us.

A police driver leaned out of the window. "Inspector, the chief would like a word, sir."

"I'm wanted at the HQ?"

I heard relief in his voice, and as soon as the driver confirmed, Singh was climbing into the rear of the Austin.

"Coming with me, Ash?"

I checked my watch: mid-afternoon. Still too much day left, so I declined the offer of a drive home.

"Same again tomorrow?" I asked.

He couldn't help himself. At the same time as he agreed, his mouth turned down with disappointment.

I watched the police car drive away and circled back through the slums. This was one of the sections I'd drawn on the map because of the crimes, but I was interested in the space between this wedge of town and the one north of the Cathay Building.

Perhaps if I'd gone to the other part of town I would have been fine. But I didn't. There was an area near Short Street—a row of factories—that I found particularly intriguing. Oddly, there was never any crime around there, and I wanted to know why.

I didn't last long before two identically dressed Chinese men in brown suits stepped out onto the pavement, barring my way.

They said nothing and I stepped left to avoid them.

They moved left.

I sidestepped right and they blocked my way again.

I opened my hands in a gesture of surprise. "Can I help you?"

The men looked at me with dull eyes, unfriendly but equally uncommunicative.

"You want me to go back?"

No response.

I heard a car, and my peripheral vision picked out a dark green shape. I didn't look because I wanted my eyes on the two guys in front of me.

A second later I regretted that decision. Before I could turn at the sound of footsteps behind me, I felt a gun jabbed in my spine.

The goons in front took this as a signal to pull their guns.

"Whoa," I said, raising my hands, "I'm just passing through and I'll be on my way."

"Shut up and get in the car," the man behind me growled. The gun jammed harder into my back, and I now turned and saw that the green car alongside us was a Humber Hawk. Its doors were open and there was a man inside.

I recognized him: Wang, Andrew Yipp's henchman—the man he used for his dirty deeds.

# EIGHTEEN

At gunpoint in the back of the Humber Hawk, I was driven to an industrial region in a sector between Rochor River and Kallang River.

Yipp had a warehouse out there where the ground was barren and the air smelled of diesel. I'd been there before when I first investigated Yipp and had seen his labourers repackaging cargo and loading sacks into wagons.

Wang was on my right and one of the goons in the brown suits was on my left. Three of us crammed along the rear seat with both men aiming guns at me. The man on my left had his weapon in his left hand but it was his wrong hand. On the street, both goons had held guns in their right.

"Is this a meeting with Mr Yipp?" I asked casually, wondering if I had any options. I could snatch the gun from the man on my left. Would Wang react fast enough?

I looked at him.

Wang said nothing, his eyes cold and dead.

After a gate, we stopped outside Yipp's warehouse and the goons got out.

Now Wang spoke. "Move!" he said.

"Is Mr Yipp inside?"

"You're lucky he isn't."

"Why?"

"Get out!"

I slid across the seat, my eyes on Wang, and eased out of the car.

Wang and the driver got out on the opposite side and Wang nodded to the Judas gate in the warehouse doors.

"Through there?"

"Move!" he growled.

One of the brown suits went first and then I was pushed through to find him aiming his pistol at my head.

"Give me an excuse," he said with a heavy accent.

I stepped aside and the other three men came in. Then I was pushed into the first of several offices set against the side wall.

As I entered, I deliberately stumbled and went down. I planned to pull the Beretta from my ankle holster, but before I could complete the move, Wang leapt forward with the agility of a cat and stepped on my hand.

"Take his gun," he snapped at one of the goons, and my Beretta was soon in another man's hand. Wang ground his heel on my fingers and then stepped back.

Grey light filtered through darkened windows and I looked up at his leering face.

"What's this about?" I said, rubbing my crushed hand.

"You want to die?" Wang asked, snarling.

I looked at four guns pointed at me, shook my head and started to stand.

"Down!" he snapped like I was a dog. "Stay down!"

I squatted on the floor. "There's been some kind of a mistake," I said, hoping I sounded calmer than I felt.

"No mistake."

"I was just walking. I didn't mean…"

Wang spat. "Shut up. Do you think this is about your pathetic investigations? This is about you and Miss Yong."

"Su Ling? What about—?"

"Don't deny your interest. She is Mr Yipp's *niece*"— the way he said it gave double meaning; he knew she was more than an adopted niece—"and you do not choose to *see* her." Again the double meaning. I briefly wondered why he didn't just come out and say "have sex with" or something cruder. Maybe it was for the benefit of the goons.

"I'm not," I lied while trying to assess the situation. I thought Wang had picked me up because of my task from Norris. What did he know about me and Su Ling? She certainly wouldn't have told him.

Wang signalled for the goons to close in, an implied threat of violence. "You were seen in the vicinity of her apartment on Hock Lam Street."

I shook my head at the ridiculousness of the comment. "It's a small city."

"Early in the morning. You stayed with her. Don't deny it."

I was sure he didn't know. He was fishing. I'd made the mistake with Norris, believing he knew my plans, and I wasn't going to make the same mistake again.

Wang waited for my admission. When none came, he motioned for his men to move again.

I knew what was coming and sprang to my feet, hands up ready to block and punch. Three against one in a confined area.

At first, I held my own and knocked two down but they were soon up again, ducking below my punches and favouring kicks, which I struggled to defend against.

When a savage kick caught my right knee, I crumpled and Wang laughed. They were upon me then, like wild animals on a wounded prey. Instinctively, I curled and protected my vital organs, my hands covering my head.

I'd fought Wang and his goons when we first met. Su Ling had intervened then. I'd also been locked in this room before too and Su Ling had come to my rescue with a key. As the blows rained down, I held out a vain hope that she would again.

She didn't stop them.
No one came.

# NINETEEN

Did Yipp know she was lying to him? Did he know about Ash? Did he know about the plans? Su Ling had watched him all day and he'd given nothing away. Wang, on the other hand, had made a strange comment first thing.

He was on his way out and said, "Enjoying yourself?"

It wasn't like someone asking if you were having fun because of the New Year. It was more like someone saying, "I know what you're up to."

If he knew about the apartment on Hock Lam Street, why not say so?

She kept herself busy but couldn't help returning to the question. Did Wang know? Did Yipp know?

At the end of the day, Yipp called her into his room.

"I'm going to visit you tonight."

"It's still my red moon—as you know, it can last for days."

"I don't care."

Her mind spun. How could she get out of this? "But it's Friday, not a mah-jong night."

"I don't care," he said again. "Chenguang knows. She's known for years."

He didn't call her the old goat, Su Ling noted.

Then it came to her and she spoke confidently. "I have a date with Sir Graham Pendall."

"Why?"

She stopped him, held his arm and looked earnest. "His reward. You remember I slept with him to influence the commission's recommendations?"

"Of course."

"I promised I would do so again, once he delivered."

Yipp's jaw tensed and she knew he was assessing the truth of her statement. It was reasonable, he would realize that.

"You should have sought my agreement first."

"You are right, and I apologize. I'd forgotten about the promise."

"Delay him."

"We need the recommendations enacted. We need him to follow through and deliver."

"Hmm," Yipp said, and she knew the argument was almost won.

"And remember, it's my red moon," she said, "so I won't actually sleep with him."

"Then he won't be satisfied."

She kissed Andrew Yipp on the cheek. "Don't worry, Uncle, he'll be satisfied."

★

Su Ling had asked her assistant, Jinjing, to call Sir Graham Pendall and set up the appointment. However, Pendall hadn't been available and Su Ling then told Jinjing to call Major Lamb. But he declined because of a prior engagement.

Su Ling had panicked, fearing that Yipp would discover her lie, but then Pendall had called back. He'd immediately agreed to a liaison and said they should have dinner at Raffles.

She arrived fashionably late and wore an attractive yet unrevealing dress.

"I was thrilled to hear from you," Pendall said.

"I promised I would."

He grinned lasciviously, causing a knot inside her stomach.

"I have a room booked upstairs," he whispered after his first glass of Burgundy.

"I'm afraid…"

He looked crestfallen at first and then confused.

"But, my dear… your promise."

"I wanted to see you," she lied with an alluring smile. "We are very pleased with the outcome of the review and I just wanted to ensure you knew it was appreciated."

"But…"

"It's that time of the month."

"Ah…"

After the first bottle of wine, he ventured: "We could do other things. It would be a shame to let the room go to waste."

Su Ling batted her eyes. "Perhaps. But let's enjoy this meal and your company first, my lord."

They talked about everything except for politics, which he no doubt considered beneath her, and she plied him with more and more wine.

Finally, she could delay it no longer, and when he took her arm, she found herself propelled towards the stairs.

"I've had a delightful evening," she said outside his room.

"And it's not over yet." With an ungentlemanly push, he had her inside and his hands on her breasts. Soon they were over her stomach and then on her buttocks. The man had hands like an octopus.

When he started to lick her neck, she pushed him away and held him at arm's length.

He was practically drooling.

"Darling Graham," she said, "not like this."

"But…"

"Isn't it more exciting to woo a girl? Isn't the tease better than reality?"

A baffled expression crossed his eyes and she guessed the wine was having an effect—especially the last one where she'd slipped in a little something extra.

"You are tired," she whispered, moving back in, "let me ease your tension."

He grinned, thinking she meant something sexual, but she didn't. Coaxing him onto the bed, she removed his clothes down to his underwear and began massaging his neck and back.

"Is this good?" she asked. "Better to enjoy this and imagine tomorrow."

"Tomorrow?" he asked groggily.

"I'll see you tomorrow. Hopefully, my red moon will have passed."

"Yes," he mumbled.

"But you still have to woo me."

Whether her words registered, she didn't know, because he was now asleep.

She slipped out of the hotel and flagged a taxi to take her to her official home above the mah-jong bar. A trishaw started immediately afterwards and followed. She glanced through the rear window and knew he was tailing her. There was no one in the back. No genuine trishaw rider would leave Raffles without a passenger. However, despite the streetlights, she couldn't see the man's face. Not until she got out of the taxi and saw him pull up near the mah-jong bar.

He was one of Wang's men.

# TWENTY

When you're beaten like that, you feel the initial blows, each agonizing contact. Kidneys, legs, arms and head— but mostly the kidneys. It was far worse than any punches I'd taken in the boxing ring.

When I was fighting, Sammy, my first boxing coach, had taught me to ignore the incoming pain. A punch by the opponent usually meant there was an opening for a counter. Ignore the pain.

Although I had no chance to counter-attack, I could still imagine being in the ring. Bob and weave and counter. Immediately, I was back in the boxing gym in Manchester where I'd learned to fight. I was getting a pounding from a bigger kid and I could hear Sammy screaming at me from the ropes in his harsh accent.

What was that kid called? Buster, that's right. A bully with a hard punch and dirty tricks.

"Bob, weave, counter!" Sammy shouted.

It worked. I rolled with Buster's punch to my cheek and caught him with a left hook that took him down. I'd ached for days after that fight, but it had been the moment Sammy had decided I'd be one of his best fighters. He imagined I'd be a professional one day and I still remember his face when I told him I was off to university.

"I want a proper career," I said, and later regretted that I hadn't let him down more gently. A hard Liverpudlian with the skin of a rhinoceros, I thought. I'd been wrong. And I'd not only let him down but I'd joined the army then left to become a freelance investigator. Proper career? It was a good job Sammy didn't know.

While I was thinking about my old coach, it suddenly registered that the beating had stopped and there was silence.

I opened an eye and blinked rapidly before I realized it was dark rather than a problem with my sight.

This was later, much later, and I was alone.

I gripped the wall to pull myself up and breathed with relief. My body felt like it had been through a meat grinder, but nothing was broken.

My gun was on the floor. I tried to pick it up with my left hand but the pain stopped me, so I switched to my right. It wasn't loaded.

I looked through a crack in a window and could just make out the yard in front of the warehouse. No green Humber Hawk. Wang and his men had beaten me until I'd lost consciousness and then left.

Wracked with pain, I edged towards the door expecting to find it locked. It wasn't, and I slowly made my way across the warehouse and out into the yard.

A sliver of moon gave no light, but an orange glow from the street helped me find a stick that I could use as a crutch so I could stagger to Kallang Road. Home was less than three miles away but I couldn't walk that far. I flagged down the first car that came down the road and shocked the driver at the state of me.

He wanted to take me to the Alexandra Hospital but I insisted that he drop me at my place on Beach Road.

★

The sun rose on Saturday 6th February and I stayed in bed. In fact, it was midday by the time I decided to venture outside, walking stiffly but still grateful that everything still worked.

I took a ride to the office, where Madam Chau immediately berated me for not telling her where I'd been. Then she looked at me properly and gasped.

"I'm all right," I assured her as she flapped around me. "I'm all right."

"You've been in a fight," she said, stating the obvious.

I smiled. "You should have seen the other man."

"Did you kill him?"

"I'm joking."

She didn't laugh.

"There were four of them. Yipp's men."

She gasped again. "I warned you, Master Carter."

"I should have listened to you, Madam Chau."

She nodded firmly, like I'd stated one of the universal truths, and then busied herself making me sweetened tea. Once I was sitting with my drink, she fussed around me, checking my bruises, then said she'd be back within the hour.

While she was gone, I read my post and messages. The one that interested me the most was a call I'd received from Karthik Srivats, the husband of the police typist.

The message simply said that his wife was still missing. There was no number, so I would be unable to call him back.

Since returning to Singapore, I'd been so distracted with my plans and diversionary tactics that I'd forgotten about the Chinese gold case and the missing typist.

What had happened to Mrs Srivats, and was it connected with the case?

When Madam Chau returned, I asked her to place a call to Chief Inspector McNaughton, but she had something more important to do first.

I'd had one of her Chinese medicine poultices before, only this time she'd made a pot of it and insisted on smearing it on all of the bruises she could see and then those she couldn't.

My lower back caused the most discomfort and I raised my shirt so that she could administer the cream. However, that's where I drew the line, and I refused to let her see the state of my legs.

After promising that I would use the cream myself, she retreated and placed the call to Kuala Lumpur.

McNaughton wasn't available but I spoke to his apologetic assistant. The man didn't have an update for me when I asked so I left a message reminding McNaughton about the dead policeman.

"Now you go home and rest," Madam Chau said. She leaned out of a window, shouted down below, and then turned her attention back to me.

"There's a trishaw waiting outside. Go straight home. I will visit you later."

I thought about protesting, but her scowl deterred me.

So I eased myself down the stairs—much harder, I found, than climbing them—and got into the trishaw. However, rather than home, I instructed the rider to take me to Secretary Norris's office.

Ten minutes later, Norris welcomed me into his private room.

"Good God, man, what happened?"

"Yipp's men beat me up."

Norris leapt out of his chair. "Then we've got him!"

"Not Yipp. He wasn't there. It was four of his men. You can't pin this on Yipp."

Norris sat down, frowning.

I said, "It was a message."

"A message?"

"Telling me to keep away."

"You think you're getting close? I heard you had a map and were out looking at locations with Inspector Singh."

Of course you did, I thought, smiling inwardly.

I nodded. "We were looking at the location of reported crimes and trying to connect them to Yipp's activities. My theory is that we don't catch him for one of the old crimes, we find something he's doing now that he hasn't been caught for."

"Like what?" His eyes gleamed with anticipation.

"I don't know. I'm working on it. I have five more days, right?"

"Yes."

"Good. I need to rest now, but hopefully I'll be well enough tomorrow and we'll start again. We'll find something that reveals his criminal activity."

"Good man."

"Sir," I said, being obsequious, "Could you tell me one thing in return. It's been bothering me."

"What is it?"

"How did you find out about me and the girl?"

"You gave it away. I read your face."

"But before that? I know Arthur Pope didn't tell you," I said.

He tapped his nose. "Walls have ears, Carter. Walls have ears. And remember, you only have five days left."

★

So I'd been right. Someone at the Singapore Club had told Norris about my meetings with Pope and he had no idea she would be leaving the island so soon.

I applied Madam Chau's strange poultice and slept for the rest of the afternoon, disturbed only when my receptionist called at my door.

She'd brought me chicken broth and heated it on my little stove before leaving me with instructions to stay in bed and rest tomorrow too.

I took her advice because I needed my strength. Tomorrow would be the New Year's Day parade, and in the early hours afterwards, I'd smuggle Su Ling off the island.

# TWENTY-ONE

*Saturday 6th February*

Su Ling had an organization chart spread out on her desk. "I've mapped out every official role," she said to Andrew Yipp.

"You haven't told me about your date last night."

"Do you want to know the graphic details?" She knew he didn't.

"I'll come to your apartment tonight."

"Again, it's the wrong day."

"I told you, I don't care anymore."

"There are two more reasons. It's still my red moon and I promised I'd see Pendall again."

"Why?"

"Because we didn't do anything yesterday."

Yipp knew what she meant, but looked less than convinced. "I hope you haven't got feelings for the old man."

"How could I love someone with a penis that looks like a strangled turkey?"

"Doesn't every man's look the same?"

"Of course not! The rest look like strangled chickens… unless they're this big." She held her finger and thumb about two inches apart and Yipp laughed. He knew she didn't mean him.

Then he asked, "And mine?"

"A swan," she lied, knowing he'd like the reference to its length and remembering what her sex teacher had told her. *Massage his ego. Tell him he has a big cock.*

He said, "Why are you smiling?"

"In a good way—thinking of you."

"When you are with other men, remember you are mine," he said.

"Of course. They can only have my body."

He nodded then looked at the chart on her desk. "Why have you done this?"

Always the businessman.

"It's useful. I can see the seven arms of your empire."

"Except for the illegal ones—most of those men are off the books."

"Of course, but it's important to see who has authority and who is coming up. Succession is important."

"I suppose." He pointed to the chart, touching his name and then Su Ling's, which was off at the side. "Who is *your* successor?"

"Jinjing."

"Really? She's too young."

"I was seventeen when I took over in the role. She's almost nineteen."

"But you are special."

"Thank you, but I'm not saying she is ready, just that I will help her develop." She pointed to the seven lieutenants, the ones heading each division. "Every one of these men should have a successor... in case one dies."

"You know the way it works... if one gets killed then there will be another who naturally fills his shoes. That's the way it's always been."

"But what if that man gets the job for the wrong reason?"

"Like what?"

"For being a thug. We need business leaders and managers, not thugs."

He scrutinized her. "I'm not stupid," he said. "Don't treat me as such."

"I apologize. I just don't like him."

He shook his head. "Wang is not a problem. He's loyal."

"I'm sure you are right, but there are many dead kings who believed their successors were loyal. All I ask is that you watch him. Just be prepared."

"I'm always prepared." He walked away from her desk but then turned back. "And make sure you satisfy Pendall's strangled chicken tonight."

★

She met Pendall for dinner at Raffles again and went through the same routine. Afterwards, he managed to get her into the bedroom and tried to press himself on her. He forced her onto the bed and got his hand between her legs. She could feel his erection through his clothes and knew then that he'd somehow avoided the potion she'd slipped in his last glass of wine.

She remembered his bony elbows from two years ago when he'd climbed on top.

His hand moved higher, forcing between her thighs, touching her knickers.

"It's not finished," she said calmly.

"Eh?"

"My lady's problem. Almost, but not quite."

"I don't mind." He drooled on her neck and his pawing pulled her dress away, revealing a breast.

"Slow down," she said and slipped a leg between his.

He was panting now.

She raised her knee and used a move that Chichi, the sex teacher, had shown her when a man is taking his weight on one arm. She flipped him onto his back. But rather than roll on top, she rolled off the bed and stood up.

"No!" she said.

He looked startled at her firm tone, but then he smiled when she placed a hand on his member that pushed up under his trousers like a tent pole.

"Tomorrow, my love, I promise."

"Not now? But I ache so much I could burst."

She kissed her fingers then touched his bulge.

"Tomorrow I will make you burst like never before. Hold on one more night. Let's do it and enjoy the New Year's celebrations together."

Without waiting for his agreement, she straightened her dress and walked out of the room.

Outside, she checked for the trishaw but didn't see one follow. However, when she asked to be dropped at the end of the road and walked to the mah-jong bar, she thought she saw two of Wang's goons loitering, watching.

One more day, she told herself. Just one more day.

# TWENTY-TWO

*Sunday 7th February*

The pain and discomfort gave me a bad night, and when I finally got out of bed I ached even more than the day before. My ribs hurt if I breathed too deeply, but again I was grateful that I'd survived the beating. The fact that it was the day of the New Year's parade seemed to give me energy. Looking for lunch, I walked to an area off Beach Road that we called the Satay Club. It wasn't a club or even a building, but a group of men cooked chicken satay over small stoves in the street, and lots of people came here to eat.

I ate mine sitting on the sea wall with the sun on my back feeling the muscles relax.

"Captain Ash Carter?"

I turned to see a petite Chinese woman with a pretty face but severely pulled back hair. Linda Wu, an erstwhile reporter from the *Straits Times*. I regularly read Miss Wu's well-written articles. She didn't do investigative journalism, but she came close, with probing questions that were less politically sensitive than most of her peers.

She raised her packet of food. "Best satay in Singapore."

"It is."

"I'm surprised you risk it. Street food isn't known for its hygiene."

I smiled. "Like you said, it's the best satay on the island. I consider myself a fully-fledged member of the club."

"I didn't come here to ask you about your taste in food."

"What can I do for you, Miss Wu?" I asked as she closed in on me.

"Call me Linda."

I nodded but didn't offer the same courtesy in return. Not yet. Not until I knew what her motives were at least.

"Banana money…" Miss Wu said, and she looked around as though checking that no one could overhear. "What do you know about it?"

The only person I knew who mentioned banana money was my receptionist. In the early days she had been worried about our finances. I think she called it banana money because I didn't always invoice for my work or wouldn't get paid.

"Not much, why?"

"I heard that's how you were paid. You've been paid in banana money."

Again I thought of Madam Chau. Had she said something? "It's just an expression," I said. "Where did you hear it, Miss Wu?"

"Linda. Call me Linda." When I nodded, she continued: "Where did I hear about banana money or where did I hear that you were paid in the currency?"

"Whichever you prefer, Linda."

"I'm sure you know that the term refers to the money printed by the Japanese as currency during the war. Called banana money because of the banana tree on the front. After the war it was useless."

I nodded.

She continued with calculating eyes: "What happened to it?"

"I don't know."

"There were millions of dollars' worth."

"Millions of dollars' *worth-less*," I corrected, trying to be humorous.

"Perhaps," she said. "What do you know about it?"

I shook my head. "Honestly, Miss Wu, I know nothing. As I said, any talk of banana money here was a joke."

She kept looking at me through narrow eyes like she didn't believe me.

"Is that all, Miss Wu?"

She shrugged her petite shoulders and stood. "I suppose it has to be, Captain Carter. But if you hear of anything—if you come across anything that might point to where the money went—please do let me know." With that, she strode away, leaving me with a lunch that had gone cold.

★

I took a ride to my office and was surprised to find Madam Chau at her desk.

"It's Sunday," I said. "You need to take time off."

"I knew you'd come in today despite your injuries. How are you?"

"Fine."

She looked at me with disbelief.

I changed the subject by telling her about my meeting with Linda Wu and the questions about banana money.

"Have you mentioned it to anyone?"

"Of course not, and don't trust that reporter," she said to me, but then she said that about a lot of people. Madam Chau had a pretty low impression of most people's motives. Maybe she was right.

After letting her fuss over my bruises and put a fresh bandage around my left hand, I headed for the research office in the government building. I disposed of the bandage as soon as I arrived.

With the files out, I put my head down and carried on with my deception of investigating Yipp.

"Oh dear," a voice said after an hour. I looked up to see Major Lamb staring at me, his face full of sympathy. "How are you?"

"I feel like I've been run over by a tank."

"You look like you've been run over by a tank."

"Thank you, Major."

"You'll be saluting me next, Ash," he joked. "Do call me Rupert."

I nodded. "Have you any update for me regarding the houses I asked about?"

"Yes, everything as expected. All of the houses were dangerous and dilapidated, with a tendency to collapse at any moment. Really nothing out of the ordinary, just part of the general programme."

I nodded again.

He said, "I hear congratulations are in order."

"For what?"

"The arrests at the factory off Selegie Road."

★

Minutes later, having hurried faster than my aching body demanded, I was in Secretary Norris's office.

"What did you do?" I demanded.

His lips twitched into a smile beneath his moustache. "My job as Secretary for Internal Security."

"Did you arrest Yipp?" I asked, incredulous.

"No, but the next best thing. We arrested some of his men and the police will now interrogate them. They'll admit Yipp's criminal activity and then we'll have witnesses."

I shook my head. "It's a mistake."

"Not if we get him—and I believe you were right about the factory. I saw your map."

*Damn!* I'd left my map in that subterranean records room at the police station. I'd highlighted the area as suspicious since criminal activity didn't happen there.

Norris was still talking. "We also found out where Wang picked you up."

"I'm surprised you didn't arrest him as well," I said sarcastically.

Norris shook his head. "You aren't very good at this, are you, Carter? I'm not going to arrest Wang for allegedly beating you. It's Yipp I'm after."

I headed for the door. "You've made a mistake," I said.

"We'll see. But just in case, I expect you to keep working on the investigation."

★

"I am so sorry, Ash," Inspector Singh said when I turned up at his office. "Secretary Norris put pressure on my boss who put pressure on me. I had no choice."

"I understand."

He popped a mint humbug into his mouth and sighed. "I'm relieved. I dreaded that you would be angry with me. And then you might hit me."

I didn't think he was being serious, but I said, "I'm in too much pain. You've got off lightly this time, my friend."

He grinned and insisted that I join him for tea and tell him all about the incident with Wang.

"You were fortunate," he said when I finished.

"I don't feel fortunate."

"You know what I mean."

I patted my pocket where I now carried my Beretta. "If it happens again, I'll be quicker with the gun."

"And how are your fingers?" He pointed to my bruised left hand that Wang had stepped on.

"It's good enough for a trigger," I said, unconsciously flexing the fingers. "Would I get in trouble for shooting him before he starts asking questions?"

"Only if you do it in public."

I nodded and smiled. It was the unspoken rule within the police. Mete out any justice in private. If Wang were found dead with no witnesses, no one in authority would come asking me any questions.

However, Yipp would undoubtedly know who'd killed his henchman and I had no doubt he wouldn't let me get away with it.

Perhaps Norris wanted that. Perhaps he was jiggling his stick in the hornets' nest in the hope that Yipp would come after me.

"What did you find in the factory off Selegie Road?"

"Nothing except for a thieves' market."

"Stolen goods? Is that all?"

Singh waggled his eyebrows. "Politics. What can I say?"

"Norris thinks it'll lead to evidence against Andrew Yipp."

The inspector finished his tea and set down his cup. "From what I've heard, Secretary Norris is under as much pressure as he's putting on you. He needs results because the governor wants results."

Naturally, the governor was concerned. The political situation could shift like quicksand. If the People's Action Party was a real threat then everyone in the administration up to the governor would be worried. Unlike communism, this wasn't a threat against the state, it was a threat against the Crown.

I left the police station having convinced myself that Norris had either acted to be seen to act or stirred things up hoping I'd draw Yipp out.

Of course, that was the last thing on my mind. All I could think of was meeting Su Ling tonight in Arthur Pope's warehouse and making sure she was safely away from the island. Then, in a few days, I'd join her in the Philippines.

# TWENTY-THREE

Su Ling passed Wang on her way into Yipp's office. The henchman gave her a lizard's smile, but she nodded politely in return.

"You've been lying to me," Yipp said as she entered. His back was to her so she could only see his reflection, dark in the window.

"I would never—"

"Wang tells me you've been seeing Captain Carter."

"You know that's not true!"

"Do I?"

"I've been entertaining Sir Pendall at the Raffles Hotel for the past two nights. Last week I saw Major Lamb."

"And afterwards?"

"Which one?"

"Where did you go last night, after Pendall?"

She breathed. Thank goodness she'd had a break from Ash. "I went home to bed. If you need proof—" She gave him the name of the bar manager where she lived. "He's seen me. He knows I've only been there."

"I will check."

She shook her head with disappointment. "You should ask yourself why Wang would lie about it."

"Precisely! Why would he lie?"

"Because he hates me. He hates that we are so close… He hates that you love me."

She was sure Yipp's features softened.

"I *am* yours, Uncle," she said softly. "Only yours."

He turned suddenly and put his arms around her.

"Don't betray me, Little Flower."

"I couldn't."

"Tonight. Let's celebrate tonight."

"I'm supposed to see Strangled Chicken tonight."

"What? Again?"

"He's still waiting for me to have sex with him. Let me have dinner with him, then I'll let him down again and come to you."

Yipp finally turned and looked into her face. "Good."

She said nothing, wondering if he was imagining them in bed together, perhaps questioning her true feelings.

Finally, from nowhere, he said, "Tell me about Major Rupert Lamb?"

"What about him? You know I had to date him." She thought quickly. "Are you asking me whether I have feelings for him as well? Is that what Wang has said—not just Carter, but Lamb as well?"

"He rang for you."

"Did he?" A lump stuck in her throat. Did Yipp know she'd tried to have dinner with Lamb instead of Pendall? Did he guess she was just making herself unavailable?

"He's been good to us," Yipp said.

She figured he was talking about vacating the factory. Lamb had provided the replacement building, no questions asked, no recompense demanded. Except...

Yipp said, "Cancel Pendall. The horny old chicken can wait. You'll have dinner with Lamb tonight." He paused. "Then you'll come and celebrate New Year Day Five with me."

"I'll arrange it," Su Ling said, feeling an unbidden sensation of disgust, knowing that traditionally Day Five was the day when taboos and forbidden activities could be celebrated. She bowed and immediately went to find her assistant then took her where they couldn't be overheard.

"I've got to have dinner with Major Lamb again," she said.

"What about Sir Graham?"

"We won't tell him, but would you turn up in my place?" Jinjing was a pretty girl and he would surely be contented.

Her assistant had a question in her eyes.

Su Ling said, "Tell him I'll see him tomorrow."

Jinjing smiled knowingly.

"I should warn you that he is a randy old man," Su Ling said, touching Jinjing's hand. "Be careful, he'll try to get you into bed. I can't expect you to do that for me. You'll have to use all your wits to get out of it without offending him."

"I'll do what's necessary."

"Get him drunk, but if he manages to get you into his bedroom, and if the worst comes to the worst, tease him like hell. He's so randy he's likely to explode in his pants. And remember, promise that I'll see him tomorrow. Promise that he'll have the best night of his life."

Jinjing smiled and nodded.

"Now I need you to call Major Lamb. He's requested dinner with me tonight at Hotel de la Paix. Confirm I'll be there for eight."

# TWENTY-FOUR

The New Year's parade started with the army coming down from Fort Canning on the hill behind the police headquarters. It began with the sound of a marching band that got closer and closer to St Andrews Road where the main carnival waited for them.

When I saw them in their splendid red uniforms, they were led by an army motorcyclist and followed by General Gaskill, the Commander-in-Chief for the Far East, looking proud and regal with a Union Flag bearer and baton-twirling sergeant major.

Behind them were the representative squads from the various units and armed forces. At the back were the military police from Gillman Barracks. A large number of the men were on duty, patrolling the streets, marshalling the parade and generally watching for trouble.

Taking up the rear was a military police Land Rover, and there I spotted my friend Captain Robshaw riding shotgun. He saw me and saluted and I threw a casual one back at him.

I walked onto St Andrews as the people's parade tucked in behind the Land Rover. Suddenly the air was filled with a cacophony of music and firecrackers, celebrating the start of this part of the pageant. The crowd surged and I was swept along, moving as quickly as my aching limbs allowed.

Acrobats swirling giant red flags led the people's parade. The words *Health*, *Prosperity* and *Happiness* were written in gold, in English and Chinese. Then behind the flag-wavers came three floats that cruised past advertising local businesses, and then a troupe of lion dancers. The large golden head snapped at the air while the acrobats danced behind, bringing the creature to life.

After this were fire-eaters, and then acrobats forming human towers, before another business float rumbled past.

We crossed over Anderson Bridge—a mass of people and vehicles, surely testing its impressive tensile strength. Then I was in Fullerton Square, with bunting and colourful lights, where the crowds congregated, swirled and surged.

People squashed all around me and I was pressed hard into a pretty young girl—too hard.

"I'm so sorry—" I started to say, but one minute she was looking into my eyes with a smile, her hand sliding teasingly across my chest, and the next she vanished into the rambunctious mass of bodies.

Despite the palpable excitement in the square, I managed to move up Battery Road and find a spot on a wall where I wouldn't be crushed.

I'd missed this last year since I'd been in mining country. My friends and I had seen the New Year's celebration in Ipoh, the state capital of Perak, but it wasn't a patch on this. People claimed that the Singapore parade and carnival was the best in the world, better even than Hong Kong's. I didn't know, but an hour of light, fireworks, dancing and music left me forgetting my aches and pains and wondering how hard it would be for me to leave this amazing city.

★

Major Rupert Lamb was waiting for Su Ling at the table in Hotel de la Paix. She arrived fashionably late, at a quarter after eight, and thought he looked uncomfortable, nervous perhaps.

Lamb jumped up, and when he kissed her hand, she noticed he seemed clammy.

"I hope you aren't unwell, Major," she said as the waiter helped her into a chair.

"Unwell? I er…"

"Oh, I do apologize for my rudeness."

He waved down her apology. "I'm a little warm from walking too fast," he said. "I thought I would be late due to the parade, but it turned out that I wasn't. I'm not as fit as I used to be, you see."

She made a polite comment about how young he appeared and that he was bound to be as fit as a twenty-year-old. He liked that and she continued in a similar vein, encouraging him to talk and then flattering the man.

His favourite subject was Thailand and his experiences as a diplomat.

"It must have been difficult," she said.

"It's a country of two halves. The Thais declared war on the Allies during the war. Did you know that?" He chuckled. "Most of the Allies didn't! However, Thailand signed a mutual alliance with the Japanese and allowed free movement."

"You said they are a country of two halves," she prompted.

"Old Siam is still there—in spirit. I suspect because of the gentle revolution the king still considers himself King of Siam."

"But he has no power."

"That's right. My, I forgot how sharp you are, my dear… as well as exceptionally pretty."

She kept the conversation going for two hours, and despite his occasional patronizing comment, she found it an easy way to spend the time without watching the clock and wondering where Ash was at any given moment.

After he'd settled the bill, Lamb said, "I've got something to show you upstairs." She noted his words were slurred after three bottles of claret, two gins and a dessert wine. She hadn't bothered to slip anything into his drink because he was harmless—not at all like Sir Graham Pendall.

"It's a lovely night. I thought we might take a stroll along the esplanade," she said. "We could enjoy the carnival atmosphere on the *Padang*."

As he walked out of the dining room, he nodded to a few fellow dinners and spoke loudly.

He's terribly drunk, she thought.

When they reached the lobby, her heels clicked and he placed a hand under her elbow.

"These tiles are awfully slippery," he said. But then instead of heading for the exit onto Coleman Street, he steered her towards the staircase.

"Major?" she said.

"You must see this—" His grip tightened, and had he been anyone else she would have been alarmed. However, this was a gentleman. He wouldn't force himself on her.

What will it matter? she decided, and she let him guide her towards his room.

# TWENTY-FIVE

At midnight I was sitting in the Land Rover with my friend Captain Robshaw. He wore his straw-blond hair longer than most soldiers—just within army tolerance—because he liked to flick it back. He'd catch a lady's eye, flick and smile.

He was driving and now I was in the passenger seat. We circled the known trouble spots, encouraging any rowdy soldiers to calm down. Officially the MPs should have been arresting people too, but tonight Robshaw, at least, was showing a great deal of tolerance.

We stopped at the end of Bugis Street, which was officially out of bounds for the soldiers. A blitzkrieg of beer-drinking revellers had swept through and we spent time clearing away a few drunken stragglers. Normally the MPs would put them in a cell until they sobered up, but not tonight. Robshaw helped them on their way, calling trishaws and sending them back to barracks.

After the hard work, we swept around the *Padang* and stopped to enjoy a dance competition—or perhaps it was a fight—between two dragon dance troupes. We leaned back in the seats soaking up the atmosphere and I could imagine sipping on a cold Tiger Beer.

Robshaw said, "I probably shouldn't tell you this, but there's a wealthy businessman who has a house in Tanglin near the barracks. He has a pretty seventeen-year-old daughter."

I swallowed hard. Robshaw could be talking about Arthur Pope and his daughter Amelia. What was he about to tell me?

Robshaw continued: "Anyway, the businessman came home one day to find a squaddie leaving his home with a smile on his face. The businessman immediately confronted his daughter and warned her to keep soldiers at arm's length. The girl promised she would.

"A few days later, the businessman came home to discover his innocent daughter with a soldier. His pants were around his ankles and she had his manhood in her hand."

"Manhood?" I asked. "It's not like you to be so sensitive, Robbo."

He widened his eyes and nodded. "Not only was she playing with his manhood, but her knickers were off. The poor businessman was so shocked that he couldn't speak straight away and chased the soldier from his house. When the man returned, he told his daughter she was grounded for a week. And if he ever caught her with her legs apart and knickers off again, she'd be sent away."

By this time, I was more relaxed. No way could this be Amelia Pope. I was certain she'd never behave so brazenly. No, this was someone else, or simply exaggerated gossip.

"Where did you hear this?" I asked. "An official report? At the barracks?"

Robshaw shook his head and spoke seriously. "I've not finished. So a week goes by and the businessman comes home to find a squaddie pumping away behind his daughter, who is bent over a table and fully clothed.

"'What the hell?' screamed the businessman as he gasped for breath. 'But, Daddy, I've kept my legs together and knickers on.'

"'No! No! No!' shouted the father. 'Blow those bloody soldiers!'

"The girl stood up indignantly, straightening her skirt. 'Blow them? But that's what I was doing until you told me to use my hands with straight arms.'"

Robshaw guffawed as I shook my head.

When he composed himself he said, "Ash, you've been so damned serious, I thought a joke would cheer you up."

"Do I need cheering up? I've been enjoying the evening."

"All right, so what's the story about the bruises," he said. "You said 'boxing ring' when I first asked, but that's not true is it?"

"No. Just a spot of trouble." I paused. "There weren't any tigers in the parade this year. The wild animals are part of the attraction, I always think."

"Someone in the crowd got mauled last year," he said. "Big cats have been banned."

"Shame."

"Yes, but you're still avoiding the question about the bruises. What was the *spot of trouble*?"

"I attracted trouble."

"Well that's no surprise—you attract trouble but you can normally deal with it."

"I do," I said, smiling.

"But not this time," he said, looking at me, demanding an explanation.

"Four of Yipp's thugs. Armed and ugly, hell-bent on giving me a beating."

He nodded. "Know who they were?"

"At least one. Wang, Yipp's muscle. I guess I could work out who the others were since they'll be under Wang."

Robbo blew out air. "Tell me when, and we'll rough him up."

"Not wise," I said, "but thanks for the offer."

"Why isn't it wise? He gives you a message and we give him one back."

"You'd be prodding the serpent."

"Is that another manhood reference?"

"No, it means if you want to defeat your enemy, you don't make him angry."

"So we kill him."

"No! Robbo, promise me you won't do anything foolish."

"Spoilsport," he said, flicking back his hair as he exchanged eye contact with a belle. "So many pretty girls in the city and so little time. Bet me ten shillings that I can't get her address."

I snorted, thinking he was joking, saw he wasn't and decided to go along with the fun. "As long as she's not a tart," I clarified. However, she was a white girl and she didn't look like a prostitute.

He was out of the jeep in a flash and walked a short distance with her, acting charming and debonair. At first, I was sure he'd fail. She looked flattered but demure, and then he was suddenly writing something into his notebook. After a peck on her cheek, he practically skipped back to the jeep.

"Genevieve Paquette," he said, almost beside himself with pride. "I'll be walking her out tomorrow evening."

"Pretty girl, pretty name," I said. "I'm impressed."

He held out a hand. "Ten shillings, if you will."

I dipped into my pocket where I keep my money clip.

The clip and the money were gone.

# TWENTY-SIX

I cursed my carelessness. I'd never been pickpocketed before but realized there had been ample opportunity tonight. All those people crammed around, bodies pressing up, easy targets.

I'd lost a couple of pounds, which was quite a lot, although I was less concerned about the money and more about the money clip. It had been a gift from my mother: silver with my initials—it'd been our secret because she knew I would change my name to her maiden name as soon as I could. Of course, that was before I went to university and before she'd taken her own life. In my darkest moments, I didn't blame my father for her death, I blamed myself. What if I hadn't left home? What if I'd supported her?

Foolish thoughts about changing the past, and now I had lost the most precious thing she'd given me.

★

Captain Robshaw dropped me at home around 2 am and I put on a disguise of dark clothes and a cap. Then I went out onto my balcony that looked out to sea and went over the side. An electric shock of pain shot through me as I landed on the ground, and I had to pause and catch my breath. Of course, I could have gone out through my front door, but you never know who is watching.

On Beach Road, I walked east, past Middle Road and a playground. I found a trishaw rider laying on a bench, smoking and undoubtedly worse the wear for alcohol. However, the rear seat of his bike had a vanity cover, so I paid him half in advance and pulled the covers around me.

He dropped me in Kampong Bintang, which was beyond my destination, and I paid the remainder of my fare, grateful that we'd made it despite his drunken state.

This was one of the worst areas of the city, full of hawkers, street hoodlums and the unemployed. People spilled onto the street, lounged, squatted or shuffled aimlessly.

No one gave me a second glance as I joined Havelock Road looking just like anyone else, hunched and acting like a hobo. Finally, I came to the warehouses on Alkaff Quay.

The centre of the city was still alive with late-night revellers, but out here, the buildings loomed dark and silent.

After a couple of people disappeared, leaving me alone on the wharf, I quickly located Arthur Pope's warehouse and slipped in through a small unlocked door into absolute darkness. I'm not sure what he had in there, but I immediately smelled something akin to rust and straw. Crates were piled up in rows, ready to be carried out to waiting boats, and I used a torch to examine each one for markings.

Because I'd told no one that I wouldn't be leaving tonight, Pope had arranged for two boxes. They looked like large coffins, but a quick inspection revealed the air holes at one end. Two boxes, each with a single X on. Su Ling hadn't arrived yet.

It was almost three in the morning.

I located a comfortable hiding spot, sat down to wait, and found myself thinking about Su Ling. She was beautiful, but that's such an easy, perhaps vacuous word. Su Ling had grace and poise. When I first saw the way she moved, I'd been attracted. And beneath her dress was a perfectly sculpted body and silky skin. The impossible length of her legs suited the fashionable cheongsam with a long slit, not quite revealing, teasing. And between the sheets, Su Ling was both athletic and assertive.

I pictured her across from me, looking into her intelligent eyes, full of life, full of promise.

I considered myself a scientist, a rational man, but I knew love was irrational and inexplicable. Not really. Desire I understood, and I certainly wanted Su Ling, but there was so much more. I was attracted to strong women, I knew that from my previous relationships. Su Ling was confident, she knew who she was and how to deal with the misogynistic world in which we live. She decided what she wanted, despite the obstacles, and she got it.

I was what she wanted. Initially, Yipp thought he was using her to control me, but she'd wanted our relationship. Afterwards, she tried to protect me by pretending she didn't care, but I remembered our impassioned tryst in a hospital storeroom. That showed me her true feelings, and I shouldn't have run away afterwards. I shouldn't have gone north and stayed in Perak.

And then she'd tracked me down and asked me to find her mother. She hated Yipp, her so-called uncle, and was looking to blame him. He was her abuser—I did not doubt this—and yet she needed a reason to betray him.

I tried to understand this attitude, but I couldn't really. It seemed akin to me forgiving my father and yet looking for a way to break the bond. I'd heard of victims who developed feelings for their captors and knew it had happened during the war. The only rational explanation I could find was like a whipped dog who longs for a kind hand from the man who feeds him.

And yet Su Ling was no whipped dog. She'd explained it as respect, and what Asians called *face*. To betray Yipp would mean a loss of face for her.

Escape was the only solution, and yet the more I thought about it, the more I wondered why she wouldn't lose face by running away. She'd said it was because we'd start a new life. No one would know her. No one would judge her for her past—for anything other than who she was.

I checked my watch: ten minutes before our agreed deadline of 4 am.

*Come on, Su Ling! Where the hell are you?*

A couple of minutes later, I checked the time again. My palms were sweating. In the silence of the godown, I could hear my heart like a bass drumbeat.

The deadline came and went. I started pacing the warehouse, thoughts swirling in my head. What had happened to her?

Had Andrew Yipp found out or had she just been detained?

Maybe she'd still come. Maybe she'd just be very late.

The big twin doors opened to the dock just after five. Dim lights came on and men started loading crates onto wagons and rolling them down to waiting bumboats.

Everything went, including the two boxes marked with single Xs. These labourers wouldn't have been told the plans; they didn't care what was in the boxes.

I watched the crates go and be stacked onto a boat. I wasn't inside. Su Ling wasn't inside.

They were empty.

At least that's what I thought.

# PART TWO

# TWENTY-SEVEN

*Monday 8th February*

I went home and slept deeply for almost four hours. Maybe I'd have slept for longer if rapid banging on my door hadn't roused me.

"How are you feeling this morning, Master Carter?" my receptionist enquired on my doorstep.

I doubt she wanted to hear about my disappointment last night. She'd have told me to keep well away from Su Ling. So instead I told her that my aches were improving thanks to her cream and that I had overslept because of the celebrations.

She nodded critically like I wasn't allowed to enjoy myself and take a day off recovering. Then she said, "You have had two telephone calls: one urgent and one not."

I waited for more details then prompted, "The urgent one?"

"From Mr Pope. He said he needs to speak to you. I've made an appointment at his office in Commercial Square in"—she checked her watch—"precisely thirty-six minutes."

"And the other call?"

"From that chief inspector friend of yours in Kuala Lumpur. He said that the lady has still not returned to work."

"No more detail?"

"No," she said indignantly, "otherwise I would have said. The chief inspector also said you were interested to hear about a police officer."

I nodded rather than have her bark at me again for speaking.

"He said there was a policeman killed three months ago. He was alone in a rough part of the city"—I could see Madam Chau trying to recall McNaughton's exact words—"somewhere he shouldn't have gone. He should only go with support. So he was shot in the back of the head by a hoodlum. No witnesses… and found in an alley two days later."

"Thank you. Is Chief Inspector McNaughton expecting a returned call?"

"He didn't say." She looked at her watch. "You now have thirty-four minutes to clean up and attend your meeting."

★

Arthur Pope sat at his desk looking pensive. I wafted through blue pipe smoke and sat on a chair across from him.

"She didn't turn up," I said. "But you already know that."

"Yes. What happened?"

"I waited for her in your warehouse but she didn't turn up. I don't know why."

He stood to relight his pipe, rapidly puffed at the embers and then sat back in his chair.

"What should I do with the box?"

It struck me that he said box rather than boxes, but I ignored the discrepancy. "I'm sure we'll try again," I said.

"I'm sure there was a hitch. If you are still willing to help... Could we try again?"

"Of course, dear chap. I think we can arrange it for"—he checked a schedule—"there are a few opportunities over the rest of the month. When you are ready, I'll confirm exact dates and times."

"Thank you."

He was looking at me hard, still pensive and still blowing out smoke.

"The box," he said. "What do I do with it in the meantime?"

I shook my head, not understanding. "Can't you just store it in the warehouse?"

"No," he said, and finally set the pipe aside. "My dear chap, it's not the actual box I'm concerned about. It's the money inside the box."

# TWENTY-EIGHT

I stared at a box marked with an X. "Hundreds of Malay dollars?" I said with disbelief.

We were back in the warehouse on Alkaff Quay with the lid removed from one of the boxes. Pope had pulled out packing straw and revealed bundles of notes. I'd picked one up and estimated thirty notes of mixed denominations.

"Ten bundles," Pope said.

"Hundreds of dollars," I said again.

"Getaway money, I think it's called. But you didn't know about it, did you?"

"No."

He said nothing. The implication was obvious: if I didn't know about it then I hadn't put it there. Pope certainly hadn't provided it, which left only one other person.

Pope said, "Your girlfriend?"

I nodded.

"Why didn't you get in the crate? Were you waiting for her?"

I hadn't told Pope that we'd changed the plan. He expected we'd leave together but I was staying behind as a distraction.

"She came here before you," he said. "The money was meant for you."

I shook my head. "She came but was somehow disturbed. She needed to leave the warehouse before getting in the box."

He looked at me quizzically. "Are you sure she intended to leave, Ash?"

"Yes," I said with certainty, although his challenge immediately made me doubt myself.

"You're the detective. Let's hypothesize that she didn't intend to leave. Why put the money in the box?"

"Exactly," I said. "Something happened."

"Does she think you're in danger?"

"Yes, but—"

"Bear with me. What if she wanted you to have the cash?" He raised his eyebrows but I wasn't sure what he meant. He waited then gave a palms-up shrug. "What if the money isn't hers?"

That made sense. I suspected she'd appropriate—a much nicer word than "steal"—the money from Andrew Yipp. I was running, so I suppose she thought I could take the cash.

I dropped the wad into the box like it had burned my hand. Then I picked up the box lid and slotted it into place.

"You should return the money," Pope said.

If I did that, Yipp would know for certain who'd taken it. Although Pope had said "Getaway money", I didn't think he was right. Maybe Yipp wouldn't even notice it gone.

"Would you keep it for me?" I said. "Give me time to decide what to do with it."

Pope nodded as we walked out onto the quay and shut the Judas gate behind us.

"Don't worry," he said. "I can make it disappear—until you need it that is."

★

I went back to work, spending time at my office and researching at the government building. I had a routine of going to a tiffin house on Collyer Quay. It had been there that Su Ling had managed to get the note into my pocket that day I went to see Major Lamb. Or at least she'd had someone else slip it in unnoticed.

I ate lunch and stayed there a long time, but I saw no sign of Su Ling and had no secret message stuffed into my pocket.

She was lying low and I decided to act as if nothing had happened. Yipp might be watching me, and Secretary Norris certainly was.

I was back at my desk, reading letters when a policeman knocked on the door. He'd been sent by Inspector Singh and invited me to attend the morgue at Singapore General Hospital.

A police car waited outside and we arrived at the hospital after a short, fast drive.

"What is it, Ishaan?" I asked as Singh greeted me proffering a packet of boiled sweets.

"Sherbet lemons... ah, you don't mean the sweets. You mean, why have I called you here?"

"Right."

"There's a body I'd like you to see." He led me down concrete steps into a cold basement that smelled of chemicals. The floor tiles were slippery where they had been washed down recently.

A body lay on a table beneath a sheet.

For a nightmarish second, I wondered if it was Su Ling beneath the sheet, but without preamble, Singh was already lifting the end to reveal the face of a woman.

Not Su Ling.

I started breathing again.

He said nothing and looked at me as though waiting for me to comment.

I shook my head, not understanding. "What did she die of?"

He ignored my question. "Familiar, Ash?"

I looked harder. She had fine features and pale skin, probably mixed-race, possibly Eurasian. Even in death, I could see she'd been pretty: good bone structure, rose petal lips, long eyelashes. She looked like a hundred women I'd seen in the city, although something tugged at the recesses of my memory.

"I'm not sure," I admitted. "Why?"

Singh dropped the sheet so that it now lay just below her clavicle. I could see bruising on her neck, particularly dark around her larynx.

"Strangled," I said. "Looks like the thumbs dug pretty deeply at the front. But..."

As I pointed to what I'd noticed, just above the bruising, Singh whipped the sheet away. He revealed the naked body like he was performing a magic trick.

"But there's a larynx," I said, my eyes moving down the table and seeing the complete body. "It's a man!"

"It's a man. The face looks like a woman's and he was found wearing ladies' clothing. But it is indeed a fairy."

I shook my head again, still not getting why I was here in this place, where even the smell of bleach couldn't hide the stench of decay.

Singh popped another boiled sweet in his mouth. He was looking at me, so I said, "He was murdered—strangled with some force, which suggests our murderer is a man."

"And you don't recognize him even though you now know he's a man?"

"What are you implying?"

"Nothing, my friend, just asking a reasonable question."

"Why is it *reasonable*?"

"Because we found"—he dug into his pocket—"this."

145

In his hand lay a curved piece of metal about three inches long. Silver.

"Your money clip, I believe," he said. "It's got your initials."

And then I remembered the face. In Fullerton Square during the parade, a pretty girl had bumped into me and then disappeared. She—or rather, he—had been my pickpocket.

# TWENTY-NINE

"What's her name?" I asked, pocketing my money clip.

"Unknown," the inspector said, looking at me critically.

I shook my head. "I honestly don't know him. My clip was stolen last night and I think it might have been this chap dressed as a woman. We bumped into one another during the parade. I've never set eyes on him/her before."

Singh nodded, his eyes more relaxed.

"There was no money found in it? I had a few pounds…"

"Nothing. Well, at least nothing by the time I saw it. You know how it is: either the cash was taken by the murderer or by someone else."

I did know how it worked. There was a good chance that the first policeman on the scene pocketed the cash.

"Where was the body found?"

"North Boat Quay at sunrise. Was asked to move and didn't. Just sat slumped in a doorway like he was asleep."

"But strangled with some force," I said again, thinking about it. "Thumbs pressed hard below the larynx. Vicious, possibly personal."

Singh pulled the sheet back over the naked body.

I continued: "It's like our murderer was stopping him from speaking. You know, maybe subconsciously."

Singh started walking away.

"Do you want me to help with the investigation?"

Singh stopped. "How long have you been in Singapore, Ash?"

"Two years."

"How many people are there?"

From my work with the government, I knew the official figure. "Just over one point one million."

"Probably more, since most censuses miss the illegals and squatters," Singh said, walking towards the stairs. "Let's get out of here and into the fresh air. Even sherbet lemons can't mask the smell."

When we were on Outram Road he spoke again. "On average there are about thirty deaths a day."

I whistled. It seemed a lot, but I'd never really thought about death rates.

"And do you know how many of those are natural deaths, Ash?"

"No."

"Nor do I, but I would guess about twenty. The police don't have the resources to investigate ten suspicious deaths a day."

"How many do you investigate?"

"Depends on the colour. It sickens me to admit it, but there's a huge difference between a white man's death and a Chinese one. It's part colonialism, part a matter of wealth—although they are probably one and the same."

He opened a new packet and offered me a sweet. For a change, I took one, a mint that stuck to my molars.

"You sound frustrated, Ishaan."

"Worried, I'd say. I worry about policing. I worry about fairness and justice for all, and I worry that there's an uprising just around the corner. It's like a heated pan of water and at any moment it's going to boil over."

We kept walking and talking until we reached the Singapore River. We crossed over Read Bridge onto

North Boat Quay and then walked along just past Clarke Street.

He stopped by a wooden door on the corner with Canning Lane that looked a hundred years old with all of its paint peeled away.

"I'm not sure of his race, but he probably had Chinese blood in him." Singh shrugged. "And a *kathoey*—" I knew the expression. It referred to the third gender.

"You don't know that."

"A pretty boy dressed as a girl? He was a sex worker all right."

"Will you investigate?" I asked, going back to our earlier conversation. We started walking along the quay towards Hill Street police station.

"It's not likely. You'd probably have more luck investigating the murder of a dog. This one won't just be about resources, Ash. This will be bottom rung—the lowest priority."

"Put two men on it," I said.

"Ash—"

"I'll also help."

"You're wasting your time," he said, and I'm sure he was right, but at that moment I felt like I had time to waste. I was treading water waiting for a signal from the woman I loved.

★

Inspector Singh left me just as the skies opened and warm rain fell. For fifteen minutes I sheltered by the doorway on North Boat Quay and found myself imagining the boy slumped beside me. Had he been killed here or just dumped?

I could visualize hands around his thin neck, not just squeezing but pressing hard. The boy would have struggled. Of course he would. He might not have been able to make a noise, but he would have undoubtedly caused a scene.

I looked around through glorious sunshine and steaming pavements.

Two people struggling on this quay. Day or night, I was pretty sure it would have been obvious. During the day, hundreds of people could have been witnesses: men on the boats, men working the docks, civilians eating and walking along the river. The view from Read Bridge was partial, but anyone on Coleman Bridge would have seen the struggle.

And at night it wouldn't be much different. Granted the river traffic would have stopped, but this was Chinese New Year, fifteen days of celebration. The streets at night were almost as busy as during the day.

No, he wasn't killed here.

"Sir?" A voice disturbed my thoughts. A young Chinese man stood two paces distant, watching me.

"There was a body here," I said hopefully. "Did you see the body they found in this doorway?"

"No, sir. Would you come with me?"

I blinked my surprise. "I'm sorry?"

"Sir, Mr Andrew Yipp has requested a meeting."

# THIRTY

I went up to the twelfth floor of the Cathay Building with my hand in my jacket pocket. The gun felt big and obvious, but I was about to meet the head of the biggest gang in Singapore. On the one hand, he hadn't picked me up and taken me to a remote location, but I had little doubt that Yipp could have someone executed wherever he pleased.

Wang was standing by the elevator doors as they opened. He stepped back and waved me forward. I saw him glance at my pocket and let a wicked smile play on his lips. Since he made no move to relieve me of the gun, I decided to keep him in front of me.

"Lead the way," I said, standing my ground.

"How is your hand?" Again he looked at the pocket where I held my gun.

"Recovering."

"If you make a move, I will kill you."

"I have no intention of making the first move, Wang."

He smiled and nodded. "This way then."

As he led me to Yipp's private office, I glanced around hoping to see Su Ling, hoping to confirm that all was fine. People looked back at me and I recognized the boy who was my official liaison and the girl who was Su Ling's assistant.

Neither face gave me any clues.

I'd been in the room before. Broad windows looked out over the Singapore River and the quays. Apart from a large rug and cushions, the room was empty.

A girl came in and bowed, offered me tea, and indicated that I should sit on a cushion. I knew it was impolite to decline, but I shook my head and remained standing by the window.

The girl crossed the room to the door that led to Yipp's room. After she opened it, the businessman immediately stepped through.

When I'd first met him, he'd worn the silk pyjamas of a tai chi master and I hadn't been able to gauge his age. I thought he might be fifty. Now he wore a severe business suit and over the prevailing two years I decided he looked twenty years older.

"Mr Carter," he said, never referring to my ex-military rank, "please sit."

"I'll stand, thank you, Mr Yipp."

"It is regrettable that you have come here armed," he said, moving smoothly to a cushion and sitting.

I removed my hand from my pocket.

The door Yipp had come through remained open. He clapped his hands once and I started to move my hand back before I realized he was requesting tea. The girl came in with a tray, placed it in front of her boss and poured a cup.

"Please," Yipp said, and I found myself moving towards a cushion. Green tea was poured and the cup placed before me.

When the girl had gone and the door closed, Yipp surprised me.

"I want her back."

"I'm sorry?"

He took a sip of tea, replaced the cup and looked at me with ancient eyes. "I want Su Ling returned."

My head spun for a moment. Yipp wanted her back.

When I found my voice, I said, "Where is she?"

He smiled thinly. "Where indeed?"

We sat in silence with us trying to read each other's eyes.

Finally he said, "I know about you. I know you were seeing her."

I said nothing. Wang had beaten me based on suspicion. I wasn't about to confirm my relationship with Su Ling.

Yipp said, "You don't deny it."

"I don't deny that I have feelings for her. I think we at least have that in common, Mr Yipp."

"Where is she?"

"I don't know."

"Did you plan to run away with her?"

I said nothing.

"Where have you hidden her? I know she hasn't left the island. So she is in hiding somewhere."

"Why would she be in hiding?" I asked, trying to sound genuine.

"Because of some foolish romantic notion, Mr Carter."

I said, "I don't know where she is."

"I don't believe you." That was blunt. In all my previous dealings with Yipp, he had been indirect and polite. Now I found this change encouraging. Su Ling had got away. She might not have escaped with me, but she'd found another way and Yipp had no idea.

Yipp still scrutinized me. "Will you also deny that you are investigating me, Mr Carter?"

"I won't deny that."

"You are working for Secretary Norris in an attempt to arrest me. I heard about the raid on the factory near Selegie Road."

"That wasn't at my instigation."

"It's not what people say, Mr Carter. However, I haven't operated in that premises for over a year. I used to have a packing business in there, but operate in one place too long…"

I said nothing and took a sip of tea.

"The men arrested were not my men, Mr Carter. The police will learn nothing by interrogating them. Nothing true, at least."

"You are probably right."

"I know I am, Mr Carter. I also know why Secretary Norris has done it. He is setting you up. He is using you. He thinks that he won't catch me doing something illegal but will force my hand. He thinks I'll have you killed."

The way he said it left me with no doubt that he could arrange my death at the click of a finger—or a clap of the hands like he'd ordered tea. *Clap*. Ash Carter dead.

Momentarily, his eyes seemed less tense. "Let me tell you, there's as much chance of that as there is of him catching *me* leaving the country."

I knew that Yipp's biggest rival had left the country and been exiled. But that had been because the man had been to China. He wasn't allowed to return due to the fear of communism.

"You are not a communist," I said.

"I am not."

"Secretary Norris thinks you are funding a new political party."

"But not communists."

"It doesn't matter to him. Any destabilization of the government—"

"—by democratic means, Mr Carter. There will be no revolution, but colonialism must end. We are ruled by a privileged elite. You know that Chinese make up over seventy per cent of Singaporeans. But we are not Singapore. Singapore is a rich melting pot of cultures and races and the government should reflect that."

"I'm not a politician."

"No, but you can be manipulated by one."

He finished his tea and stood up smoothly, demonstrating his agility despite his advanced years.

I also stood.

"Bring Su Ling back, Mr Carter."

Before I could respond, he was walking through his door leaving me alone in the room to ponder his words.

# THIRTY-ONE

Arthur Pope didn't ask me why I wanted the money. I waited in his office while he fetched it for me.

I had no intention of taking Su Ling back to Yipp. She'd got away. Maybe she hadn't left the country yet, but it was surely the plan and she'd surely be in touch.

The money was undoubtedly Yipp's, and our little chat had given me an idea of how to use it.

"Worth a little over fifty British pounds," Pope said as he handed me the cash. "Any news about your girl?"

"Not yet."

He patted my shoulder. "Don't worry, things will work out and we can execute the plan another time. In fact, the next best date I have is the end of next week."

I thanked him and said I'd be in touch. Then I returned to the police station and handed Singh the cash.

"Goodness!" His eyes were as big as saucers.

"I acquired it," I explained because we both knew I didn't have this sort of money to splash around.

"Acquired?"

"Let's put it to good use," I said, avoiding the explanation that it was Yipp's cash. "Let's find out who killed that boy. Is it enough?"

"When I said we didn't have resources, I wasn't implying that you should pay."

"But it will help." I paused a beat. "Ishaan, I know how these things work."

He nodded. "Hopefully. With this money perhaps we can find two or three murderers for this." Singh's smile suggested he was joking.

"Great! How many men?"

"I need to clear this with the chief first, but…"

"But?"

"Perhaps two men?"

I nodded. It sounded reasonable. After all, the two coppers would be taken off other tasks.

"When do you want them to start?"

"Straight away. The longer we leave it, the colder the case gets."

"All right." There was something in his tone that I couldn't read.

"What is it?"

He shook his head with sadness in his eyes. "I fear it was too cold as soon as our murderer walked away."

Singh went off to confirm that two men could be assigned, leaving me for twenty minutes.

"I was starting to think you'd run off with the money," I joked when he came back.

"The chief took some persuading. We can have two men but for only two days. And… unfortunately they won't be detectives… in fact, all I could get were pretty raw recruits."

I whistled through my teeth. "Expensive."

"So what's the plan?" He showed me his palms. "You know I'm not a detective either."

I'd given it thought while I was waiting—probably more than I'd questioned my own motives. "We get them doing two things," I said. "They canvass both sides of Boat Quay for witnesses—"

"People won't talk."

"They might. And secondly, we get your men talking to sex workers. Give them a photograph of the boy and see what we can find. Tell your men their objective is to get a name and an address."

We shook hands and then the inspector patted me on the shoulder just like Pope had done less than an hour before. I was getting the distinct impression people were feeling sorry for me.

"I saw Yipp earlier," I said. "He mentioned the Selegie Road factory."

Singh waited for more.

"Let's go and take a look."

A few minutes later, the inspector was opening faded blue double doors on the old place. "You still haven't told me why you want to see it," he said.

"Simply because Yipp brought it up. There's something here, something he's hiding."

We walked into cavernous darkness and Singh pulled out a torch. "No lights," he said. "We think it's been empty a long time." There were a few windows but they had been whitewashed out and provided little illumination.

I got him to shine the torch at the ceiling. "Lights but no bulbs," I pointed out. I could see wires dangling as well as other cables. Apart from that, the room was bare.

There was a large square office at one end with a whitewashed window and no furniture.

"Where was the thieves' market?" I asked.

"The end room. There are three sections and this office. The farthest section has a broken wall where they got in."

We walked back through the first room and into the second. Like the first, it was spotless. This one didn't even have pulleys and cables dangling down. Just a clean, empty room. I borrowed the torch and went along the walls, looking closely.

"Anything?" he asked me.

"Nothing. But do you notice that smell?"

"Stinky thieves, no doubt."

There was an open door then a dogleg, and we entered the final section where I immediately saw the broken wall. I also saw suitcases and piles of household goods on tatty carpets.

"We arrested the thieves. This is their garbage," Singh said.

I walked to the hole in the wall and examined it. "That goes out onto Short Street," he said.

"Looks fairly recent."

"I agree. We don't think they'd been using this place for long."

I wasn't interested in this room and so walked back through the dogleg, through the door into the middle section.

"The smell here is different," I said. "Familiar, but I can't place it."

Singh sniffed, but he'd just popped a boiled sweet into his mouth and I suspected he could only smell lemon sherbet.

"Was the door open?" I asked, pointing back the way we'd come."

"No, we had to force it."

"So the thieves were confined to the end section—and maybe afterwards. Maybe they were given access afterwards."

He puffed out his cheeks, probably trying to follow my logic. "Access after what?"

"Whatever used to be here was moved. This place has been cleaned. It's spotless. No dust, no cobwebs. What sort of factory is spotless—especially after being allegedly empty for years. And where are the squatters?"

He nodded. Singapore had a housing problem. People slept everywhere they could and this was an ideal spot.

"Food? Perhaps that's what you can smell."

"Not food," I said. "Yipp cleaned this place in a hurry. He let the thieves use the end room, but they respected him, or feared him enough to stay the other side of the door."

"All right," Singh said like he finally got it. "So if not food, what was it?"

"Something illegal."

"What?"

"I don't know," I said, "but I'm going to find out."

# THIRTY-TWO

*Tuesday 9th February*

The night dragged as I tossed and turned, unable to keep stray thoughts at bay. Where was Su Ling? Was she in danger? Was Yipp up to something and trying to fool me? Did he really know where she was? Had he found out and done something to her?

I kept reminding myself of the money. Surely that implied Su Ling had been in the warehouse. She'd put the money in the crate. No note. No other clue. What was she trying to tell me?

I'm normally a rational man so this wasn't like me. Worrying never helped anyone. I needed facts. I needed information. I needed to wait.

In the morning, the reporter Linda Wu was waiting for me on the steps to my office.

"Have you remembered anything about banana money yet?" she asked as I approached.

"And good morning to you too," I said.

"Banana money," she repeated.

"I told you I don't know anything."

I started to walk past her but she grabbed my arm, her face earnest. "Perhaps you know something you don't know."

"What's that supposed to mean?"

"Perhaps you don't realize you know something."

"Come up to the office," I said, and I trotted up the stairs. I was already at my desk, having greeted Madam Chau, before Miss Wu stepped into the room and looked critically around.

"Do you get much business, Captain Carter?"

Before I could speak, Madam Chau was on her feet and marching towards the diminutive reporter. "Who are you? And you should knock before you enter!" she barked.

Linda Wu said something in Chinese and I heard the words *Straits Times*. Madam Chau responded in kind, although her tone was still cutting. Then she turned her back on the reporter and looked at me.

"She says you invited her up."

"I did."

"I prefer that people make appointments." She tapped a black diary on her desk. "That way we have a record and a schedule."

I nodded and winked at her. "Just this once... Let's put in that Miss Wu has an appointment now, at eight am."

Madam Chau huffed her disapproval. "Let's say eight-fifteen, shall we?"

I looked at her with curiosity.

"There's something urgent and private first," she said.

I asked Linda Wu to wait outside for fifteen minutes and Madam Chau closed the door behind her.

"What is it?" I asked.

"You've had a telegram." She took it from her desk and handed it to me. The message simply read:

Check the police reports: Munsi and Batu murder

I looked at the sender's name: A New Friend. The message had been relayed to the Singapore Post Office from the General Post Office in Kuala Lumpur.

Madam Chau was watching my reaction.

I shook my head. "I don't know…" I said absently, still thinking. This was about the policeman and the Batu murder. Were they linked?

"A new friend?" she asked.

"Anonymous." Whoever had sent this couldn't risk calling me. However, I had a good idea who it might be.

The reporter knocked and stepped into the office at precisely the allotted time, which made Madam Chau nod her appreciation.

Miss Wu took the seat opposite me and without preamble said, "Have you thought any more about the banana money?"

"No."

"Why not? You've had since Sunday to think about it."

I smiled at her. "You asked me about banana money and I told you I knew nothing."

"You said you'd heard about it and thought it was a joke. Could you explain, please?"

I glanced at Madam Chau, who was listening but pretending to be otherwise occupied.

"When I first started up, getting paid was difficult. My receptionist said I shouldn't be paid in banana money."

Linda Wu swivelled and looked at Madam Chau. "Why did you say that?"

My receptionist narrowed her eyes and waited until I encouraged her to respond. "It was just an expression," she said. "We needed cash flow, and Captain Carter has a tendency towards charitable work."

Miss Wu swivelled back to me. "Why?"

"Why what?"

"Why do charitable work?"

"I didn't always issue a bill if I thought the work didn't justify it or the customer couldn't afford to pay."

"So you're saying you never actually handled banana money."

"That's precisely what I'm saying."

Miss Wu glanced out of the window and said nothing for a few seconds.

"Is that all?" I asked.

She looked back at me and I detected confusion in her eyes. "I don't understand."

"What don't you understand, Miss Wu?"

"I received a note. It said to ask you about banana money."

"Who was the note from?"

"Anonymous." She looked deep in thought for a moment, then: "You're an investigator."

"Correct."

"You have contacts, right?"

"Yes."

"Then that will be it. You don't know anything but my anonymous tip must be to get your help."

That seemed reasonable so I nodded.

She said, "With all your contacts, do you happen to have one at the Board of Commissioners."

"No. Who are they?"

"The Malayan treasury department. They're responsible for the issuance of currency now and they're based in Kuala Lumpur."

"I'll try and get you an introduction."

She thanked me and I asked Madam Chau to place a call to my friend Chief Inspector McNaughton. Within minutes he got me on the telephone with the assistant to the Currency Commissioner of the Board of Commissioners.

I placed my hand over the mouthpiece and spoke to Miss Wu. "He can see you this afternoon at three."

The reporter frowned, looked at her watch and shook her head. "Kuala Lumpur?" But then she surprised me by adding, "It's possible I suppose."

I nodded and I confirmed the appointment.

When I put the telephone down, she said, "I don't have a car."

"So you can't make it."

"You will drive me."

I almost laughed at her audacity. Then I thought about the telegram, but I also thought about Su Ling. Following up on a murder and the death of a policeman could wait. I needed to be around for Su Ling's communication. I needed to know what had happened and what she planned.

"I don't think so," I said.

Linda Wu shook her head. "You are involved somehow, Captain Carter. Someone wants this investigated and you are an investigator. And there's another reason you should join me."

"What's that?" I asked, less than convinced.

"Because there was another piece to the anonymous note. At the bottom, it said: Beware of Andrew Yipp."

# THIRTY-THREE

I drove up to Woodlands Crossing, jumped the queue as usual and went over the causeway into Malaya. Once there, I took Route One out of Johor Bahru and was soon beyond the town, heading north through the jungle.

Linda Wu sat very upright, eyes forward.

I don't like constant chatter, but I had expected some conversation to pass the time. However, whenever I asked a question I received an abrupt response. Nothing ever came back.

Eventually, I ventured, "You're not like another reporter I knew. She was constantly asking questions, trying to get personal information out of me."

"What was her name?"

"Hannah Quinn. We were in Penang. Do you know her?"

Linda shook her head. "Did she get it?"

"Did she get what?" I said, jumping to the conclusion that she meant something else.

"Did she get personal information out of you?"

"Not really."

"Was she interested in you?"

"I guess so."

"There you have it," she said like she'd won an argument.

"There I have what?"

"I'm not asking personal questions because I'm not interested in you."

I gave up and we sat in silence for over an hour, just the wind and rattle of the jeep for company. I glanced at her a few times and she seemed deep in thought, or the opposite, like she'd switched her brain into sleep mode.

When she finally spoke, I almost jumped at the sound beside me.

"Why are you in Singapore? Is it the sun, sea and sex?"

"That's an unreasonable generalization." I paused for comedic effect. "Some of us aren't interested in the sea."

"You don't sail?"

"No," I said, and figured she hadn't got the joke. This girl was hard work.

Silence again for a few minutes before she said, "I'm making an effort at conversation."

"Ah."

"When you first saw me what did you think?"

"Honestly?"

"That's why I asked," she said.

"Let's see, I noticed you're over a foot shorter than me. You're fairly young I suppose and… I thought you were pretty."

"There," she said.

"There what?"

"You're a male chauvinist."

I started to protest but she stopped me.

"It's a man's world, Captain Carter. You can't help it. When you see a woman your brain assesses her as a potential mate. When men see a woman they think she's either pretty or ugly—and subconsciously they're assessing whether they would take her to bed."

"I don't want to bed you."

"Subconsciously."

"I don't wish to disappoint you, Miss Wu, but it's neither conscious nor subconscious," I insisted.

"I'm not disappointed," she said. "Do you play sport?"

I blinked at the apparent switch in subject. "I box and I used to play rugby."

"Typical he-man activities," she said scornfully. "Again it's related to sex. Neanderthal man got the best women by being the strongest—he could protect them. He could keep them. These days you can't openly fight for your woman so you revert to Neanderthal mentality."

"I box because I enjoy it and it keeps me fit."

"You don't realize it, but it's basic instinct. You are trying to attract women."

"And I thought my success with the fairer sex was down to my good looks and charm."

She said, "The only dynamic that's changed since Neanderthal times is that money is now important too. Masculinity and money. Both needed to get the female."

"There are two sides to that coin," I said, joking about money, but she either didn't get the pun or didn't want to show that she did. I added, "Money is no good unless women accept it."

Linda turned in her seat, her face suddenly flushed. "You are such a male chauvinist! I know you're alluding to prostitution. Women have to accept money from men because they have little choice. It's a man's world, Captain Carter. The women have to rely on men to feed them. Most of the work goes to men, so if a woman wants independence, selling her body is the only way she can do it."

I started to defend myself but she was in full flow now and cut me off.

"Men take advantage if they can, and they do. Also, women may have to play along until their opportunity arises. But times are changing. The world is changing.

Women have more prospects—are getting those opportunities. The war did that for us. Especially in Britain and America. Women were needed to do the work, to aid the war effort, and they proved they could do it just as well as the men. In the future, women will lead businesses and governments. It may be a slow process but it will happen because we are just as good—if not better—than men."

She took a breath.

"It'll surprise you to hear that I agree," I said. "Maybe not that women are better, but—"

"Look at history," she said, animated once more like I'd flicked a switch again. "When women have become leaders, they have been great leaders. Take Queen Victoria and the first Queen Elizabeth. They were put in those positions because the men had no alternative, but once those women got there, they showed themselves to be independent and strong. Look into any female leader from the past and you'll find one better than any man."

"You feel very passionate about this."

"I do, and change is coming. It's a new world. Strong women are rising to the fore. Not just monarchs, but business leaders and politicians, especially in America. People like Coco Chanel and Eleanor Roosevelt."

I nodded. "This new world sounds like a better place."

"Mark my words," she said, "I doubt America will ever have a black president, but they'll have a female one before too long."

She went on to tell me about more great women of influence and power and it whiled away the time.

At one point, I said, "Why haven't I read an article in the *Straits Times* about this?"

"I tried but the editor—a man of course—rejected my piece."

"That's a shame."

169

"Not really, I'm writing a book on the subject. It's called *Women Don't Need Men.*"

"That's worrying for me—as a man."

She laughed, or at least it sounded a bit like a laugh. "Don't worry, men will still have a role. Your job will be the heavy lifting and all the menial tasks. You'll be the worker bees in the future society."

"So no more need for me to train in the boxing gym," I said.

"Oh yes," she said, and this time I was certain of the laugh in her voice. "The roles will be reversed. Men will have to keep fit and look good. You'll need the money. And if you want your independence, then maybe you'll prostitute yourself instead. Maybe you won't even have a choice. Maybe you'll be trapped in sexual servitude."

"This new world isn't sounding so good after all."

"The shoe is on the other foot."

"I hope you don't use so many clichés in your book," I intended it to be a joke but realized my mistake as soon as the words left my mouth.

"I'm dumbing it down for you," she snapped. The wind pummelled my ears and the jeep rattled, then she said, "Sorry, I guess I'm a little tense. I've not been out of Singapore before."

I glanced at her again and wondered just how old she was. Maybe she wasn't out of her teens yet. A young girl, early in her writing career—and because of her intensity and passion, I had no doubt she'd be a success. Maybe she'd even be one of those leaders she predicted.

"My editor will remove the clichés," she said.

"The same one who refused your article?"

"Oh no! My book's to be published by Malaya Publishing House. The staff there are much more enlightened."

I knew the company, on the corner of Stamford Road and Armenian Street.

"They actually publish?" I asked, and knew exactly what she'd reply.

"That's what the name says: *Publishing House.*"

"Yes, but it's a really old company. I thought they just sold stationery these days and had a book shop."

"They've started publishing again," she said, less critically this time. "They're keen on new authors and titles."

"And then what comes after *Women Don't Need Men*? Another book?"

"Possibly."

"Is there a book in this little trip—in banana money?"

"Possibly," she said again. "There's undoubtedly a story that someone wants us to uncover."

# THIRTY-FOUR

The Currency Commissioner welcomed us into his office and I got the sense that he was grateful for the visit. He had tired eyes, suggesting he'd spent years counting money and become bored with it.

"So you want to know about the Malay dollar," he said, his tone showing a surprising degree of enthusiasm.

Linda had a notebook out and a pencil at the ready.

"Before the war, the money was all printed in Britain. We had twenty-seven million"—he emphasized *million* so that we'd appreciate the enormity of it—"in one-dollar notes and almost six million in the five-dollar denomination. Do you know about the lost money?"

Linda sat forward. "No!"

"Three point two million dollars were lost. Seven hundred *thousand* one-dollar notes and five hundred *thousand* five-dollar notes. The money was shipped here of course but the Nazis sunk one of our boats." He gave a date and the name of the ship and Linda wrote it down.

"What happened during the occupation?" I asked after a pause.

"The stock was locked in the treasuries. Singapore notes—Straits dollars—stayed on the island. Malay dollars went to Penang. Most of it."

"Most?" Linda asked.

"Well, there's a bit of contention because allegedly nine million dollars was shipped to India for safety. However, after the occupation, this money was found in the Japanese treasury in Singapore. Just what happened no one knows—at least no one alive. We don't think the Japanese captured it because the ship that allegedly took it wasn't seized."

I said, "So it never left."

"That's the only logical answer," he said. "Maybe it was a smokescreen or perhaps there was a delay."

Linda said, "Or someone did it intentionally, planning to steal it."

The commissioner shrugged. "It's a possibility. We'll never know. But based on the serial numbers"—he patted a blue book on his desk—"we know that all except for one thousand one-dollar bills were recovered."

"Incredible," I said.

"What happened to them?" Linda asked.

The commissioner nodded as if he'd hoped she'd ask that question. "The Japanese found them in Penang, although we don't know what happened to them afterwards. If someone else found them, they wouldn't be any use, because all stocks were destroyed in 1946 after the Board of Commissioners"—he pointed to a plaque on the wall telling us the obvious: we were in their building—"was established. April Fool's Day," he chuckled. "Prior to April first, I'm sure you know, Captain, the finances were administered by the Army Pay Corps."

I nodded. "So what happened next?"

"You get the Malay dollars you have today, pegged at one dollar equals two shillings and fourpence."

I nodded again. I mostly used British pounds, since the currency was interchangeable. American dollars were also accepted, although the exchange rate depended on who you were bartering with—and US soldiers seemed happy with whatever they got for it.

"What happened during the war?" Linda asked. "Would you tell us about banana money, please?"

"Japanese invasion money," the commissioner said. "The Japanese issued their own dollars in the region and deemed the old dollars invalid. It meant anyone holding Straits or Malay dollars from before the occupation were suddenly penniless."

Linda frowned. "But isn't that exactly what the British did when they re-took the region?"

"Yes, but their currency was literally worthless anyway. The Japanese foolishly didn't use serial numbers, so it was easily counterfeited. Also, we think there were no real records or control, so the authorities just printed more when they needed more, leading to hyperinflation." Again he pointed to the sign on the wall. "That's why it needs to be appropriately governed. The supply needs to be controlled."

"What were the denominations?" I asked, trying to get us back on track since the commissioner seemed to have taken offence at Linda's comment.

"They had dollars and cents like us," he said. "Five, ten and fifty cents. The dollars were ones, fives, tens mainly, but there was also a hundred- and a thousand-dollar note." He shook his head. "The thousand-dollar note was created towards the end of the war and was basically a recycled hundred-dollar note. Inflation was totally out of control for them at the end."

"Did all the notes have banana trees?" I asked.

"Only the ten-dollar note had the banana tree."

Linda had been writing in her notebook. She looked up and asked, "How was the money disposed of?"

"The pre-war money was punched with a hole," the commissioner said. "It was also stamped with the word 'Decommissioned' in red to avoid any mistakes."

"But if I had any of those dollars, pre-war or Japanese dollars, they were valueless."

"That's right."

I hoped she wouldn't comment again on how tough that must have been for the general population and fortunately she didn't. Instead, she said, "You didn't say what happened to the Japanese dollars. There must have been lots."

"You are right, my dear. The Japanese treasuries in Penang and Kuala Lumpur, as well as Singapore, all held large stocks of the notes."

"Did you punch those and mark them as decommissioned?"

"No, they were all burned."

"Out of interest, could you tell me the process? I mean, were they just bundled together and set alight?"

"In a fashion," he said. "But they were all collected first. Initially, I believe there was a view that they might be honoured or that the Japanese government would be forced to reimburse the nations. So they were collected and catalogued and sent to Singapore by train. It started in Penang on the sixteenth of January 1946, picked up the notes from the capital and then on overnight to the General Post Office in Singapore."

"And from there?"

"Ah, I'm afraid that's all I know. I presume that's where the bonfire will have been once they deemed them worthless."

Linda handed the commissioner a Malay five-dollar note.

"What's this?" he said, taking it with a smile, "payment for my services?"

"Look closely."

I glanced at her and mouthed, "What?"

She looked back at the commissioner, waiting for his response. He rubbed it between his fingers as if testing the thickness. Then he took out a loupe like he was a jeweller checking a diamond for occlusions.

His lips pursed like he was thinking. Then he opened a drawer, pulled out a booklet and began thumbing through it.

He suddenly stopped and took a long deep breath, looking hard at the reporter.

"Where did you get this?"

"I was sent it—anonymously."

"What's wrong?" I asked.

"It's a counterfeit," he said. "A surprisingly good one, but definitely fake."

# THIRTY-FIVE

The Currency Commissioner said, "The quality of the paper is excellent. The print quality is flawless. The colour looks good."

"But...?" I prompted. "What makes you say it's a fake?"

"The serial number and denomination don't match. It's a one-dollar serial number."

Linda said, "You said the Japanese converted the hundred-dollar bill into a thousand. Is this something similar. Has a one-dollar bill been reprinted as a five somehow?"

The commissioner shook his head. "Wrong size. Wouldn't work." He held up the note. "Can I keep this? I'd like it analysed. If someone is printing counterfeits, I'm sure you appreciate that this can undermine the economy."

Linda agreed, and that was the end of the meeting.

"What are you going to do now?" I asked. It was almost four in the afternoon and I'd already decided I was staying over rather than dashing back. I wanted to see those police reports.

All that talk on the way up about my basic instinct and subconscious mind desiring sex with her had made me wonder if she was going to suggest we stay in a hotel together. As it turned out, it was just my Neanderthal brain playing tricks.

"I'll catch the night train," she said. "I want to imagine I'm that Japanese money being transferred to Singapore."

"And when you get home?"

"I'll visit the post office. Hopefully, my journalistic reputation will get me through the Postmaster General's door. I want to know what happened once the money reached them. And you—what will you do?"

"I've something I'd like to do," I said, providing no information. "I'll stay over and travel back in the morning."

★

I'd once stayed here with a girlfriend called Heidi Allan. I chose a different hotel so I wouldn't be reminded of the attractive doctor I'd left behind in Perak. Heidi was a strong woman and self-possessed like Su Ling, but that's where the similarity ended. After three months with the doctor, I knew I needed to move on. Su Ling, on the other hand, made me think long term like no other woman had.

I rang Madam Chau on the hotel telephone and checked whether I'd had any messages or calls, in case Su Ling had been in touch, but nothing had happened. I promised to call back at the end of the day since my receptionist liked to know I was all right. However, I really wanted another opportunity to hear from Su Ling.

Then I drove over to the police HQ and confidently asked for the records office. My government ID is only good for Singapore, but the duty sergeant accepted it, which meant the records clerk didn't even ask for credentials, assuming they'd already been checked.

I told him I wanted the files on the police detective called Munsi and the ex-soldier found murdered in the Batu Caves.

"Which one?"

"Which one?" I repeated, thinking he was asking me to specify a cave.

"Yes, there were two men murdered in the caves."

I blinked, surprised. "Two? All right, get me both."

The records clerk scurried away, and just minutes later I had three files in my hand.

I read the first Batu Caves file. This was the case I knew about. The ex-soldier found scalped in August. I picked up the next file. Another man in the caves, although he'd had his throat cut. When Peter Jihan had mentioned an ex-soldier found in Batu Caves, I thought he'd made a mistake. He hadn't. He was talking about this one. The first thing I noticed was that the initial report had been written by Detective Sergeant Munsi. So that was the link. I'd thought it unlikely that BlackJack had killed a civil policeman.

Detective Munsi's report on the second Batu Cave murder was dated 18th September, so right towards the end of BlackJack's killing spree around Kuala Lumpur.

In his report, Munsi suggested a link to the other deaths because the man was white-skinned and killed with a knife.

I pulled out the photographs and saw tattoos referred to in Munsi's report. There had been nothing to identify the man but Detective Munsi had recognized the emblem of the Manchester Rifles on the body's right triceps. An ex-soldier, undoubtedly. Judging from his comfortably overweight condition and greying hair, I decided he'd been out of the army a while, possibly since the last war. Munsi referred to him as *the victim*. In my mind, I labelled him as *Soldier A*.

The report said they'd asked at all of the local barracks and no one recognized the man. The case was still officially open but there had been no update since October last year.

However, that wasn't what surprised me. What I didn't understand was why the SIB hadn't investigated the murder of Soldier A. They'd looked into all of the others, including the scalped man found a month earlier, so why not this one? It had happened before that investigation had spun off into hunting the killer.

I looked at the pictures again and wondered if it had been investigated after all. The other killings had been gruesome: a face cut off, genitals removed and stuffed in a victim's mouth, disembowelling. In fact, one thought had been that the killer may have had medical training, such was the precision.

Soldier A had his throat slit. He'd also been stabbed in the back. The coroner's report said that he thought the stabbing was non-fatal and had occurred first.

I visualized BlackJack coming up on Soldier A, stabbing him in the back, then grabbing his head and slitting his throat. Why the initial stabbing? Surely BlackJack was skilled enough to just slit the man's throat.

I was staring at the photograph of the initial wound when the records clerk handed me a mug of tea. He looked at the picture and sighed.

"Poor Munsi."

I studied the man's face. "Why do you say that—apart from the obvious?"

"Well, he died a few weeks later. Maybe it was the curse of the caves."

"Is there a curse?"

He shook his head. "Not really. I mean, it's a Hindu religious site and Munsi was Muslim. Not exactly a sacred place for him."

I said, "Why would the victim be there?"

"Unless he was Hindu—which I doubt—I don't see why he would be."

I said, "Would you get the coroner on the telephone for me?"

The clerk seemed pleased at being involved and scurried away again.

While I waited, I read through the report on Detective Munsi's murder. He'd been shot rather than stabbed—again more confirmation that this wasn't BlackJack's doing. I looked at a photograph showing a hole in the back of Munsi's head. The coroner concluded that the gun had been within an inch of the skull.

The detective's body had been found in a notorious part of the city, and two known criminals had been arrested and charged with his murder.

I was reading their confessions when the records clerk called me. The coroner was on the phone.

After perfunctory introductions, he asked me how he could help.

"Do you remember the second body found at Batu Caves? Not the scalped one, the other white man with army tattoos?"

"Of course, last October."

September, October? Close enough, I reckoned. "Looking at the cut to the throat, would you say left- or right-handed?"

He cleared his throat, and I suspected he was visualizing the corpse.

"Hard to say. Entry point on the left, exit on the right."

"So if the attacker came up from behind?"

"Right-handed—if it was from behind.

"Easiest way to slit a throat. Less messy," I said, nodding. "What do you make of the initial blow?"

"Just below the right scapula. Struck a rib. Didn't penetrate far. Didn't cause much damage."

"The throat slash—expert or amateur?"

"Pretty amateur, I'd say."

"Thank you."

"Anything else I can help with?"

181

"That's all. You've been a great help."

I ended the call and also thanked the clerk and told him I'd finished with the reports.

"Find what you were looking for, sir?"

"I think so."

Leaving the records office, I went upstairs and found the corridor that led me into the typist room. I was pretty sure someone in there had been the origin of the telegram that told me to check the records.

The lady at the head table—the manageress—was my likely candidate.

"Hello," I said as I approached her. The room was a clatter of typewriters.

"Good afternoon, sir," she said without a flicker of recognition. "How can I help you?"

"I left you my business card," I said. "Captain Ash Carter."

Now there was recognition in her eyes, but not what I expected. She wasn't the source of the telegram.

I looked around the room. "Any news of Mrs Srivats?"

The woman blinked, and I saw her humanity for the first time. "I'm worried, sir. She's still not turned up."

Of course, she was just confirming what I already knew. I wanted to gauge her response and that of others in the room.

"Anu Srivats is missing?" I said loudly, as though I hadn't quite heard the response above the noise. No one looked up, which I found odd. It gave me the distinct impression that the typing ladies deliberately kept their heads down.

I turned back to the manageress.

"Tell me about the police reports."

She gave a small shrug as though I'd asked an obvious question. Maybe I was. "I receive the handwritten notes in an envelope." She pointed to a pile of buff-coloured envelopes on her desk. I picked one up and noticed several names and departments, all crossed off until the last one—Typing Pool. She said, "I check what's involved, log it in and allocate it to a member of staff. The notes are typed up and returned to me. I put them back in the envelope and it's returned. If there are changes or errors then the file comes back. I note the errors and re-issue it to the same member of my team."

A lady approached with a sheaf of papers. I nodded for her to proceed and she handed them to the manageress. The lady then removed a blue sheet of carbon and put a page in an envelope. There was a remaining page and she put this in another tray. Three trays in total. In, Out and the third one.

"And that?" I asked, pointing to the third tray.

"My copy. For managerial purposes. I can check for mistakes and the general quality of the typing."

I said, "Tell me about the Batu Caves report—the second one."

She frowned. "I don't read the reports, sir."

*Damn!*

A familiar face appeared at the door's window. George McNaughton.

He pushed into the room and pumped my hand. "I was told you were in here. What's going on? No, tell you what—are you staying over?"

I gave him the name of the hotel.

He pulled a face. "I suppose that's acceptable. Anyway, let's go to dinner. You can tell me all about what you're up to then, old chap."

★

McNaughton wanted to take me to the Polo Club again, but my clothes weren't suitable. Instead, he took me to an exclusive Indian restaurant that normally required a week's notice.

I'd been back to the hotel and changed and called Madam Chau in case Su Ling had been in touch. She hadn't. However, Inspector Singh had visited. His men had obtained an address for the boy who had stolen my money clip. He said they'd wait for my return before visiting the premises.

I met my friend at nine, and despite my smarter suit, I still felt underdressed.

"So," he said after we'd ordered, "tell me all about your visit to the Board of Commissioners of Currency." And I did, although there wasn't much to tell. The only thing I found intriguing was that the Japanese dollars had been shipped down to Singapore after the war for disposal there.

"What's this reporter girl like?" he asked when I'd finished. "Not attractive then?"

"Petite and pretty," I said, thinking that she would probably bite my head off for my sexist profile.

"But not pretty enough for you to... you know?" He grinned and winked.

"Only one girl for me these days," I said, and told him about Su Ling.

"Andrew Yipp's niece?" he said, almost spitting out his wine.

"The very same."

"Well you don't make it easy on yourself, do you, Ash? My goodness!"

I said, "She's disappeared. I've not seen her since last Wednesday night."

"Not avoiding you?" He started to chuckle but then saw my serious face and said, "You think Yipp's done something with her?"

I shrugged. "I just don't know what's going on. Possibly, but if it is him then he's pretending he doesn't know where she is."

He may have been joking but he said, "I'll put out an APB for her."

"I doubt she's travelled upcountry. Yipp daren't go further north than JB, and I suspect she's the same."

"The new man after Yipp's organization as well?"

"Secretary Norris," I said. "Unlike his predecessor, he doesn't think Yipp is a communist, but he's still afraid of political influence—plus there's the old thorn in the side because everyone knows he's a gang boss."

"Knows, but can't prove. Corporate structures," he said with a sigh, "the modern way of hiding a plethora of trouble."

We ate the delicious food and made small talk until the conversation turned to why I was at the police station.

"I got a strange telegram," I said, "that pointed me to the police reports."

"Who sent it?"

"I don't know."

"What was in the reports?"

"Nothing too illuminating," I said. "Except for one thing I don't understand."

He took a sip of wine, waiting for me to continue.

"BlackJack typically killed with his left hand and he was skilful."

"What makes you think it wasn't his left?"

"The initial blow. At first, I thought it was just an amateur attempt to kill, but maybe it wasn't. Maybe it made the victim freeze. You know, like a gun in the back. Then the killer grabbed him—probably around the head, pulled back and drew the knife, left to right."

He looked thoughtful and spoke slowly. "Either BlackJack pretending to be someone else or it is someone else."

"He chose the same location as another BlackJack murder." I took a breath. "I think it was someone who wanted it to look like a BlackJack murder but didn't know he killed left-handed."

"I'll let the detective inspector know," McNaughton said. "I'm not sure where it'll take us, but you never know."

I nodded. "Follow every lead."

He said, "So anything else about the case?"

"No."

"All very odd about the mysterious telegram then."

I nodded again.

"And odd about your missing girlfriend. What are you going to do about her?"

"As soon as I get back I'm going to start investigating," I said. "I'm going to find her, whether Yipp wants me to or not."

# THIRTY-SIX

*Wednesday 10th February*

Dawn was three hours away when I left the hotel in Kuala Lumpur. I'd slept badly, with thoughts of Su Ling again spinning through my mind. What was I doing in Kuala Lumpur when I should have been looking for the most amazing woman I'd ever met?

My logic had been to delay. I was waiting for a sign from her, but since talking it over with my friend, I had an awful feeling that something was seriously wrong. However, I couldn't reconcile this with why Yipp was so relaxed about it. He appeared genuine when accusing me of her disappearance. Logic then told me that he knew she hadn't left the country. Which made me wonder whether he'd known about our plans all along. Had he stopped her going to the warehouse? What then? Had she run away?

As I drove through the darkness, these thoughts still bothered me. Nothing made sense. If Yipp knew our plans then he'd have been following me. After the beating, I figured Wang would be watching, but then if Yipp knew about my movements on the night after the parade he'd surely know that I wasn't hiding Su Ling.

Where would she run to?

Yipp knew her far better than I did. He'd know everything—except for her secret apartments. I knew of three and could check those out. Maybe there were more.

Maybe she had other secrets.

And therein lay my problem. If they were real secrets, then she probably hadn't trusted anyone. I was about halfway to Johor Bahru before I remembered Su Ling's assistant Jinjing. I'd met the girl last year when Su Ling hid me. That was at one of her secret apartments and Jinjing had taken me there. That was the critical thing. Jinjing knew the location—and maybe she knew other secrets too.

I finally started to relax and the sky lightened over the hills to my left. My conscious mind stopped fretting about Su Ling because I had a plan of action. I would check her known hiding places and I would approach Jinjing.

Now that the freeze had thawed from my brain, I spent the rest of the time thinking about everything else that had been going on. They were all distractions, but deliberately so. Until I could focus one hundred per cent on Su Ling, I was happy to fill my time.

I thought about the banana money. That was a strange one. Who had sent the message to Linda Wu? What did they want her to find and what was my involvement? The message had warned of Yipp. I'd assumed that was because of me, but what if he had some connection to the decommissioned Japanese dollars?

We'd learned that before the occupation millions had been lost at sea. We also learned that most of the money had been hidden from the Japanese during the occupation, although there was the odd situation with money apparently sent to India and yet found later in Singapore.

I hadn't known any of this history, nor had I known that the British decommissioned their own dollars after the war, under the auspices of the army's Paymaster

General. Tough times for the locals. They have money, they don't, they have money, they don't. No wonder the black market was still so rife. No wonder criminality was a way of life. People needed to survive and the British had been as fiscally brutal as the Japanese.

Linda would be back in Singapore now, having travelled on the overnight train. Despite her natural animosity and chip on her shoulder about the misogynistic world, I respected her. She was driven and would be influential one day—providing she softened up a little. I had no doubt she would be on the post office steps waiting for the doors to open this morning. She'd probably be first into the building, demanding an interview with the Postmaster General.

I smiled at the thought of him inadvertently saying something sexist. She'd probably bite his head off.

A mile outside Malaya's southernmost town and the causeway, I started thinking about Soldier A and Detective Munsi.

The telegram had told me to look at the police records. I'd looked and had two thoughts: firstly, the killing of Soldier A seemed amateur. I found it hard to believe that BlackJack was the murderer. The second thought was that SIB should have investigated it. They'd investigated cases far less likely to be BlackJack murders and yet this one had been missed.

Who had sent me the telegram? They'd wanted to remain anonymous and I'd assumed it had been the typing pool manageress. Now I was sure it wasn't her. She'd have given me some sort of signal if it had been. I'd turned up at the police station on the same day I'd received the telegram. I'd have seen something in her eyes if only appreciation that I'd come so quickly.

But I had learned something from her. The typists produced everything in duplicate. The original was returned in a marked envelope, the carbon copy was retained by the manageress as a means of quality control.

*Check the police reports.*

What if the sender had meant the copies?

I put my foot down and raced across the causeway, receiving a shout of "Slow down!" from the MPs on the Singapore side.

I waved an apology as I shot under the hastily raised boom and pressed the pedal harder to the floor.

Last night Madam Chau told me a relative had died, and I'd told her to take the day off. However she was in the office when I arrived.

"I wanted to make sure you got back," she said.

"Madam Chau... You missed me!"

"Nothing of the sort," she said with a frown. "I don't like the idea of you gallivanting about. We have bills to pay."

I smiled because I think she actually imagined me gallivanting about like a pleasure-seeking playboy. I also knew she really did care about me but for some reason she couldn't admit it.

"Madam Chau," I said, "I insist you take the day off. But before you do, please would you place a call to the police headquarters in KL and ask for the typing pool manageress?"

It was almost fifteen minutes before the lady came on the line.

"Yes, sir?" she began. "I apologize for the delay, but we don't have a telephone in the typing room."

"Not a problem... I'm sorry, but I don't recall your name," I said.

"Mrs Sharon Bressen."

"Well, Mrs Bressen. My first question is this: are you aware of anyone who might have contacted me?"

"Contacted you, sir?"

"By telegram."

"No, sir."

"I gave you my business card. Do you still have it?"

"It'll still be in my desk drawer, sir."

"My second question is about the copies you keep. Please could you find the police reports typed up on the second body at Batu Caves investigated by Detective Munsi in September and also the report on Detective Munsi's murder."

There was no immediate response. I heard whistles and electronic clicks and distant voices—the sound of policemen talking as they walked by.

"Are you still there, Mrs Bressen?"

"Yes, sir. I'm sorry, sir, but all of my records were taken this morning."

I looked at my watch. It wasn't even nine-fifteen.

"Who took them?"

"A detective investigating the murders," she said.

Now it was my turn to be silent. I heard all the usual noises and finally said, "Was there anything unusual about the reports that you can remember?"

"No, sir. As I told you, I don't actually read the papers, just check them." She sounded apologetic. "There are far too many. I just don't have the hours in the day."

I thanked her and asked that she let me know if anything did come to mind. Then I asked the operator to put me through to Chief Inspector McNaughton.

"What's going on?" I asked him and then proceeded to explain that the typing pool reports had been sequestered.

"For investigation, dear chap," McNaughton said. "Thanks to you—or at least your anonymous tip-off—we think there may be something we missed. You know how the police protect their own. Munsi investigated the ex-soldier's death and was then murdered himself. Maybe the gangsters who confessed to Munsi's murder were involved in the other one. Maybe they are connected."

"Or maybe the confessions are false," I said.

"That's a possibility too."

After a pause, he said, "I thought you were moving on from the case. I thought you were focusing on finding your girlfriend."

"I am. Good luck with the case," I said, and ended the call.

Madam Chau took the handset from me and set it down. "Your appointment with Detective Singh is at eleven today. Meet him at Hill Street."

Of all the things going on, I'd forgotten about the murdered boy who had stolen my money clip. That gave me over an hour.

"I'm going out," I said, putting on my jacket.

"Gallivanting?"

"I wish. Now go home!"

I'd have to wait until dark to check on Su Ling's private apartments. In the meantime, I would visit all the places that were special to her, starting with Haw Par Villa with its landscaped gardens, pagoda and scenes from Chinese mythology. She'd left me a clue there once before. It was in the west near Gillman Barracks. And afterwards, I'd visit Mount Faber, where we'd had our first date two years ago. Where we'd lain on our backs, looked at the stars and talked about our dreams.

I walked and I searched, but I found no clues.

# THIRTY-SEVEN

Detective Singh was waiting for me on the steps of the Hill Street Station and directed me into the back of a black police car.

"Where are we going?" I asked.

"Kampong Bintang."

Of course, I knew it. It was behind Havelock Road, close to the quay where Pope had his warehouse, close to where the fire had been.

Singh said, "We got an address yesterday. Some of the ladies"—he stressed the word, implying they were anything but ladies—"on Bugis Street recognized the boy's photograph."

"Did you get a name?"

"Fagooren."

I raised an eyebrow.

He said, "Yes, it's an odd name. Not one I've heard before."

We drove over the river and down Havelock Road before turning left into the area known as Kampong Bintang. At one stage in history, this had been a separate village. Now it was a slum with crumbling buildings and staring faces.

"You needn't have waited for me," I said. "You could have come last night."

"I wouldn't risk my men here at night. Also, anyone who knows him was probably out during the dark. They'll be home, sleeping now."

"Which property?" I asked as we stopped by a row of dilapidated shophouses.

"We don't know," Singh said. He drew his service revolver and got out. The driver and front passenger also climbed out and slung rifles in the ready-position.

"Expecting trouble?" I asked the inspector.

"Better safe than sorry," he said.

We went into the first property and found a typical set-up with people sleeping fairly rough downstairs and the upper floor split into cubicles, most just divided by a curtain. Poor families crammed into a miserable existence.

The two constables each had a photograph of the boy and showed it from person to person, thrusting it in faces and slapping anyone who didn't pay enough attention. They spoke mostly in Hokkien, a Chinese dialect, but sometimes also in English.

Receiving no useful responses or recognition, we moved onto the next property. After three old shophouses, I decided to stay outside with the inspector.

"It doesn't feel right," I said.

"We have to be rough or the people won't answer."

"I meant the location. When he/she bumped into me in the square, she was beautiful: clean, well presented, well dressed. It wasn't someone from a slum."

He looked up and down the street. "The girls on Bugis Street were adamant Fagooren came from here."

I was thinking I'd give it another ten minutes when the armed police constables came out and went into the next building and we strolled towards the end of the street. A couple of minutes later the men came running out.

"Sir, we have another address," one said. "Our boy used to live here but was moved."

*Was moved.* I thought the expression unusual but let the constable continue.

"We've got an address on Canal Road."

That was back towards the centre, but not far and also off Havelock Road. We ran back to the police car and were soon outside a property on Canal Road. This one was more like an office block than a residence, but still decades old.

We jogged to the entrance, the constables with their rifles ready, like soldiers coming out of the trenches.

Inside was better than the slum houses, with larger rooms and some proper beds. There were no children, just young adults, two or three to a room.

We worked our way through four rooms, with people denying they knew the boy, but I wasn't convinced. Eyes looked more furtive than afraid. And then we heard running feet and a door slam.

Bursting into a hall, I saw eyes looking to the rear and another door. I ran for it, jerked it open and found myself in a yard. The police crowded behind me, but I ignored them. Ahead was a wall, and I'd just seen someone disappear over it.

One of the police blew a whistle, which was pointless since I doubted there were any other police within earshot. I was already moving and scrambled up and over the wall. There was another yard, full of weeds and scrap, on the other side. Then another door. I went over the wall, into the yard and then barged through the door.

The fugitive was ahead, running, pushing people out of the way, sending debris clattering behind him. Then he was at another door and out onto a street, well before I had begun progressing down the hall.

I jerked open the front door and rushed into the street beyond. Cumming Street, my brain registered. The man was running towards the river and he was moving fast.

I'm a good runner, but this man was like lightning. Magazine Road was at the bottom and he reached it before I had covered half the distance. But I kept running and turned left at the end.

And there he was. The police car blocked the road with the young man pressed against its bonnet. It looked like he'd run straight into the car and now one of the constables stood next to him, rifle pointed.

Singh stood there with his hands on his hips, grinning at me as I pulled up out of breath.

He tapped his head. "Smart."

The second constable rounded the corner behind me, bent double, and coughed as he recovered from the sprint.

I closed in on the young man on the bonnet. Little more than a kid, definitely under twenty, he looked at me with scared eyes. I guessed he was mixed-race. Slightly darker skin than the boy who'd stolen my money clip, but similar.

I waved for the first constable to put away the gun and flash the photograph.

"Who is he?" I asked the kid.

No response, just those scared eyes.

"Why did you run?"

Still nothing.

Singh said, "Get him in the car. We'll make him talk back at the station."

I checked my watch. Almost half-past twelve.

"I'll join you later," I said. "A couple of hours?"

Singh grinned. "Good, because otherwise one of my men has to walk back."

The police station was only a few minutes away and so were the locations I wanted to visit. It was lunchtime and I wanted to go to all the places where Su Ling knew I regularly ate, just in case she got a message to me. I also wanted to look for her assistant, Jinjing.

Firstly, I went to the café near my office and had lemonade while I waited. After thirty minutes I walked through the arcade that connected Collyer Quay to Raffles Place. Fairly new, it attracted girls who worked locally with shops selling business-style clothes, boutiques, parlours and, most importantly, it housed the second place in Singapore to get air conditioning: the Cold Storage Milk Bar. It was a café where shoppers and workers could cool off with pastries and a glass of milk.

I think they could have sold anything in there and it would have still been busy, such was the luxury of cool air.

There were no free tables and I figured it would take too long to be served, so I hung around outside for fifteen minutes. Jinjing didn't appear nor did I receive any secret messages, although I could feel the eyes of sixteen or so young ladies burning into me. When one came out and invited me to join her group, my heart fluttered with the hope that there would be a sign from Su Ling, but the girl was white and too posh, I decided as I declined the request.

From the arcade, I walked past a bar on Boat Quay where there was more of a melting pot of nationalities and I was therefore more likely to get a message from Su Ling. Nothing.

I then took my favourite route over the river via Coleman Bridge and wended my way towards Little India. There was a tiffin house that she and I both liked. I went inside and ate some lunch as I watched the patrons and passers-by.

My final stop was at a Chinese restaurant close to the Cathay Building. And there I spotted Jinjing eating at a table.

Once inside, I sat with my back to the wall and drank jasmine tea. The owner fussed around me until I ordered food. I didn't touch it. Instead, I tried to make eye contact with Su Ling's assistant.

Her attention passed my way, casually, like someone taking in the room rather than properly looking. Her glance didn't rest on me, but a moment later her look met mine.

I raised an eyebrow hoping for a response and got a frown. Then her glimpse flicked away and back. I waited a beat and then looked in the same direction. By the door were two men deep in conversation, but they had water and no food, and when one glanced my way I knew who they were: Yipp's men. Or more specifically, thugs working for Wang.

Jinjing's eyes moved left and right. Not looking. Shifting her eyes instead of moving her head. She was saying "no". She was saying "don't approach me".

I looked towards the street and raised an eyebrow as a question. Meet me outside?

Again the "no" with her eyes.

I waited for another signal from her, but I was still sitting there when she and her group left. No one approached and she'd said nothing more with her eyes.

I doubted she'd left anything on her table for me since she'd given no indication. Despite this, I wanted to check. However, when I stood, so did Wang's thugs.

They looked at me, I looked at them.

Trouble?

I sat down again and pretended I wanted to finish my tea. As I raised my cup, I dropped my left hand to my ankle holster and retrieved my gun.

Had they noticed? I didn't care. The Beretta went from my hand into my pocket and I stood again then made my way to the door.

I walked out onto the street, took six paces and turned around.

Wang's thugs had followed me out.

# THIRTY-EIGHT

The men stepped onto the street and then froze as they saw me, facing them with my left hand in my pocket.

After the initial surprise, their natural confidence kicked in and they squared up to me on the pavement. I could see the Cathay Building between them like they'd deliberately lined up symmetrically. I stayed relaxed and didn't move, which seemed to create a problem for them. It was as though they had orders and being confronted by me wasn't one of the scenarios they'd considered.

We were four good strides apart. I stepped forward, mainly to see how they'd react.

They didn't move. They just stood there as if barring my way. Which maybe they were.

"I'd like to go to the cinema," I said. The cinema was on the ground floor of the Cathay Building.

My words seemed to kick the one on the right into life. He shook his head.

"What? Nothing good on today?"

He said, "You're not welcome."

"At the cinema?"

The one on the left said, "In the building. Mr Yipp's orders."

"It's a free world," I said.

Neither thug responded.

"Give Mr Yipp a message from me," I said.

Their eyes narrowed.

"We're closing in on him." I took a step back. "Next time I walk into the Cathay Building, he won't be around anymore."

I was certain they'd pass the message on, although probably through Wang first. Of course it was a bluff. When you're unsure of your poker hand and your opponents', try and unsettle them. Would my comment unsettle Yipp? Probably not, but I felt better as I walked away from the restaurant and the two Chinese thugs.

It was after three and the heavens opened as I reached the police HQ. I'd been a little longer than I assumed, but at least I'd made eye contact with Jinjing and felt she had something to tell me. How and when we'd talk, I didn't know, but it felt like progress.

I found Inspector Singh, who led me to the cells.

"He's not told us much," the inspector said. "He and his friend are from Vietnam. His name is Saburo Huynh and his friend is—was—Patrice Dang."

"Not Fagooren then?"

"Ah, our foolish mistake. It was Fàguó rén. It means Frenchie—a nickname."

"Frenchie?"

"Because they're French-Vietnamese. Came to Singapore eight months ago."

He opened the cell door. There were two guards inside and the kid lying curled on the floor. It reminded me of the beating I'd received from Wang and his men at the end of last week.

One guard stepped out so that we'd have more room and the other lifted the prisoner onto a chair. One of his eyes was swollen, and blood had smeared across his cheeks where his nose had bled and been wiped.

I knelt in front of the kid.

"How old are you, Saburo?" I asked in my schoolboy French.

He blinked his good eye, possibly surprised that I spoke the language. Then he replied in kind: "Eighteen."

Older than I'd guessed.

"And you came here eight months ago?"

"Yes."

"Why? Why come to Singapore?"

"To make our fortune. There's wealth here. In our town back home, we had no opportunity. Life was hard."

"And have you made your fortune?"

"No, monsieur."

"Would you like water?"

When the kid nodded, I looked up at Singh, who was frowning at me.

"D'eau?" he said. "That's water, yes?"

"Please," I said, "could he have some water?"

Singh flexed his shoulders, and I figured he was uncomfortable. Being kind to a prisoner didn't come naturally to the Singapore police. Then he shrugged and told one of the guards to fetch water.

I waited for it to arrive and then watched Saburo gulp it down.

I said, "Did you kill Patrice?"

Even his swollen eye flew wide. "No, monsieur!"

"Then why did you run?"

"Because of the police. I knew they would beat me whether I was innocent or guilty."

I said, "Ma Francaise est un peu… comment on dit… rusty? Would you mind if we switched to English?"

A smile tweaked in the corner of his mouth as I struggled with his language. "Of course not."

"What happened to your friend?"

"I don't know."

"What were you doing on Sunday evening—the night of the parade?"

"Working?"

"What do you do?"

Saburo glanced at the police and looked uncomfortable.

I looked up at the inspector. "Would you mind if we spoke in private?"

"Fifteen minutes," Singh said, then walked out and shut the cell door behind him. A guard stayed in the corridor but was far enough away that I thought he couldn't hear.

I said, "Saburo, are you a prostitute?"

He said, "Homosexuality is illegal."

"I don't care about that, I just want to help."

"Who are you?"

"I'm an investigator. I help the police and army and government, but I'm private. I can help you."

"How can I trust you?"

"I promise." I drew a cross on my chest. "Traverser mon Coeur."

He truly smiled this time—or at least I assumed it was a smile when he showed me bloody teeth. "Your French isn't too bad."

"My German is better. Now, tell me what you know. When was the last time you saw Patrice?"

"On Sunday afternoon. He said he had a plan to get us free."

"What was the plan?"

"He didn't say."

"Free from what, Saburo?"

Then he told me his story. He and fifteen others had paid for travel to Singapore. However, despite agreeing on the price upfront, once on the boat they had to pay for food and even the use of the toilet. One man had complained and been thrown overboard. No second chance. A clear message that if they didn't accept the terms they would die.

When they arrived in Singapore they were taken to a property in Kampong Bintang and told they had to earn money to pay for the accommodation.

"There's no work," he said. "The jobs on the wharves are controlled. Chinese have priority then Indians. The other way is to have a stall or shop, but that takes money and we had none. For Vietnamese there is no work in Singapore and yet..." He looked past me at the guard. "We had to steal to pay our debts."

I said, "Patrice stole money from me."

"He was a good pickpocket, the best, but he still couldn't earn enough. We gave the goods to the men and they sold them. They decided how much we owed and how much we earned. It was impossible to ever get away."

"But you did."

"Yes, after two months Patrice and I were moved to the house on Canal Road. For the first time, we had a room between us. Two of us in a room, not eight. We were looked after, but our jobs changed. We were made to wear make-up and dress like girls. They said we were pretty and we could earn a lot of money and get our freedom."

"But the bills increased?"

"Yes, living in the new house was much more expensive."

"Did Patrice work the same streets as you?"

"Patrice was —"

A door opened and shoes clacked down the hall. I turned to see Singh walking towards the cell.

Holding up a hand I said, "Five more minutes."

Singh stopped then stepped back. "Three, and we'll wait here."

I looked into Saburo's face again and lowered my voice. "You were saying?"

He whispered back. "Patrice was prettier than me, he was popular and not working the streets."

"Did he have regular clients?"

"Of course."

"Was he with a client on Sunday?"

"I don't know. He left me to watch the parade. That's the last time I saw him."

"And he said he had a plan."

"Yes."

"Was he going to pick lots of pockets? He only had my money clip on him when he was found."

"No. We needed a fortune. It was something big."

"Who were his clients?"

"I don't know. People in high places."

"Who would know?"

He looked like he was thinking then nodded. "The boss. He told us what to do. He controlled everything."

"His name?"

"Mr Zhao."

Singh started walking towards us and I stood up.

"Look after him," I said as Singh came into the cell.

"What do you mean?"

I gave him a brief update without mentioning illegal activities, but I did tell him about the gang in Kampong Bintang and Mr Zhao taking advantage of immigrants.

"That's not illegal," Singh said.

"But it's wrong. I would like you to find this Zhao chap and get a list of Patrice Dang's clients."

Singh nodded. "It's your money." Which I guess meant there was still plenty of resource available for the cash I'd handed over.

I said, "And I'd like you to protect Saburo."

"That's not how it works," Singh said, shaking his head. "And he's just a *kathoey*."

"He might be a witness. The murderer could be someone in authority. Could even be someone here. His friend was murdered and he could be next."

"People live and die," he said wearily. "It's life."

"Ishaan!" I said, glaring at him. Then softer, "Please."

"All right. For a few days, but this isn't a hotel. He stays in the cell."

"Make him comfortable and post a guard outside; make sure he's safe."

Inspector Singh wasn't happy when I left him but he promised to let me know as soon as he had the client list.

Outside, steam was rising from the pavement, the rain and clouds having blown away.

When I arrived at my office, Madam Chau was there. I challenged her and she said, "I've been and returned."

"You should take time off."

"I'll go to the death house tonight. And I didn't know where you were all afternoon."

I shook my head but realized arguing with her was futile.

"Anyway," she said, "that reporter has been trying to get hold of you. Miss Wu said it was important."

# THIRTY-NINE

*Thursday 11th February*

Linda Wu had returned numerous times and each time my receptionist had made an appointment for later.

"You're finally here," the reporter said as she came in.

I waved her to the chair opposite. "Did you manage to meet the Postmaster General?"

"I did. At first, he was reluctant, but I told him it was government business and I was helping you."

Although I admonished her with a shake of the head, I couldn't help admiring her audacity and tenacity.

She said, "He wasn't here straight after the war and has only been in the job for four years. But he did know the story of the Japanese money. He had a ledger with records showing that it arrived by train on the seventeenth of January 1946, just like we'd been told."

"How much?"

"He had an exact number. It was millions of dollars like we expected."

"Why do I think you're going to tell me something we didn't expect?"

She smiled.

"What happened to the cash next?"

"It was sent to the post office for destruction."

"Right, but that didn't happen. So what did?"

"Disposal was contracted out to the Malayan Publishing House."

I stared at her. "The building on Stamford Street—the people who'll publish your book?"

"The very same."

"All right. The obvious question is why?"

"Because they handled the printing of the dollars during the occupation. They printed and they destroyed."

"Is there evidence?"

"Only that someone from the publishing house signed for the notes and took them away."

"I presume you've been to see them for their version?"

"Yes, and I discovered that the Malayan Publishing House before and during the war was not the same company. The current business took over in 1947 and knows nothing about the money."

"Or claims to know nothing."

She shrugged. "Before you get too excited, that's not the most interesting thing."

"What is?"

"I mentioned counterfeiting to the Postmaster General and told him about my fake five-dollar note."

"And...?" I prompted. She was drawing this story out and loving it.

"He said that it was a different size. None of the Japanese notes could have been reprinted into the Malayan five-dollar note because of their size."

"I suspect you're about to tell me what could have been."

"The pre-war red ten-dollar notes."

"Which were decommissioned," I said.

She tapped her nose.

"What does that mean?"

She said, "What did the Currency Commissioner in KL tell us?"

"The pre-war notes were hole punched and stamped 'Decommissioned' in red."

"By whom?"

"Well the army's Paymaster General was in charge of currency, so I guess it was the army."

"Good guess, but you're wrong."

I waited for her to continue.

"They were stamped by the army but the hole punching was by the post office, who collected the notes."

She paused and I waited. This girl liked to tease with her stories.

"Not the post office in KL, but Singapore. So the same thing happened with the decommissioned Malay dollars as with the Japanese dollars. These ones were sent by train to Singapore and logged as received on June second 1946."

"And then hole punched?" I said, guessing that wasn't what happened.

She blew out air. "Well, the Post Master General said he had no evidence the notes were ever hole punched. They may have been, but it's not recorded. What is recorded is the collection of the notes for disposal by—"

"The Malayan Publishing House."

"Correct."

"So the publishing house got all of the old worthless Japanese and Malay dollars?"

"Millions and millions of worthless dollars."

"Interesting, but do you know what happened to that company if it's no longer the same one?"

"No," she said, "but I know someone who might."

★

We took a short ride south to the *Straits Times* Printing Works on Cecil Street, and when we went inside, I immediately found the smell familiar: warm printer's ink and paper. We went into a long room with six huge typesetting machines in a row, each with a white man hunched over a keyboard. I noticed the scraps of paper and lots of other detritus on the floor.

"Is this what you aspire to?" I asked Linda.

She pulled a face before whispering, "Being a white male or typesetting? Neither. I'm a writer. There's no creativity in here."

We walked down the line but the men were so focused on their work that no one looked up. At the end, a door and then a staircase led up to a small room.

An elderly man sat hunched on a rickety chair eating a sandwich.

"This is Old Bill," Linda said. "He's in charge of the photographic library."

The man set his meal aside, got up with some discomfort and shook my hand. "Bill Teags. I also act as caretaker."

After introductions, I said, "Looks like you have your work cut out for you, Bill. It's a mess down there in the workshop."

He nodded. "They drop their rubbish everywhere. These creative types"—he raised his eyebrows—"but there's no point in clearing it until they're done for the day."

Linda said, "I was telling Captain Carter about the Malayan Publishing House, how it was occupied by a different company during the war."

Bill nodded. "Yes, the Brits left of course—me included—and didn't come back until afterwards. While the Japs were here, a Chinese firm occupied the publishing house. Not just the building, but they took over the printing—working for the other side."

I said, "They didn't have much choice. You dance to the tune of the piper if you want to survive."

Bill Teags nodded slowly before saying, "But these chaps were opportunists. They saw an empty building with printing equipment and moved in."

Linda said, "But not just any old *chaps*, eh Bill?"

The old caretaker looked from her to me. "No," he said. "It was that man, Andrew Yipp. It was his business that took over. He was the one printing the banana money. He was the one making his fortune during the war, working for the Japs."

# FORTY

I took Linda to the factory on Selegie Road where I'd walked through with Inspector Singh, where I'd seen the broken wall and the thieves' market area and then the two rooms, the one with the hanging cables and the one between the two.

"Spotless," she said as I opened the main doors for her to see inside. "As an old factory, I'd expect a mess."

"Worse than the *Straits Times* typesetting room," I said.

"Much worse."

I led her to the totally empty middle section and opened the door.

"What do you smell?" I asked.

She sniffed. "I can't smell anything except warm air."

"Ink and paper," I said. "I didn't recognize it until I was in your printing works. You probably can't smell it because you're so used to it."

She laughed. "No, I didn't even know the printing works smelled of anything but body odour." She sniffed loudly. "No, I honestly can't smell ink, but I do smell tea."

"It's ink," I said. "Here's my theory: I think Yipp moved out of the Malayan Publishing House and set up here shortly after the war ended. Maybe the end of 1946, before the current company moved into the building on Stamford Street. Maybe around June 1946."

She said, "When the decommissioned money came to Singapore. They collected it and brought it here."

"—and carried on printing money," I said.

"Oh!"

I thought she'd be more impressed with my theory, but then I realized she'd seen something. We'd walked from the middle room back into the first section with the office. Now she headed for the office with the whitewashed windows and then stopped in the doorway. I came up beside her and saw what had attracted her attention.

There was an overturned chair and a large dark stain on the floor.

She stepped forward and touched it, then turned to me.

"Blood," she said, her eyes wide. "A lot of it. Someone was killed here recently, I think."


We went directly to the police HQ. Linda had to wait in Inspector Singh's office while he took me to see the chief superintendent. I told him about the blood and our suspicion that the factory had been used to print counterfeit money.

"What do you expect me to do about it, Captain?" the superintendent asked me through a moustache so bushy I could barely see his mouth move.

"Question Andrew Yipp."

"Based on what? Suspicion? All I've heard so far is that you think he owned the business that printed money for the Japanese. And you think he moved it to the old factory on Selegie Road. All we found there was a bunch of thieves, not a counterfeit money-printing operation."

"But it looks like someone was murdered."

"And again you provide no evidence against anyone. It's all hypothetical."

"Except for the blood."

"And we will investigate it," he said. "But until you bring me something concrete against Andrew Yipp, I am not going in there with hobnailed boots causing unnecessary trouble."

"Sorry," Singh said after we left the superintendent's office.

"Not your fault," I said. "And he's right. We need evidence."

"On a happier note, I picked up your Mr Zhao for questioning." When we got back to his office, Singh handed me a scrappy notebook. "This is Zhao's. It's got all sorts in there, including appointments for your murdered *kathoey*."

"Let's just call him Patrice Dang," I said, ignoring his repeated addition of *your.*

Linda perked up. "What are you talking about?" she asked, but I didn't answer. Instead, I looked through the notebook but then gave up because it wasn't in English.

Singh said, "I don't recognize any names but I'll write them out in case you do. One thing I noticed though, there's a change in pattern."

I handed the book back, intrigued.

"There are more transactions after your... Patrice starts... until two months ago. The business picks up. Then it drops off again."

"You think he was killed because of that—because Patrice wasn't bringing in the money anymore?"

"Zhao won't talk, so that's my theory."

"But Saburo said that Patrice was popular and not working the streets." I nodded in the direction of the cells. "Let's have a quick word with him."

Again, Linda wasn't invited to join us, and she sat with a sour face as we left the office. When I saw Saburo's cell, I was happy that he'd washed the blood from his face and looked more comfortable.

A quick question about Patrice confirmed that he had been as busy, if not busier than ever.

"Mr Zhao was doing well."

"As we thought," Singh said.

Saburo continued to look at me. "But Patrice had one main customer for the past two months."

"You told me Patrice had a plan," I said. "Did it involve this main customer?"

"I think it may have."

"Who was it?"

"I don't know, but someone important."

Afterwards, in the corridor, I asked Singh to take me to see the so-called boss, Mr Zhao.

"We had to let him go," Singh said apologetically.

"Why?"

"He's done nothing illegal. He employs these people. You may not like his practices, but it's not against the law."

"Homosexuality is," I said.

"Of course, but he doesn't have anything to do with that according to him. He sends his boys out to work and they repay their debts."

I shook my head, thinking. "Put pressure on him," I said. "Get his financial ledgers—because even crooks like him keep financial records."

"And that will tell us what?"

"I don't know, but at least it'll confirm whether Patrice was still earning and if not, then maybe you have evidence of motive."

★

I gave Secretary Norris an update, and he was excited by my theory about Yipp.

"We're getting closer," he said, his eyes gleaming with anticipation. "Get the evidence against him."

"I'm doing my best," I said.

"I know."

His tone surprised me. I was even more surprised when he invited me to dinner at the Singapore Club. "If you don't have plans," he added.

I did have plans but that was later. The distraction of dinner served my purposes, especially if it meant appeasing the secretary and protecting Su Ling.

I'd left Linda Wu outside Secretary Norris's office and hadn't expected her to still be there when I came out.

"How did that go?" she asked when I reappeared.

"Pretty much the same as with the chief superintendent. We need that evidence before they'll risk going after Yipp."

I walked back to my office, and she came with me since it was on the way to the *Straits Times* works.

"One day it'll all be different," she said.

I said nothing.

"Imagine meeting the most senior policeman and finding it's a woman."

I nodded.

"Imagine going to the Secretary of Internal Security and it being a woman. One day it will be."

"Hopefully not everyone in authority will be a woman," I said.

"Why not? It sounds ideal to me. The world would be a much kinder, fairer place."

"Maybe," I said. "But then the roles will have been reversed and that won't be fair to men."

"Still sounds ideal to me," she said and laughed.

She left me and I went up to check whether Madam Chau had taken any messages. Had Su Ling or her assistant Jinjing called?

No.

I headed home and changed into my dinner suit and arrived at the Singapore Club at the allotted time. I'd eaten snacks here before but never been in the formal restaurant.

Arthur Pope was at a table with three other gentlemen and nodded when our eyes met. Whether he thought it strange that I was dining with Norris I don't know, because I read nothing in his face.

The food was exceptional, but I couldn't help being aware that all the diners were male, as were the staff. One day, I surmised, women would be members of this exclusive club.

Towards the end of dinner, I said, "I trust you are happy with my progress."

"That's why we're here," he said, raising his glass in a toast to me. "I hope this celebration isn't premature."

I said, "I wasn't happy with your threat last week."

If he was taken aback by my bluntness, he didn't show it. "My dear fellow, I would have never arrested the young lady. I just needed you motivated and"—he took a slow sip of wine before smiling—"it worked, didn't it?"

"It did."

"Without proof, I could no more have arrested her than I could her boss."

I said, "She's innocent. Whatever he's done or been doing, she isn't—"

He waved me down. "Don't worry, don't worry. Let's just enjoy this fine food and relax."

Before we left, as he puffed on a thick cigar, he said he wanted to tell me a story. It turned out to be a traditional Chinese proverb about a young peasant lad called Ma Liang who tended cattle for a rich man.

"The boy worked hard but only had dry bread to eat. The rich man wasn't very good to the people who worked for him. One night Ma Liang dreamt that an old man gave him a magic paintbrush and asked that he help the poor people. When he awoke there was a paintbrush in his desk.

"Ma Liang made some paint from plants and decided to paint some hay. Miraculously the painting became real and he fed the hay to the cattle. The river was dry. He painted water and that too became real, and the animals and people could drink. After that, he painted cattle to help them till the land and food so that they would have enough to eat.

"The rich man heard of this magic and sent people to lock Ma Liang in prison and take the paintbrush. But it wouldn't work for him, so he told Ma Liang to paint him a mountain of gold. Which the boy did. But he painted it surrounded by sea. The rich man was furious and insisted that the boy paint a ship.

"When the man sailed off, the boy painted a big wave that destroyed the boat and killed the rich man."

"An interesting tale," I said when he finished. "I presume there's a moral to the story."

"Oh, I don't know with these Chinese myths and fables. They're all a little strange and fantastical." He took a final puff of the cigar and stubbed it out. "But I can tell you this, Ash Carter, I'm certain you're right. Andrew Yipp has a magic brush and been painting money. I'll get him and he will be punished for it."

# FORTY-ONE

I knew three of Su Ling's secret places, and after midnight, I came out of my apartment on Beach Road and went to the *Padang*, where the New Year's fair was still in full swing. I did a little aimless strolling, in case anyone was watching, before I ducked away and crossed the river.

After five minutes of switching direction and making sure I wasn't followed, I crossed the river again and cut through to Hock Lam Street and Su Ling's apartment, where I'd recently stayed with her.

I found the key and slipped inside. Using a torch, I scanned all the surfaces, hoping to find a note or at least a clue. The room looked unchanged since I'd last been there. I turned the place over and found nothing.

My second port of call was a room above a shophouse north-east of the city, off Princep Street. It took me forty minutes of slinking from shadow to shadow to get there. At one point I thought I was being followed but lost whoever it was through a warren of streets.

I didn't have a key to this second room, but I knew the shopkeepers and they recognized me when I appeared at their clothing and hardware shop.

Su Ling had told me she trusted these people, and when they took me upstairs I asked whether they had seen her.

After a lot of sign language, I concluded they had no idea where she was. The room she used also revealed nothing.

The third place was north of this shophouse. She'd told me the address although I'd never been. I found it after another fifteen minutes of switching back and forth then located a hidden key.

This room smelled musty, and I figured it'd lain empty for months. A quick search again revealed nothing, and I descended into a dark alleyway feeling tired and disappointed.

The only other place I knew was her official residence above the mah-jong bar in Chinatown. She'd taken me there two years ago, but it was far from secret. There was also no way I could gain entry without Yipp finding out. Of course, it struck me that if he was looking for her then that would have been the first place he'd have checked.

After three streets and two turns, I flagged down a trishaw and told the rider to take me home. There was no need for secrecy any more.

I heard firecrackers close by, and despite recognizing the sound, instinct made me glance in that direction. Lucky that I did because I caught sight of another trishaw following.

"Go left," I said in the limited Chinese I could speak.

Before the next road, I said, "Go left again." As we turned, I glanced back along the road and saw the trishaw. No passenger, so definitely a tail.

Leaning forward, I held out a fifty-cent note, which the rider snatched.

"Take the next right. I'll jump out but you keep going straight," I said.

We turned and I dived from the bike into shadows.

Seconds later, the other trishaw came around the corner. The pursuer stood up in his pedals to accelerate just as I dived at him, hard. We flew over the bike and thudded to the ground, his body under mine.

Two rapid knocks to the head with my gun and he stopped squirming.

Sitting on his chest, I pinned him by the throat and pointed the gun.

"Who are you working for?"

He jerked, trying to throw me, but I pistol-whipped him again.

"You'll regret it," he spat.

"Who are you working for? Simple question."

"Wang." If hatred could kill, his eyes would have stabbed me as he forced out the name of his boss.

"Why?"

"Because he wants to know where you are and what you are doing."

"Why?"

"Because you are *húndàn*," he said, insulting me.

"I'd like you to give Wang a message from me," I said, getting off him and pulling the man to his feet.

The gun was in my weaker right hand. I jerked it and he looked. At the same time, I threw an uppercut with my left that took him off his feet and sent him sprawling in the dirt.

"Tell Wang to stay away. Don't forget I can get the army behind me. If Wang wants trouble. I'll give him trouble."

I don't know whether he actually heard my rant because he didn't move, but it eased my tension.

His trishaw lay on its side and I picked it up and got on. The adrenaline was pumping fast and I used it to pound the pedals all the way back home.

I left it near the Satay Club and expect someone acquired it within the hour. Then I walked the short distance home and unlocked my front door. Until the trouble with Chen's gang last year, I'd left it unlocked.

Now I needed two keys. Despite this, I realized my security wasn't adequate. Su Ling had sheltered me the last time I'd been in trouble. I could use one of her secret places, but since Wang's men had been following me, there was a good chance they'd found the apartments.

No, this time I would go to Gillman Barracks, the military police base where I was always welcome. I'd just started to pack essentials when I heard a noise outside, a clatter.

It came from the beach side—the opposite side to my front door.

I flicked off the light, drew my gun, and took one step towards my balcony doors just as they burst open.

# FORTY-TWO

I dived for cover and aimed, ready to shoot the intruder.

"It's me!"

Jinjing stood, framed by the doors like a shadow. Her clothes were black and tight-fitting. Only her face showed.

I got up and put the gun away. "What the heavens?"

"Sorry."

"I could have shot you!"

She closed the balcony doors and sat on a chair.

I went to switch the light back on, but she stopped me.

"I mustn't be seen, but I needed to see you."

"I'm glad you came," I said, sitting across from her. "Tell me—where's Su Ling?"

She took a breath. "I don't know. That's why we need to talk."

"What do you know?"

"I know about the two of you." She paused. "I know about your plans."

"Our plans?" I tried to sound intrigued. Jinjing may have been Su Ling's assistant, but I didn't know how far I could trust her. If Yipp wanted to find out what I knew, using her would be the smartest approach.

But she surprised me. "My mistress told me you were planning to escape. You had arranged to smuggle her away after the New Year's celebrations on Sunday. There's a warehouse on Alkaff Quay owned by Arthur

Pope. You would be taken from there in the early hours and transferred to a ship. Su Ling didn't tell me which one or where it was heading just in case... in case Mr Yipp forced it out of me."

"She didn't turn up," I said.

"I realized that when you came looking for her. Mr Yipp thinks she's in hiding or you are protecting her, but that doesn't make sense." Again she paused, and when she spoke again I heard a tremble in her voice. "She's disappeared, and I'm worried."

"I am too, Jinjing."

She nodded at me then shook her head like she couldn't understand what was going on.

"Tell me what you know," I said. "Tell me what she was doing on Sunday night."

"Do you know about the other men?"

I swallowed. "Pardon?"

"Oh, I don't mean like you. I mean Mr Yipp made my mistress entertain certain men now and again as a favour. She was in much demand."

"I didn't know. The last time I saw her was a week ago. She left early in the morning."

"She had dinner with Sir Graham Pendall on Friday and Saturday evening. I think she was avoiding Mr Yipp."

"Pendall, you say?" My mind spun for a moment. Pendall's committee had recommended constitutional changes that would have massive ramifications. Secretary Norris had told me he was worried about a new political group funded by Yipp. If Norris was in Yipp's pocket..."

Jinjing broke into my thoughts. "But my mistress didn't see Sir Pendall on Sunday. She had agreed to but Mr Yipp insisted she have dinner with someone in the government called Major Lamb."

"Lamb!" I shouted, and her eyes flew wide with panic at my exclamation. Lowering my voice, I said, "Sorry. What's Lamb got to do with Yipp?"

"I don't know. Property I think."

I nodded. "Go on. What happened?"

"Well, Su Ling met Major Lamb for dinner. Eight o'clock at the Hotel de la Paix."

"And afterwards?"

"I don't know."

"What about Sir Pendall? Did he just accept Su Ling wouldn't keep her appointment with him?"

"I took her place." In the dim light, I saw her swallow at the memory. "Su Ling promised she'd see him the following night, but of course she disappeared."

"What might she have done after dinner with Major Lamb?"

"I don't know. The fair, perhaps?"

"Is there anything else you can tell me, Jinjing?"

"She didn't... I mean... doesn't trust Wang. She thought he'd been following her."

I nodded. "His men have been following me."

"Find her," she said.

"I will."

Now it was her turn to nod, then she got up and walked to the balcony. "What will you do?"

"The first thing I'll do is visit the major and see where that leads. Please go through her diary and think about her recent activities. Is there anywhere she might have gone?"

"I will. But contacting you is difficult."

I looked out to the dark sea, calm and speckled with the reflection of the night sky. "Send me a coded message. Don't use your name, just write a number on the paper, like a five, and put your message in every fifth word of an innocuous note."

"Captain Carter," she said earnestly, gripping my arm suddenly. "Don't assume she's hiding. Something has happened to her."

In a smooth athletic movement, she swung her legs over the railing and dropped to the ground below. She melted into the darkness as if she'd never been there. Which made me think of Su Ling.

She'd just disappeared.

Like she'd never been there.

# PART THREE

# FORTY-THREE

*Friday 12th February*

I caught a few hours' sleep at Gillman before driving back into the city. Major Lamb was not available. Apparently, an urgent committee meeting had been called. So, I found his assistant and first asked for a list of all the properties that had been *re-appropriated* in the name of Planning and Development.

"Send them to my office," I instructed. "And when the major comes out of his committee meeting, would you ask him to join me urgently at the Hotel de la Paix?"

I then travelled to the hotel and presented my government identification to the receptionist, who promptly fetched the manager.

The obsequious little man bowed and gestured like the Frenchman he pretended to be.

"Could you tell me if Major Lamb ate dinner here on Sunday evening?"

The manager checked his register. "Oui, Monsieur, Sunday the seventh. A table for two."

"Please describe his companion."

"A most beautiful lady," he said. "I remember her well. Tall, of Chinese-English mixed-race. Quite easily the most attractive young lady here that evening." He smiled.

"Long dark hair. Shapely, but not too much, if you know what I mean?"

"Did she wear her hair down?" I asked, knowing that Su Ling normally tied it up.

He looked uncertain for the first time. "I believe so, oui."

"Her dress. Do you remember that?"

"Royal blue, I think. Oui, royal blue and white heels."

"A cheongsam?"

"Non, Monsieur. Not a traditional Chinese dress. Which is a shame."

"Why so?"

The manager smirked. "Long beautiful legs—she would have looked even more spectacular."

I did not doubt that he was describing my girlfriend and felt a sense of relief that she hadn't worn something revealing on a date with Lamb.

I was therefore taken aback by the manager's next comment. "The major had a room here that night."

"A room?" My chest constricted.

"He stayed here. The lady too." He tapped his nose.

"The lady you just described stayed the night at this hotel?" I said slowly.

"Oui, Monsieur."

"Major Lamb is married."

The manager tapped his nose again then placed a finger on his lips, implying that his lips were sealed. However, he was comfortably telling me everything.

"All night?"

"Oui, Monsieur."

"Would you just stop saying that!" I barked. "You're no more French than I am."

The manager pulled a shocked, then guilty, face.

"It's part of the image," he said, suddenly sheepish. "I'm sorry."

I suspect I overreacted based on the news he'd just delivered. But it didn't make sense. Su Ling should have been making her way to Alkaff Quay, not making love with Major Lamb.

I took a calming breath. "Did she enjoy breakfast with the major?"

"No, the major breakfasted alone."

"How do you know that the young lady stayed the night?"

For a second I thought he looked uncomfortable before he composed himself. "She left by the back staircase and the staff exit."

"You saw her?"

Again the discomfort. "Yes." Then he looked past me and beamed. "Ah, Major Lamb! What a delight to see you, Monsieur."

Lamb nodded curtly and then offered his hand to me and indicated that we should withdraw to the lounge.

"Private," he whispered.

After we'd sat and he'd ordered a brandy, he said, "You requested a meeting."

I nodded.

He said, "Why did you ask my personal assistant for a list of re-appropriated properties?"

"It's for Secretary Norris," I lied. Lamb couldn't deny a request from my boss. He inclined his head, accepting my explanation, and I added, "But that's not why I wanted to see you."

"It isn't?"

"On the day of the New Year's parade—Sunday—you were here. You had dinner with Su Ling Yong."

He nodded cautiously. "Andrew Yipp's niece, a charming and most beautiful girl."

After I questioned him, he then went on to provide the same detail as the hotel manager. Exactly the same. Word for word except for one fact. He said nothing about her leaving.

I said, "Can I be clear? She went to your room?"

"Yes."

"Did she stay with you all night?"

"It would be inappropriate for me to be too specific—must protect the girl's reputation, you know? Plenty of diners and the manager saw us leave the dining room and go to my bedroom."

"Be specific. What did you do in the bedroom?"

"I'm married."

"It doesn't seem to stop you, Major."

He cleared his throat. "She stayed all night."

"And…?"

"We had sex."

I nodded slowly.

"And in the morning?"

"She left by the rear entrance. The one the staff use."

"You have a witness?"

"Yes, Gustav, the manager. Shall I get him to confirm?"

I shook my head. "He already did. I was interested in his observations, very detailed, and also convenient that he witnessed her leave."

Lamb said nothing.

I said, "Where did she go after she left?"

"I don't know," he said slowly. "Home I presume. Why ask that?"

"Because she disappeared."

Suddenly Lamb's eyes flared, his neck reddened, and he opened and closed his mouth like a fish out of water. When he could finally speak, he said, "She didn't stay all night."

I blinked at him. "I'm sorry?"

"I elaborated a little."

"Protecting her reputation, Major?" I'm sure he heard the sarcasm in my tone.

Lamb stood up and shouted. "Gustav!" Then to a bellboy: "Get the manager here immediately."

The little manager scurried over and bowed. "Oui, Monsieur? Is there a problem?"

"I've been found out," Lamb said matter-of-factly. "Tell the captain what I told you."

The manager cleared his throat, looked from Lamb to me, back to Lamb for confirmation and then back to me. "The major told me what to say."

I nodded. "Was any of it true?"

"Oui, Monsieur... I mean... yes, Major Lamb dined here on Sunday the seventh from eight pm until around ten-thirty. Then they went up to the major's room."

"Did you actually see that?"

"Ah, no, you are right. I saw the major lead her upstairs."

"Anything else?"

"No, Captain."

"Did you see her in the morning?"

"No."

"As far as you are aware, did anyone see her leave?"

"No."

I waved him away and turned my attention back to the major.

"What are you playing at, Lamb?" He must have noticed my disrespect at dropping his rank, but he didn't deserve it.

"I persuaded the girl to come upstairs with me, for appearances' sake."

"Appearances?"

"She's beautiful. I wanted people to be jealous. I wanted them to imagine her in my bed." He sighed. "I know, I'm a foolish old man."

"So tell me the truth. What really happened?"

"She refused to enter my room and did leave by the back way—partly because I asked her to and partly because she said someone might otherwise follow her."

"Did she say who?"

"Someone who works for Andrew Yipp. Wang, I think his name was?"

"Wang," I repeated. "He's a nasty piece of work. So she didn't give you any hint of where she was going?"

"Not a thing."

"All right," I said. "For the time being, I'll assume you're telling the truth, but if I find you're lying…"

He shook his head and started to protest his innocence, but I was already striding out of the lounge and out of the hotel.

★

"Mysterious," Inspector Singh said when I told him about Major Lamb and his lies. We were sitting in his office drinking tea. "But you should stay away from that girl. Mixing with her and investigating Andrew Yipp can't end up well."

"You're right, my friend," I said. "I'm just curious about where she is. So, if you hear anything…"

"Of course." He slid a ledger across his table to me. "You wanted Mr Zhao's financials and here they are."

"Have you arrested him?"

"And charge him with what?"

"Murder?"

"I don't think either of us believe Zhao murdered his golden goose."

"Is that what Patrice Dang was?"

Singh reached over and tapped the book. "Looks like a lot of money came in, and a good deal of it was from him."

"Then charge Zhao with handling stolen goods."

"I have no evidence. All I have is a man in a cell who is probably a homosexual and under our *protection*."

I nodded, thinking.

"The chief says we have to release Saburo. And before you protest, the money you gave us has just about run out. He promised you two days and you've had four. There are other priorities."

I thumbed through Zhao's ledger. I could see the money coming in and that it had picked up considerably six months ago—presumably coinciding with Patrice's arrival.

Singh was saying, "We've spoken to three of the fifteen names we got—the clients—but they aren't saying anything, certainly not admitting lewd and inappropriate sexual behaviour or deviancy. And we're out of money."

I was half-listening. "The outgoings," I said. "Did you look at what they are?"

"No." He took the ledger back. "I'll get them translated. You're interested because—?"

"Because there are regular payments, most weekly, and seven weeks ago one stopped. I wondered what it was."

"How urgent?"

"I'm not rushing off anywhere," I said, unsure what my next move was. At the moment all roads led to Wang: Jinjing mentioned him; Su Ling mentioned him to Lamb; plus he was following me. However, I had nothing to go on and I wasn't ready to roll out the army like I'd threatened.

"I'll find someone," Singh said, leaving me alone in his office. A minute later he returned with a nervous Chinese constable.

"Land space, sir," he said.

I squinted at him. "Land space?"

"Perhaps, like floor, sir?"

Singh shooed the young man away and raised his eyebrows. "Floor?"

"Or rent," I said. "Find out why Zhao stopped paying rent."

My jeep was parked outside the police station. I jumped in and immediately noticed a piece of paper in the footwell. I picked it up and read:

Please help. Must ask your opinion. Miss Chen makes good tea?

The number in the top right-hand corner was four.

Jinjing had left me a message: Ask Chen.

# FORTY-FOUR

Chen Guan Xi was dead. He'd been Andrew Yipp's biggest rival—the head of another Chinese secret society. Chen had been exiled after visiting China, but he still managed to operate out of Singapore. Seven months ago, finding myself trapped between them I'd set them up for a showdown on the small island of Blakang Mati. I'd planned for them to kill one another; instead, they both survived. Chen had finally been arrested in Singapore and been locked away.

Just how he died in prison, I don't know, but I suspected Yipp had something to do with it.

So when the message said Chen, I figured it was Christian Chen, Guan Xi's eldest son, who had taken over the family business.

Because of my involvement with his father, I'd steered clear of Christian Chen, but now I had no choice but to ask him about Su Ling.

Before travelling to his offices in the east of the city, I let Madam Chau know where I was going.

"If I'm not back within the hour, call Colonel Ambrose," I said. Lieutenant Colonel Ambrose was the CO at Gillman Barracks and I had no doubt he'd send at least fifty MPs charging in to rescue me.

I was already leaving the office as she shouted after me, "The reporter wants to see you again."

"Then make an appointment in an hour or so."

I jumped in my jeep and hammered east, over the Singapore River, past my apartment, then onto Kallang Road and over the Rochor River. Chen Guan Xi's gang operated this side of the river. It wasn't a perfect dividing line between the secret societies because I knew Yipp had buildings in Kallang, but it was a pretty good guide.

Guan Xi hadn't operated out of an office since he wasn't supposed to be in the country. Instead, he seemed to flit between properties—mostly residential and always one step ahead of the authorities. Until I tricked him, that was.

Christian Chen was a public figure with a playboy reputation. His office wasn't prestigious like Yipp's, but it was impressive nonetheless, situated within the wedge between Kallang Road and the northern side of Crawford Street. A red-brick building built just before the war, it had Chen's Emporium Ltd as the banner across the top, visible when approached from the west or south. I'd never checked, but I suspected Yipp could see it from his office. Like Chen was taunting his rival.

I parked my battered jeep next to smart new cars and walked into the reception.

Chen didn't make me wait. Within a minute I was standing in his office, facing the young man. Two guards stood at my back and I had no doubt they were armed. One was large, maybe an inch taller than me, and more solidly built. The other was short and wiry, with the face and snarl of a junkyard dog. I suspected the junkyard dog was the more senior. Large was the muscle.

They had patted me down with overly physical moves, letting me know that violence would be an easy transition for them. But they were less intelligent than they were rough. They checked everywhere except my ankles and I went upstairs with my holstered gun. Which gave me some comfort.

Christian Chen wore a white three-piece suit and a matching white trilby with a crimson ribbon. He scrutinized me through round glasses.

I said, "Did you put the hat on just for me?"

"You have a nerve coming here, Captain Carter," he said. "I can't decide whether you are stupid or brave."

He stared at me like a gunslinger waiting for the first move.

I said, "It's about Su Ling Yong."

Chen's eyes betrayed nothing. "Why come to me?"

"In case you know what happened to her."

"What happened to her?"

I shook my head. "When was the last time you saw her?"

Chen's jaw twitched. "Captain Carter, I am only tolerating your presence because you did me a favour."

"I did?"

He raised his hands and then pulled a fake smile. "All this is mine because of you. My father would never relinquish control despite his difficult situation. You killed his right-hand man and you may as well have killed him. So you actually did me a favour. Now I'm the boss of Chen's Emporium." The way he said it was like emporium meant empire.

I nodded. "And that's why I'm here."

"Being the boss of a legal company is not the same as being the head of an illegal society."

"Of course," I said, noting the same crimson dragon motif on the carpet that had signified old Chen's gang. "You are legitimate."

He appeared to relax and perched on the edge of a desk, thinking. Then he waved his two men out of the room.

"A king who usurps a king must always watch his back. A king who has the respect of his followers needn't fear those who protect him."

I nodded. I'd heard so much about the importance of respect and keeping face. Christian Chen had wanted to take over but needed to bide his time. I wondered how much the German—old Chen's henchman—had to do with it. Would he have been loyal to the son if Christian had killed his father? Maybe not.

He said, "Why are you asking me about Su Ling? I am not Yipp's rival—except for in business."

I nodded but heard the lie.

He continued: "So why would I know anything about Yipp's niece?"

"I'm not suggesting any foul play. I just want to know if you've seen her recently."

He thought for a moment then seemed to come to a decision.

"Yes, she came to see me."

"When?"

"About two weeks ago."

"What did she want?"

Again he paused, possibly wondering how much to tell me. "She had a business proposition. But don't expect me to divulge it."

"Can you tell me anything?"

"I can tell you that she is a good negotiator—for a woman. I only entertained her because I could never speak so frankly with her boss."

"What was it about?"

Chen wasn't a great poker player. I could see him thinking the truth, then thinking he wouldn't tell me, then deciding to lie.

"You must know that I own Happy World." It was the entertainment park in Kallang, right by the civil airport. I didn't know, but he continued without waiting for a response. "The Chens are patrons of the Society of Chinese Artists and the Ee Hoe Hean Club."

"I didn't know that," I said.

He smiled because that was undoubtedly true and he was building up to the lie.

"Entertainment is the future, Captain Carter. I'll grant you it's always been important, but it will boom and I want to control it. I'm buying the Rex Cinema hall and we discussed that. But the main negotiation with Su Ling was for the purchase of the Cathay Cinema and the dance hall."

"Really?" I said.

"I know it seems fantastical."

I didn't believe him but nodded anyway. "All right, so you discussed the sale and purchase of the cinema. What else?"

"That's it."

"Can you tell me anything that might explain why she has disappeared?"

"Perhaps Yipp didn't like her deal. Perhaps she didn't have his authority and he's killed her." Chen laughed like he'd delivered a humorous punchline. "Have you thought of that, Captain Carter?"

"He hasn't killed her," I said, and was sure of it. "But I don't know about his man, Wang."

Chen's small eyes narrowed. "His henchman. Wang Kim Lo? The world would be a better place without him."

"Can you tell me anything about him?"

"He's been with Yipp for four years and killed more men than his predecessor killed in twice that time. It's also likely that he killed his old boss to take the job."

"Where was he working before Yipp?"

"I heard that he came from a small gang on the mainland."

"KL?"

"Johor Bahru. His brother is a small-time crook."

"What's his brother's name?

"Wang, of course." He laughed. "Wang Jon Soo. Rumour has it that Yipp's Wang is still involved."

"In what way?" I said.

"Su Ling is missing. You're the detective, you connect the dots."

"Thank you," I said.

"I've decided," he said, standing up again and straightening his white suit, "you are both brave and an idiot."

"Probably."

"And if you do find Su Ling, let her know that I helped. Let her know that our deal remains."

# FORTY-FIVE

"You're still alive!" Madam Chau said when I returned to the office. It was hard to tell, but I think she was relieved.

"For the time being," I said. "I'm going up to JB."

"Why?"

I ignored the question. "I expect to stay overnight."

"I'll book a hotel."

"No need."

She frowned at me.

I said, "If I'm not back here by midday tomorrow. I want you to tell Inspector Singh that I think Wang did it."

"Just the name Wang?"

"He'll know who I mean."

"What about your appointment with the reporter?"

"That will have to wait," I said, but as I left the building, Linda Wu approached on the street. She had something rolled up under her arm.

"I've got maps," she said. "Yipp moved the money-printing business out of the factory on Selegie Road to somewhere else."

"Right," I said, climbing into the jeep.

She got in beside me.

"You can't come with me," I said.

"Where are you going?"

"I'm looking for Su Ling. There's a chance someone in JB will know where she is."

She didn't budge, her eyes on me like a cat's, curious and assessing.

Then she said, "How's your Hokkien?" It was the most common language spoken by the Chinese. Most people on the island didn't speak multiple languages, probably because there were so many. Business people spoke English but the common folk stuck to their native tongues.

"I know a few words."

"You'll need a translator."

With the engine idling, I said nothing, just sat there.

"It could be dangerous. No, it will be dangerous," I said after a minute's silence.

"You're a male chauvinist, you'll feel obliged to protect me," she said, and from her tone, I couldn't tell whether she was being funny or not. "Do you have a photograph of Su Ling?"

I hadn't thought of that. Everyone in Singapore knew her or about her. That wouldn't be the same on the mainland.

When I said I hadn't, Linda told me to drive. "Don't worry, Old Bill will have one."

At the printing works, she made sure I came with her—presumably so that I wouldn't drive away—and obtained two good photographs from Bill Teags's picture library.

By the time we got back in my jeep, I'd decided to let her come along. I went via my apartment and picked up a small bag.

"Do I need an overnight bag?" she asked.

"No, I'm not planning to stay."

She must have wondered what I had in the bag, but she didn't ask and I drove quickly up to the crossing with Linda trying to find out why I was looking for Su Ling. I told her she was my girlfriend and was missing. That's all I would say.

"There's more to it," she probed eventually. "Why aren't you telling me?"

"More to it? Is there?"

"The niece of Andrew Yipp, your missing girlfriend? Come on! And you said it could be dangerous."

"Will be dangerous."

"Exactly. So, who are you afraid of? Andrew Yipp?"

"His henchman Wang."

"I know him. Nasty-looking—evil eyes and a scar on his cheek that makes him look like he's smirking."

"That's the one."

"Do you think he's killed her?"

I shook my head. "No, I'm going to JB because I'm hoping she's there. Maybe he's hiding her."

We drove in silence for a mile or so.

"Does that make sense?"

"I don't know what makes sense anymore. And I've given up trying to second guess Yipp and his men."

She tapped the roll of maps that she'd wedged between her legs. "Well, hopefully, we can work out where he moved the money-printing press to."

"How?" Maybe I would have worked it out if I'd given it my full attention, but I was more focused on finding Su Ling, and, at that moment, jumping the queue onto the causeway.

"By looking for reasonable and empty properties. There can't be many suitable places in the city," she said, and I nodded half-heartedly.

On the other side, when we stopped for lunch, she spread the map on the table and we spent thirty minutes eating and pointing and circling potential locations.

"What are you thinking about," she said towards the end.

"All the slums we have. It's a city of two halves."

"But with big plans for improvement," she said. "I know. We've done a few pieces on it for the government."

"The Planning and Development department," I said, and told her that I'd had a few complaints about the re-appropriation of properties.

"Understandable," she said. "Whether you live in a palace or hovel, a home is a home. It's your shelter. No one likes it taken away, especially since re-appropriation means being moved on rather than rehoused. When you think about it from the individual's point of view, it can be pretty harsh."

"Did you report the individual's point of view?"

"I didn't cover it, and no, the articles just reported the positive angle: new, cleaner housing."

"Fewer collapses, fires and deaths?"

"That too."

She stared off for a second, then spoke in a disappointed tone. "We should have considered the other side."

"Next time. It's only just begun," I said, then tapped Hive Street on the map. "I had a complaint from here. They're old buildings, but not as bad as some in Kampong Bintang. In fact, I went into a property close by and it wasn't too bad—not on the verge of collapse like others down Havelock."

"What are you thinking?"

"I don't know. Something niggles."

"It's an odd area, with the oil refinery at one end, a sugar factory behind and then a vacant biscuit factory. It's like a section that's become trapped. Commercial behind and around then the merchants and quays on the other side towards the river."

"Yes."

"And?" She looked at me like I had all the answers.

"As I said, I don't know."

"Possible location for money printing?"

I finished my food and called for the bill. "I think we're looking for somewhere clean. The old factory on Selegie was virtually dust-free. I can't see these old buildings providing the right environment."

I went to pay the bill, but Linda insisted on paying for her share.

"I like this new world," I said.

She smiled. "Now, what's the plan?"

"I'm going to the police station. We need to find criminals and they'll know where I should look."

"I'll walk around for a while," she said. "No point in us both talking to the police. So I'll use the photograph of Su Ling and see if anyone recognizes her."

That suited me, I thought I'd be better off without her anyway—especially if I came across any gang members. However, she made me agree to meet her at 6 pm by the town hall.

★

I drove her into the old colonial centre and dropped her in the main square. Then I headed back the way I'd come to the police station headquarters that overlooked the crossing.

I hadn't been here for sixteen months, and even then George McNaughton had been my only contact. At the public reception, I showed the desk sergeant my Singapore government ID and asked for the chief inspector.

A long and hot wait followed before I was shown into the man's office.

"Chief Inspector Eric Stanford-Jones," he said pumping my hand. "I've heard of you."

"Only good things I hope."

"Mostly." Stanford-Jones smiled and offered me a seat. We made brief small talk about our military pasts before I got to the point.

"I'm looking for a missing person. There's a possibility it involves criminals based here."

He nodded sagely. "Tell me more."

"Well, that's it. Except there's a suggestion it's connected to a hoodlum called Wang. He works for Andrew Yipp."

"I know of Andrew Yipp. The businessman, big in Singapore."

"His henchman is called Wang Kim Lo."

Stanford-Jones shook his head. "But that's not a name I've heard. Three groups are operating within the state— which means in this town mainly. They're not on the same scale as your gangs in Singapore, simply because we don't have the wealth."

"Are they connected to the Singapore gangs?"

"Undoubtedly, although I couldn't tell you who or how. There are three main criminal activities here: smuggling, usually into and out of Singapore, which is typically about handling stolen goods and passing them off as legitimate. Then you have the usual extortion of businesses, although that's harder to prove since the business owners treat it like rent. Then you have the drugs business. Opium is as big here as it is in Singapore—well, on a like for like scale, you understand."

"What about kidnapping?" Which was an outcome I'd considered.

"Never come across it. What are you thinking?"

"That she might have been taken for a ransom."

He studied me for a moment. "Who is this girl? An Englishman's daughter?"

"Andrew Yipp's niece."

He laughed out loud. "Goodness, man. No one in their right mind would kidnap anyone related to Andrew Yipp! He'd tear their heads off."

I nodded and wondered how long it would be before Yipp decided my head needed to be separated from my body. If he really thought I'd hidden her, I probably had limited time. "I'm sure you're right," I said, "but someone's done it and my working theory is it's this Wang chap."

Stanford-Jones opened a map and showed me where the gangs hung out. As with Singapore, there were clear demarcation lines. Three gangs: east, west, and a northern swathe.

I thanked him and stuffed the paper in my pocket.

"Good luck." He pumped my hand again. "Don't expect me to give you any backup if you cause trouble."

"I won't."

Then, as I opened his door to leave, he said, "McNaughton."

"Yes?"

"You know he's in KL now. A chief inspector, no less!"

"That's right. Promoted after he helped me crack a case."

Stanford-Jones shook his head.

"Sir?" I said, hovering in the doorway, wondering at the expression on his face.

"It's always who you know rather than what you know," he said. "Just take care and don't get into trouble, Captain. Have a good day."

# FORTY-SIX

Looking for criminals during the day is like fishing in a muddy puddle. I drove the streets and looked for bars where gang members might meet. The central region followed Main Street and had thriving businesses. If they were paying protection money, it didn't seem to impact their trade.

I continued to the town square with its smaller version of Singapore's government sector, and then north until I reached a power station. The map said this area was called Kibur and was the edge of the northern gang's territory. I went right, to the east side, crossing a river and eventually joining Route One. Again, by the main road, I saw healthy trade taking place, but in a street beyond, I found hovels and squats that looked perfect for low-level criminals.

When I came across a police depot, I decided I'd come too far. This was the last place they'd choose to hang out. So I turned around and wended my way back south.

I saw children playing in the street, drunks and stoned men lounging in doorways. I passed rundown shops and a garage and kept going until the properties petered out near the causeway where Route One met the eastern coastal road.

The garage had interested me and I drove back to it. Outside were piles of tyres, oil drums and other seemingly typical debris. There was an old Ford, possibly a Model A, but burnt out and almost unrecognizable. There were a couple of ancient trucks in the yard as well. But what made me think about it and return was the solitary petrol pump.

This garage was in the wrong place. Route One was a short distance away and heavy with traffic. This old garage with its faded signs and junk couldn't expect much business. And yet the petrol pump looked like it was used and I'd seen people inside the garage.

As I watched, forty yards away, I saw cars go in and come out again. I saw an odd person walk in with a cart. Anyone who entered, exited again after a few minutes.

Not drugs, I thought, because of the transport. Not smugglers, because of the small scale. Stolen goods, I decided. A drop-off point. Maybe from people travelling right down the country. Perhaps the petrol pump was for customers requiring emergency fuel.

I kept watching and eventually two men came out in identical brown clothes. In Singapore they would have worn suits, but here the criminals weren't so wealthy—at least not the juniors.

I jumped out of the Land Rover and followed at a safe distance. The men lit up and chatted and laughed and then split up. I chose one and followed until I was happy we were far enough away from the garage. Then I ran.

When I hit him I was going full pelt, and I grabbed the back of his shirt as he went over. With his legs behind him and weighing next to nothing, he was easy to drag into the shadows.

I spun him around and looked into his scared face.

"Whose gang are you in?"

He said nothing. Then he started wriggling, trying to get free of my grip.

I pinned him hard against a wall, my forearm on his throat.

He started jabbering at me in Chinese.

"Whose gang?"

The stream of frantic Chinese continued.

"Do you know Wang?"

No reaction to the name, but still the jabbering. He was so panicked I doubt he'd have made sense in any language.

"Wang Jon Soo!"

I must have said it five times and was cursing that I'd tried to do this without Linda as translator. A handful of people were watching. I glanced at them and judged none to be a problem. Just idle curiosity I thought.

Pulling out the map, I tried one last time, practically shoving it in his face.

"Where is Wang's gang?"

Eventually, I just released the scared kid. He practically slid down the wall before bouncing up and round me. If he'd run in the direction of the garage, I might have been in for trouble. But he didn't.

I stood for a moment, looking at the spectators, before an elderly man shuffled forward. His clothes were in tatters and his skin hung off him like he hadn't eaten for a month. But he showed no fear as he approached and held out his hand.

At first, I thought he was begging, but he pointed at the map in my hand.

I passed it to him. "Wang's gang?"

The man said something in Chinese and pointed to the paper. The west side. He drew a circle with his finger between a cemetery in the south and a place called Kampong Tarum.

As I took the map back, he turned and started to shuffle away. It took me two strides to catch him and I thrust some notes into his hand.

"Thank you," I said, hoping he understood. I think he did because when I left him standing there, tears streamed down his dusty face.

I drove back to the town square, crossed the rail line that divided the town and kept going west. I passed a hotel called the European and Oriental. Undoubtedly the best hotel in the area, I'd stayed here when the government was paying the huge bill.

The hill with the Grand Palace of Johor was to my left with the straits just over the rise. The wharves were further along from there but the old man hadn't included them in the area of interest. I found the cemetery and then worked my way north through the streets.

Where Kampong Tarum started I wasn't sure, because the one-time village had become merged with the rest of the town, as happens with urban expansion. However, I knew when it finished, because the properties stopped and trees began. They rose, covering one of the numerous hills around the peninsula.

I'd thought that the east side seemed poor, but this sector was an expansive slum—attap huts and corrugated roofs sat between crumbling brick structures.

The same desultory faces I'd seen in the east watched me pass. I drove slowly looking at properties and assessing until I reached the cemetery again. Then I circled it clockwise, and it wasn't until I was three-quarters of the way around that I noticed some green paint on the cemetery wall. Three lines that overlapped, forming a rough triangle. Chinese writing was of course everywhere, but seeing this green triangle made me think. Since I'd been in the west of the town, I'd seen a lot of similar signs. I'd seen none in the east.

This was a marker: a gang's territory. A block later and I not only saw the green square again, but the row of buildings looked perfect. I saw a bar and long shop front.

It had Chinese lettering across the top and then English all the way underneath: *High Glass Shanghai Leather Trunk Merchant. Dealers in German Dyestuffs, Paints, Leather Suitcases & General Merchants.* I wondered if anyone had ever pointed out the spelling mistake—Glass instead of Class—but suspected few English speakers used this shop. Which is what made it suspicious.

Along the front was a step, and I counted nine men sitting and smoking. They had probably been chatting but now they all watched me pass. They *really* looked, like they were assessing and checking that I kept going. Which I did. Until I was out of sight.

I deliberately didn't turn around. Instead, I looped back until I met the rail line again and then drove into the town square.

An hour later, Linda found me in a café watching the sun low in the sky.

She plonked herself down next to me and rubbed her feet. I ordered her lemonade and it arrived before she spoke.

"I didn't find anything," she said with a sigh. "No one recognized Su Ling's photograph. At least, no one admitted they did. How did you get on?"

"The police told me that three gangs are operating here. East, west and north. I didn't see evidence in the north but I found a gang member in the east."

"And he talked?"

"He talked a great deal. Only I didn't understand a word."

She smiled.

I said, "But an old man recognized Wang's name and pointed me in the direction of the gang in the west."

"And?"

"And I'm sure I found their base, or at least one of them."

For a second I thought she looked concerned as she asked, "Did you speak to someone there? Did they speak English?"

"I didn't. I'm going back there after dark." I paused a beat before adding: "And you're coming with me."

# FORTY-SEVEN

To kill time, I took Linda Wu to the European and Oriental Hotel. A sweeping drive leading to a British colonial building that had grand windows and staff outside wearing uniforms, hats and white gloves. The whole effect was like something from a hundred years ago, the height of the empire when all British men from Singapore were kings.

I booked a table for dinner and Linda wanted to look at the map of Singapore again, trying to pinpoint Yipp's new money-printing shop. However, I made her put it away because it would have been unseemly in such a setting. We might have been asked to leave and then I wouldn't have been able to relax before confronting the gang based about a mile away.

Small talk with Linda wasn't easy so I set her off talking about her favourite subject: the rise of women, although the demise of the privileged white male seemed equally important.

Dinner looked exquisite, but neither of us ate very much, and to the manager's distress I ordered no wine. We didn't talk about it, however, I knew we were both thinking about the next few hours. What would happen, what would we learn? Despite thinking I should eat, I had no appetite.

She said, "I'm impressed at how calm you are. Your girlfriend has been missing for how long?"

"Five days."

"You think a gang has her—she might have been murdered. And yet you're calm."

"Inside I'm worried like hell," I said, "Panic won't help. I need to stay focused and channel the fear."

"Did you learn that as a boxer?"

I nodded.

She smiled encouragingly. "I'm glad you're worried. It means you are human."

"I'm human all right," I said. "I worry and I bleed—in fact, my body still aches from a beating I received a week ago."

She looked surprised. "From?"

"Wang and his goons."

"Ah." She nodded like it explained something, but it didn't.

When the bill came, she said, "I'll pay half."

I shook my head. "When two men dine together, they don't split the cost."

I saw her swallow and guessed she was thinking about the expense. "All right, I'll pay."

"When I had dinner with Secretary Norris at the Singapore Club yesterday, he paid."

"Why? Doesn't that make you indebted to him?"

I said, "When I had dinner at the Jockey Club in KL with my friend Chief Inspector McNaughton, he paid. Then, two weeks ago, I returned the favour. It's easier that way. If you're invited out—like my dinner with Norris—then the host usually picks up the bill. If it's between friends then you work something out. It's more casual—like an unwritten arrangement."

"So you're saying that insisting on splitting the bill is what—insulting?"

"Awkward and unnecessary. I understand your reasoning, but in a world of equals, you should be happy for me to pay."

She nodded. "Providing you let me pay next time."

"That's how it works."

"Between friends. Nothing more."

"Right."

She nodded again and smiled. "In that case, thank you."

I had a change of clothes in my bag, and before we left the hotel I put on an outfit that Jinjing would have approved of. I looked a little like she had when she'd come to see me last night: all in black. Except I didn't wear a hood that covered most of my face. I did however have two guns. Under a loose-fitting, lightweight jacket I wore a Sam Browne belt with a service revolver on the right and my Beretta holstered on my left hip.

When I reappeared from the changing room, I received a few queer looks from hotel residents and staff alike. Linda, on the other hand, smiled appreciatively.

"You look ready," she said.

I felt like a gunslinger, and the adrenaline was already making my fingers tingle, but I was indeed ready.

★

Since the New Year, the moon had been waxing and was now about a quarter full, but cloud cover meant it was very dark.

"What's the plan?" she asked as I parked a street away from the shop selling Shanghai leather.

"You stay here."

"How can I translate if I'm here?"

"I'll bring someone to you. They'll talk and you'll translate."

Despite the darkness, I could see she was looking at me like I was crazy. "And just how are you going to do that?"

"With stealth and surprise. I'll just grab one of the gang and no one will be the wiser."

"All right," she said dubiously.

I said, "We'll keep the engine running. Sit in the driver's seat and be ready just in case."

I slipped out of the jeep and she scooted over into my seat. First of all, I walked to the junction so that I could see the bar.

Light spilled out into the street. There was lots of activity, men sitting at the tables like they were debating the latest crime but also men going in and out of the places where the windows had been blacked out.

From there I circled to the rear, where I found a track that fed small yards. I looked and waited and saw no one. There were cars back here but no guards—as far as I could tell. I figured this gang didn't fear attack from anyone, although the cars were probably set for a quick getaway, should the police show up at the front.

Keeping close to the wall, and moving slowly in case someone was lurking in the darkness, I edged to the rear of the bar. Through a gate I saw kitchens and storerooms, people cooking and preparing. Low-level staff, not key gang members, I decided. No point in grabbing one of them. I also realized that I wouldn't be able to get in without walking past a whole bunch of workers, so my plans wouldn't work.

I moved on.

The next yard ran the whole length of the leather shop with a faint light coming from rear windows. I saw no movement inside, so picking up a stone, I clattered it into the darkness and waited.

After a minute of nothing but night sounds, I crept to the building and placed my hand on a door handle then listened through the wood. Nothing.

I figured the door would be unlocked based on my getaway theory and was right. It opened easily and I slipped inside.

I was in the back of the store. It wasn't crammed with leather goods as suggested by the frontage. Here were piles of boxes—storage rather than a shop.

I saw movement ahead but decided against entering. With all the boxes, I could easily walk into a group of men, and since I had no real sense of where people might be, I slipped back into the yard.

Moving along the rear lane, I repeated the same trick with the stone. After no response, I went into the next yard and listened at the door. Faint voices carried through the wood. There was a keyhole with no light coming through. And the door was unlocked.

I opened it a crack and looked in before entering a dark corridor. The voices were louder but still sounded like they were beyond a closed door.

With my Beretta in hand, I walked softly down the corridor.

The first room I came to was a toilet. The next was an unmanned room with a round table that looked set ready for a game of cards or perhaps mah-jong.

I kept going and came to the next door, which was closed. Chatter from the other side was the source of the voices I could hear. I listened and figured there was one main guy and at least three others.

I then heard footsteps from above on wooden stairs.

Quickly, I slipped back and ducked into the games room and closed the door to within an inch of the jamb.

The footsteps came towards me, past the door and then stopped.

I darted into the corridor and down towards the rear. At the toilet door, I jolted it open. A man who had just started peeing looked at me angrily, and then with alarm as he realized I wasn't one of the gang.

He opened his mouth, but before he could shout, I slammed his head into the wall, spun him around and clamped my palm over his mouth.

A second later, I was pulling him roughly out through the back door.

He'd been dazed but shook himself out of it fast. As we went into the yard, he kicked out, missed me, but slammed into the door. It shot wide open, bounced on its hinges and slammed shut.

I didn't wait to find out if that alarmed anyone. With one hand around his neck and the gun jammed in his face, I ran him out onto the dirt track and past the cars.

Only six paces along, I heard sounds behind me, people rushing out. Lights must have come on but I didn't look back. Then I heard shouting.

I kept on running and dragging my prisoner all the way to the street and then back to the jeep.

I practically threw the man into the rear and piled in after him. At the same time, I shouted at Linda.

"Drive!" However, she was already pumping the throttle and we lurched forward.

Wild gunshots filled the air, but we weren't hanging about to give them a clear target. Linda sped away, first west and then south and then east. I had to hit the Chinese guy three times to stop him fighting beneath me.

"You've done this before," I shouted to Linda over the noise of the racing engine and wind.

"Never," she shouted back breathlessly.

We crossed the main road and into the east gang's territory. That's when I said we could stop. I was sure there would be men in cars out there looking for us, but for five minutes or so, I figured we were safe. We were near a street light so I could see my prisoner. He returned my gaze with hatred and frustration.

"What's that smell?" Linda said, turning around in her seat.

"He pissed himself," I said.

"Charming."

"Don't blame him. He was in the middle of it when I grabbed him."

I got off the man and he tried to escape before I hit him again with the gun.

Holding up the picture of Su Ling, I said, "Where is she?"

He screamed back at me, and I knew it was pure invective before Linda summarized.

I held the gun to his head.

"Yes or no. Do you recognize her?"

Linda immediately translated what I'd said.

He clenched his teeth and said, "Yes," in Chinese.

"Where is she?"

"He says he doesn't know," Linda said.

I pressed the gun harder against his temple.

"Guess," I said, and Linda translated.

I heard a name and repeated it. "Tambatan?"

Linda spoke to the man and then translated his words. "Near the docks. A place called Tambatan House."

"She's there?"

He said, "Maybe," which Linda translated. Then he smiled and spoke English. "It's a brothel."

# FORTY-EIGHT

I threw him out onto the street. He was in the wrong part of town so his main concern would be getting back to the west rather than raising the alarm. As he scurried away, I climbed into the driver's seat and sped off.

"So much for stealth and surprise," she said.

Within a few minutes, I'd arrived at the docks. They were nothing like Singapore's, being more of a fishing port than for major trade, which made sense since the water in these straits wasn't deep enough for most cargo ships.

I drove the length of it, noting godowns and low-rise sheds. After a mile, it ended and I turned, taking the next road and doubling back. Halfway along, I spotted a likely building and pointed.

"The Chinese over the entrance—" she said. "It's the name, Tambatan. That must be the place."

There were red lanterns along the frontage and curtains at the windows with light bleeding around the edges.

I kept going.

"Around the back?" she asked.

I took the next left and then left again. It was a typical residential street, not a slum but no sign of money either.

I stopped fifty yards away from where I judged the back of the house to be.

"Same as before," I said, leaving the engine running and getting out.

She nodded. "Stealth and surprise."

Walking on the opposite side of the street, I gauged the activity. The smell of cooking vegetables and rice mingled with the harsh odour of fish from the dock. I could see people—shapes mostly—in the homes opposite. A man on a bicycle laden with boxes passed and I saw bicycles parked, but no cars.

I walked past the back of the target property and then slunk back, hugging the darkness.

A dog barked close by and I heard laughter. But no sounds came from Tambatan House. There was no light either. Which was good because it had no yard and anyone looking might have seen me approach the back door. Then it opened outwards and light spilled across the road as a man stepped out. I was the other side of the door, and when he shut it he stood a mere six feet away from me, his eyes not yet adjusted to the dark.

I could have executed the same move as before: grab him, drag him away and get him to talk. But Su Ling might be inside and I was wasting no time.

I stepped forward and punched him just as he raised a cigarette to his mouth. His head jolted back, hit the wall and he slumped to the ground.

With my Beretta drawn, I stepped over him and through the door. As soon as I was inside I could tell it was a cheap brothel. The smell of stale sex and dirt assaulted my nostrils and made my heart thump with fear. Was Su Ling here?

I imagined the layout: a reception area at the front, rooms for the girls in the centre, and a bathroom, possibly an office, at the rear. I figured the door directly ahead went to the girls' rooms. Opening it slowly, I stepped through and saw a row of drawn curtains acting as dividers for the rooms.

I heard groans and grunts and saw a curtain twitch, then a man walked into the central aisle. In case he looked my way, I stepped through the first curtain on my left.

Before me on the floor was a naked girl and a man standing over her with his trousers down. I hit him behind the ear with the Beretta, and as he dropped like a felled tree, I dashed to the girl and stopped her screaming with my hand clamped over her mouth.

"Su Ling?" I whispered into her frightened face.

She shook her head and I eased my hand away. She continued to stare at me as I pulled out my girlfriend's photo.

"Su Ling Yong?"

The girl shook her head and I backed away. A quick check outside and I ducked through the next curtain. This girl was alone and seated. She looked at me through unseeing eyes and I figured she was stoned. Maybe the first girl had been too, just not as bad.

This one started to remove her cotton gown, exposing her nakedness beneath.

"Su Ling?" I asked, showing the photograph.

She looked at me, then at the picture and blinked. Did she recognize her? She looked at me again like she was focusing for the first time. But it wasn't at me.

A hand snatched my shoulder, hard. A Chinese man behind me, now shouting.

I spun, caught him with my left elbow. He threw a wild blow at my head and I hit him again. As he went down, I punched him in the back of the head.

The girl was screaming. I rushed out of her booth into the corridor. Curtains twitched, but now I hurried, looking into each section, hoping to find Su Ling.

If a man appeared I hit him. If it was a girl I checked what she looked like before moving on.

I got to the end. No Su Ling. Which was both good and bad news. Good that she wasn't in this whorehouse, but bad because I hadn't found her.

I went back down the line, holding up the photograph to the girls who had come out.

Two of them showed more response than the others, maybe recognition, I wasn't sure. However no one spoke English.

Another girl screamed and I swung around and saw a big guy who had burst through from the reception and was barging girls out of the way. As he charged towards me, he had a machete raised and was making threatening noises.

I glanced behind at the exit and then back at him. No time.

"Out of the way!" I shouted, hoping the girls would understand. Then I fired. Twice. Centre mass. Even as he crumpled, another man crashed through the door. I shot him too.

Somewhere I thought I could hear a car horn, but it was lost in the screams of the girls and gunshots. A man from the booth beside me lunged with a chair. It glanced off my back as I turned and put a bullet in his forehead.

The reception door opened again and now I could see a whole bunch of crazed men coming in.

I'd been backing up and now I grabbed one of the girls—the one who'd shown the most interest in Su Ling's picture. I fired and fired again, counted fifteen then switched to the service revolver. All the time, I was walking the girl rapidly backwards, hoping my shots into the doorway would stop the attackers.

What must have only been seconds felt like long minutes until I was backing through the door, out into the street.

Linda was right there with the Land Rover.

I lifted the girl into the back and jumped in after her.

She was panicked as hell, but I had to be rough. She fought me ineffectively, her arms flailing and bouncing off my arms and head. But I didn't care, Linda was already racing down the road and I held the girl down as gunshots rang and echoed around us.

At the end of the street, a T-junction gave Linda two options. Ahead was a hill. Left towards the end of the port or right, back towards Kampong Tarum, and potentially the gang's heartland.

She went left.

As we hit the port, I looked left and could see three cars outside the brothel. Men milled around them and the next instant they were in the cars and racing our way.

Linda needed no encouragement. She tore away, making me cling onto the seat in front of me. The acceleration made the girl stop slashing out in favour of saving her own life.

When we came to a turn away from the water, Linda took it and then we were doubling back.

"Linda!"

"Don't worry!" she shouted back. "I studied the map while you were inside."

A second later and after a skidding turn, we were going north and then west. I could hear engines screaming their complaints as our pursuers raced after us, but I could no longer see them.

When we came out again on the road that would lead to the port, I was concerned. What if they hadn't turned off? But we were going north-west, outside the town now, following a twisting river. And then our headlights picked up the first warning sign.

"What is it?" I yelled.

"Leper Hospital," she called back. Then she was turning off the road and heading for a silhouette of a giant building.

Before we got there, she slammed the jeep hard right behind an outbuilding that loomed up unexpectedly. The engine and lights went off.

I realized the girl was making a lot of noise so I held my hand over her mouth. For a second I thought I could hear a car over the sound of river birds and cicadas, but I saw no lights. Then, after it had stopped, I spotted three sets of lights bouncing along the road. Heading straight for us.

# FORTY-NINE

Three sets of car lights and three car engines raced up, but they didn't turn into the hospital grounds.

I breathed out as the rear lights faded into the distance.

"They wouldn't come in here. Not unless they had to," Linda said, her voice shaking with adrenaline.

"Good move," I said, thinking about the other engine I'd heard, but then I dismissed it.

"Stealth and surprise back there?" she asked.

"Things got complicated."

"I saw them arrive. I tried to warn you."

"I heard the horn," I said. Then: "Su Ling wasn't inside."

"I guessed. What about this girl?"

"Desperation," I said, easing my hand from her mouth. She immediately started to gabble, and I asked, "What's she saying?"

"She's scared. First the shooting and the kidnapping and now the leper hospital." Linda then spoke to the girl and back to me. "I explained that we aren't bringing her here. That you are desperate to find your girlfriend."

I took out the photograph that was now crumpled from being stuffed in my pocket. Linda fished the torch from the glove compartment and shone it for me.

"This is her," I said. "Please look closely."

Linda repeated what I'd said and the girl took the photograph. Then she said a few words.

I wasn't hopeful, but Linda asked her a barrage of questions and got some longer responses.

"Let her go," Linda said to me, and as soon as I released my grip, the girl leapt out of the jeep and ran into the darkness.

"Hopeless," I said.

"Odd."

"Odd? What do you mean?"

"I didn't understand her. She said a woman was being held by a poisonous flower."

My mouth went dry. Surely not? I'd heard something similar sixteen months ago.

I climbed out and took the driver's seat from her. Then I reloaded my Beretta. It was another delaying tactic and I finally brought myself to speak.

"Linda, what was the name of the flower?"

"Rafflesia."

"Oh my God!" I fired the engine into life and reversed back to the driveway we'd ducked off. I swallowed. "Did she mention a school?"

"Yes, but—"

"Rafflesia School at Bukit Zarah," I said. "I know it!"

★

We were off the map of Johor Bahru, but I knew where I was going. The road we were on would eventually join Route One, but it was the obvious route. After a short distance we came to a crossroads and I went left on a rough track heading west. It twisted and turned around hills and over rivers until I found the road I was looking for. This track went directly north for about four miles through jungle until it reached a village called Pulai Perdana. The name had stuck in my memory because *pulai* meant island, and all I could think is that originally this place was based on the river, but it had grown and grown and I saw no river now.

I'd stopped here for directions sixteen months ago. Despite the darkness, I knew which way to turn, going first west then north to the base of a long winding hill.

Without my headlights, I eased up the track that would become a driveway.

The closer I got, the more my heart pounded.

There were thick trees on either side. Even with my headlights on, I wouldn't have been able to see around the bends for more than fifty yards. As it was I was relying on other lights in the gloom to betray someone's presence.

I saw none.

Had Wang's gang figured out what I was doing? Did they realize who I was? If so, those three cars were probably up ahead.

Halfway, I stopped and bumped the jeep into the undergrowth.

"What are you doing?" she asked, concerned as I raised the Beretta.

"I'm going the rest of the way on foot. It's too risky."

She was going to complain, but I wouldn't listen and told her to get out and wait in the trees.

"Hide until I come back."

"You're crazy," she said, whispering louder than me.

"Probably."

"Give me one of your guns."

"No."

"I'm not staying!"

I started to walk away, but she was out of the jeep and following.

"You aren't leaving me behind again," she said.

"It'll be dangerous and I can't protect you."

"I'm not asking for protection and I *can* use a gun." She was alongside me now with her hand out. "Let me have one and I'll cover you."

271

The service revolver was heavier with fewer bullets, but I'd be damned if I was giving her the Beretta. I pulled out the revolver and handed it to her as we walked.

"Just don't point it at me."

"Thanks," she said. "Now what's the plan?"

We were a hundred yards from the gates, and I took her into the trees so that we could approach more cautiously.

Moving slowly now, careful of the noise underfoot, we cut through to the perimeter wall.

"Give me a boost up," she said.

I'd thought about climbing a tree. "It's ten feet high!"

"Give me a boost."

I relented and offered my hands as a foothold. She was quickly on, then pulling herself up and looking over the top.

"Dark," she whispered when she dropped down again. "There's a big house and gardens."

"Cars?"

"None."

Damn! We'd come so far, following lead after lead only to find a dead end.

She said, "But I saw movement."

"People?"

"Possibly. A person, probably."

"Where?"

"Along the side, at the end of a drive."

The garage, I thought.

"OK," I said, "let's go in."

We tracked back to the drive and came to the gates. I remembered them well. Stone eagles, mounted on top of the brick gateposts, glared down at us. The metal gates were open and damaged, like a truck had driven through them. Which it had, sixteen months ago.

There was a guardhouse to the right, and I confirmed it was empty before slipping behind and hugging the wall.

There were burnt sections along here. The front garden had once been pristine with box hedging, but that had been mashed through by the truck and burned as well.

I couldn't see the damage to the lawns but I could just about make out the broken windows.

"Where did you see the person?" I checked.

"Down there."

She pointed to the right of the building—which I knew had once been a beautiful *istana*—in the direction of the garage. Just as I'd predicted. In fact, now that I looked in that direction, I thought I could see a sliver of pale light between the garage doors.

"The plan," I said. "You stay here. If you need to warn me, fire the gun. If you are in peril, fire the gun."

"And if I see someone about to shoot you?" She looked at me and I wondered if she was enjoying this. "Shall I fire at them?"

"Only if they're nowhere near me."

"What will you do?"

"Go into the garage."

"How long do I give you before I come looking?"

I shook my head. "Linda, it's not a game. You give me ten minutes. If I don't reappear, you get out of here. No matter what. Understood?"

"Yes, sir."

I suspected she was being facetious, but I ignored it and slipped through the long grass all the way to the building that I knew was a garage.

It was big enough to hold three cars and still have room for a workshop. There was definitely a faint light inside, and I kept away from the main doors, instead circling around the back and coming out facing the rear of the old school. The garage had a side door here, and again I saw the light. I could also see the gardens, untended since I'd last been here. Not destroyed by the truck or fighting, but overgrown and shapeless.

I listened at the door before opening it a crack.

That's when I received a blinding blow to the back of my skull.

# FIFTY

I staggered, falling into the garage, but wasn't knocked out. Instinct kicked in and I rolled and sprang unsteadily to my feet, ready to shoot.

But instead of confronting my attacker, I faced Linda.

"What the hell?" I hissed at her. "Why did you—" But before I could finish my accusation, she opened the door wide and I saw a body on the floor.

"He was following you," she said. "So I followed him."

I got it finally: he'd snuck up on me and hit me and she'd done the same to him.

"Stealth and surprise," she said, demonstrating a blow with the weighty service revolver. "I thought it better than shooting him."

Feeling the rapidly ballooning lump on the back of my head, I figured the pain was worth it.

I found twine and an oil rag, bound his hands and feet and stuffed the rag in the man's mouth.

"OK, now wait here," I said.

"Where are you going?"

"Just going to check this garage," I lied. "You keep guard."

The garage had a single very dim light on. Linda glanced at the solitary car parked in here and then frowned and shrugged. I let the side door close and then checked the car. It was cold, so not one of those following us from the brothel. Behind it was the workshop area. I stepped over and located the hatch in the floor. I eased it open, cringing at the creak and groan of the old hinges.

A four-rung metal ladder descended into a passage. I went down. At the bottom was a tunnel barely wide enough to squeeze along and too low to stand upright in.

Three paces and the tunnel turned through ninety degrees. I stopped and checked around the corner. Faint light came from behind me, from the garage. Faint light appeared at the end of the passage, fifty yards or so distant.

I edged along it, listening, and glancing behind and then focusing ahead.

Thirty yards.

Down there was like being in a tube. Sounds were deadened and directionless. And the light at the end was like a lure, offering hope, but also the unknown.

Twenty yards.

What I did know was that there was a room ahead, a hidden cellar beneath the school that had a cell, maybe dating back to when it had been occupied by the Japanese in the war.

Ten yards.

The light came from a lamp. I could see pale orange strips where the light glinted off the metal cage.

Four yards.

I saw movement. A man walked across my field of vision. He yawned and sat down near the lamp. There was a rifle on his lap, side on to me: a guard covering the stairs, not the tunnel.

I stepped into the room.

"Hands up!" I bellowed. "Drop the gun!"

The Chinese guard swivelled, shocked, started to raise his rifle then thought better of it.

"Drop the gun! Drop it now!"

Whether he understood the words, I don't know, but he got the tone and let his rifle clatter to the ground.

Closing the gap at a run, I grabbed him, spun him and delivered a knockout blow with the butt of my Beretta.

As I'd run across the dimly lit cellar, my peripheral vision had picked out something in the cage. Something piled on the floor. Clothes? A body?

Unable to breathe, I rushed to the cell door. Close up, I could now see the pile was a person huddled on a thin mattress.

"Su Ling!" I shouted.

The bundle moved. Alive, but I still couldn't see who it was.

Dashing back to the guard, I searched his pockets and found a key. It fit the lock and I darted into the cell and pulled a blanket away. I saw bare feet and bare arms—a woman. A royal blue dress.

I rolled her and revealed the face of the woman I loved. "Su Ling!"

My joy crashed into worry. Her skin was clammy and her eyes stared blindly. Sick or drugged, I didn't know, but the latter seemed most likely.

There was a cup of water in the cell and I forced drops between her lips and lifted her. I carried her out of the cell, to the staircase. With her head on my right shoulder, I could hear her laboured breathing.

I was talking constantly, saying reassuring things that I didn't feel.

"It'll be all right. It'll be all right. I've got you now. You're safe, Su Ling."

I think she understood because I felt her respond, snuggle in and breathe more easily. Once upstairs I made my way through the hall, through the grand lobby. My footfall echoed through the giant empty house.

Then I reached the main doors, kicked them open and stepped into the cool night air.

At once, lights burst on: two sets of blazing headlights aimed at me, dazzling me.

My gun was holstered but I wouldn't have been able to reach it without dropping Su Ling, and I couldn't do that. I stood still, waiting, hoping that the lights wouldn't be followed by a barrage of gunfire, thinking that each second I stayed alive was good news.

Silhouettes blotted the lights and I counted eight men closing in. Then I saw them all pointing guns. It wasn't until they were ten yards away that I saw their Chinese faces. I didn't know them, but equally they looked as confused as I felt.

*Stay alive, evaluate. Act when the opportunity presents itself.*

Were these Wang's brother's men? Had they finally found me? But if so, why the confusion? Surely they knew Su Ling was being held in the school.

"On your knees," one man said, his voice a heavy Chinese accent.

I didn't move. "Who are you?"

They were six feet away now and forming a semicircle around me. Six guns pointing into the centre. Foolish options went rapidly through my head and I dismissed them.

*Stay alive.*

The man who had spoken in English then spoke in Chinese and another set aside his weapon. He stepped forward and took Su Ling from me. Gently and with respect.

"Who are you?" I asked again.

"On your knees!" the one in charge barked. Without Su Ling, I could do something. Once on my knees, my options would rapidly shrink to zero.

But before I could act, my gun was snatched from its holster and a barrel jammed in my ear.

"On your knees!"

I went down. And that's the last thing I remember.

# PART FOUR

# FIFTY-ONE

*Saturday 13th February*

Su Ling retched and emptied her stomach of the very little that remained.

Fingers of daylight played though a curtain that moved gently in a breeze. She saw curtains she didn't recognize. A room she didn't recognize. And she was in a comfortable bed she didn't recognize.

An elderly woman got up from a chair. "Drink this," she said and handed Su Ling a bowl of something foul-smelling. "It'll make you feel better."

Su Ling gulped it down and tensed her throat so that it didn't come straight back up.

"How do you feel?" the woman asked, taking the bowl and then mopping Su Ling's brow.

"Better," Su Ling said, despite the nausea and pounding headache. "Where am I?"

"Safe," the woman said. "Outside Johor Bahru in a safe house."

Su Ling smiled at her.

The woman said, "Mr Yipp will be here soon. He's coming to take you home."

An hour later, she awoke to find Andrew Yipp standing over her bed and holding her hand.

"Are you all right, Little Flower?" he asked.

The nausea and headache were gone. She felt weak and disorientated but that was all. He handed her a glass of water and she sipped it.

"Much better," she said.

"Are you ready to come home?"

She thought then smiled. "Yes. Take me home."

"Good. The lady will get you dressed. Take your time, but I also want to know what happened."

"Of course."

"What's the last thing you remember?"

"I had dinner with Major Lamb. I left the Hotel de la Paix and was going to the fair when he stopped me."

"Who?"

"Wang."

"What did he want?"

"He said he would take me to you." She took another sip of water. "As you know, we were going to meet last night."

"Last night? It was six days ago!"

She stared at him. "Where have I been?"

Yipp's face was tense. "Tell me what you remember. What did Wang do?"

"He made me get in the car. I remember that. There was someone else in there. I remember we drove and he was taking me away from the city. That's all. I have flashes of places, dark and damp, feeling sick and everything spinning around." She rubbed her neck. "My neck and shoulder are sore."

"Do you remember being rescued?"

"I... Was I carried? Was that you?"

"Yes, I found you."

"Thank God," she said. "Thank God you saved me. Now, please take me home to sleep in my bed."

He nodded. "Yes, my love. But there's something I must do first."

# FIFTY-TWO

I'd been beaten by Wang's men, I'd been hit on the back of the head with a gun, and now I'd been hit with something else. My head had been a punchbag recently and my brain felt jarred.

I woke up realizing someone was shaking me.

"What?" I said groggily.

"Where are we?" Linda's voice.

I opened my eyes and it took a second to understand. The darkness was total, but I recognized the smell. "We're under the house," I said. "It's a cellar."

"What happened?"

"I went through a tunnel and came out in this room. There was a guard, and I found Su Ling in a cell."

"We're in a cell now," she said. "It's locked."

"I figured."

"Was she all right? Where is she now? There's no one else down here as far as I can tell."

"I think she'd been drugged. I don't know if she'll be OK and I don't know where she is. I carried her outside and men were waiting. They took her and knocked me out."

"The gang found us."

"I don't know," I said. "I don't understand what's going on. Tell me what happened to you."

"I was waiting for you outside the garage. I heard a noise and went to investigate. The next thing I know is I wake up here with a lump on my temple. I know less than you."

"Why leave us alive?" I said. "I'd killed at least five back there in the brothel. They should have killed us."

"Maybe it wasn't the gang from JB."

"That's my theory."

She didn't say anything for a few seconds and I heard her breathing, trying to stay calm perhaps. I wondered if she'd been on the verge of panic. Then: "How do we get out, Captain Carter?"

"Let's work our way around the cell. Let's check every join, every hole where the rods go into the rock. There's bound to be a weakness." To be honest, I was sure there wasn't. This cage had held lots of people in the past. It had been built as a prison cell by the Japanese. Could it have weakened in less than ten years? I doubted it, but it was worth a try. Plus it gave Linda hope.

★

The hope lasted about twenty minutes, although we couldn't see so it was hard to judge the time.

Linda was getting agitated now she had nothing to do. I lay down, staying calm and thinking. From a young age, I'd been in similarly bad situations. A solution always presented itself.

The only metal I had on me was my belt buckle. Pulling the belt off, I handed it out for her to take.

"Make noise," I said. "Rattle it on the cage. Hopefully, someone will hear." She started banging, making more noise than I expected. I doubted it would do any good but it kept her occupied. The downside was I wanted to close my eyes and rest, but she got into a rhythm of banging and shouting. Torture may have been preferable.

After a while she stopped and listened, then she started up again. I don't know how long this went on for, but it felt like many hours.

And then we heard a noise followed by footsteps in the house. Suddenly she went quiet. I couldn't even hear her breathing.

"Good or bad?" she asked.

"It doesn't matter," I said. "We have no choice." That's when we both started shouting for help.

Within seconds, light flooded into the room. Boots clattered on the stairs, then legs appeared, then what seemed like an army of men. But they weren't the army, they were the police, all carrying guns, all looking nervous.

Ten minutes later we were sitting outside on the stone front steps with blankets around us and drinking water. It was after three in the afternoon. We were offered fruit and I realized how hungry I was. So we just sat there, looking at the damaged garden and a line of police cars and wagons in the drive. Policemen milled around, although I suspected they were awaiting orders rather than investigating anything.

A car pulled through the broken gates and stopped at the back of the queue. Chief Inspector Eric Stanford-Jones got out and strode directly for us but then stopped as he received an update from a sergeant.

"Good God, man!" he said approaching. "Are you all right?"

I shrugged off the blanket, stood, and shook his hand. "We're fine."

"And lucky," he said.

I nodded.

He had his hands on his hips and he looked at me critically. "I don't fully understand what happened. We have two men shot through the head here, execution-style. One was tied up."

I said, "I tied one up but didn't shoot anyone."

"Tell me what happened."

"Have you found anyone else?" I asked, thinking of Su Ling.

"No, just two dead Chinese men. Tell me what happened."

"I found the girl I was looking for—"

"Andrew Yipp's niece?"

"She was in a cell under the house."

"A coincidence that it's this property," he said, referring to the case when I'd first met George McNaughton, "but good you found her. Is this her?" He looked at Linda and I shook my head.

"This is Linda Wu from the *Straits Times*. She was helping me."

"So, Yipp's niece?"

"We arrived then someone else came. They took her and left us here."

He said, "It was a good job your secretary knew where you were."

"My receptionist?" I said slowly.

"Chau, she said her name was. Told me you were here."

"Right," I said, wondering how she knew.

He said, "So you didn't kill the men here?"

"No."

"What about the men in Tambatan House near the port."

"Ah," I said. "Self-defence. I started asking questions and they attacked me."

"Lucky for you they were known gang members. As were the others."

"The others?"

"A place in Kampong Tarum. Looks like you wiped out the whole gang."

"A huge leather shop?"

"*High Glass Leather* something," he said.

I nodded. "I know it, but it wasn't me. I didn't kill anyone there."

He looked at me through critical eyes, maybe not believing me. "I told you, Captain, I didn't know Andrew Yipp's Wang. That was true, but I do know a Wang— Wang Jon Soo. I didn't want you to start a war but it looks like you both started and finished it. Wang Jon Soo was one of the men killed at Tarum."

"It wasn't me," I said again.

"There was also a body dumped in the Grand Palace gardens. People must have seen it happen, but no one is talking. Throat slit, execution-style. Know anything about that one?"

"No."

He held out a photograph. A close-up of a man's face, very pale, drained of blood, but I recognized him immediately.

Wang, Yipp's henchman.

# FIFTY-THREE

It didn't make sense. I was missing something huge. I reckoned that Yipp had killed Wang for being involved with the kidnap of Su Ling.

Hunting Wang's brother had led me to the brothel and then the school. Which implied that the Johor Wang was involved. I figured Yipp had attacked the leather shop in Kampong Tarum, so he thought the same.

Johor Wang's gang had chased us from the brothel and yet they hadn't come to the school looking for me. Why? Surely that was the obvious place—unless they hadn't realized I was looking for Su Ling.

Then I dismissed that thought because of the first goon I'd captured and interrogated in Kampong Tarum. I'd told him and left him alive.

I thought back to when we'd been hiding at the leper hospital. I'd heard the sound of a car on the road as we hid. It had been before I'd seen the lights of the Wang gang cars chasing us. So was someone else following, and if so who?

Could that have been Yipp's men, since I figured they were the ones who had arrived and locked me and Linda in the cell. They hadn't killed us, and I later found my two guns in the footwell of my Land Rover.

Considerate, and yet they'd left us in that dungeon—to die. Another apparent contradiction.

I dropped Linda at her home near Scott's Road. She'd hardly said a word on the way back and I wondered if shock had set in.

When I popped into the office, Madam Chau tutted and shook her head.

"I thought you'd be happy that I'm alive," I said.

"But yet again, you are only just. One of these days you won't walk through that door. And by the way, you look awful. What are those clothes you're wearing?"

She was right of course. My clothes were the black ones I'd put on at the hotel and they were now dirty and dishevelled.

"Don't worry, I'll clean up. I just wanted to let you know I was back and to thank you."

Her demeanour didn't change. She was still grumpy.

I said, "So how did you know where I was? I had no idea I'd end up at the school."

"I got a call first thing. A man's voice, Chinese by the sound of it. Wouldn't say his name."

I nodded. Now that made a little sense. Yipp had instructed his men to leave me there but notify someone. One of his employees had called her and she'd instructed the Johor Bahru police.

She touched a pile on her desk. "You have some letters and a document from the Planning and Development department."

The list of properties I'd requested from Major Lamb. "Thank you."

She glowered at me. "What are you doing?"

"Working. It's Saturday." I went to reach for the envelopes and Lamb's document on her desk, but she barred my way.

"I know that, but you need to rest," she said. "Go home! That's an order."

I thought about it as she continued to glare. Of course she was right. I was in a bad way and needed rest.

"Fine," I said. "I'll see you on Monday."

"You had better rest, Master Carter!"

"I will," I assured her as I left. But thought: after I do something important.

★

Cleaning myself up, I headed out into the city and found a baker's delivery boy who looked trustworthy. I asked him to deliver a note addressed to Jinjing and read:

Bread from the bakery, Teck How Lee? The price of rolls is always best. If order them, she can get discount.

Not a great sentence, but I hoped it would seem like bad English and get the message to Su Ling's assistant. I wrote the number six at the bottom and sent the boy off to the Cathay Building.

Thirty minutes later he returned with a reply.

The best flour is fine. No bread needed, I see. Or rolls today. Thank you. Perhaps another day or tomorrow? I can order at night.

There was no number, although I was pretty sure what the message was, and the boy confirmed it as I paid him.

"The lady said five shillings."

Five shillings was a ridiculous amount. It was a clever message. The number was five.

Her message: Fine. See you tomorrow night.

I was so relieved that Su Ling was all right and might visit me, I almost gave the kid five shillings, which he wouldn't really expect. Instead, I handed him twenty cents and he skipped away, contented.

Now that I knew, Su Ling was all right, I could follow Madam Chau's instructions. I went home to my place on Beach Road and rested. I figured, now that Su Ling had been found and Wang was dead, I could relax. I didn't need to stay at Gillman Barracks anymore.

The following day, with the anticipation of seeing Su Ling later, I visited the Hill Street police station.

"Why are you smiling?" Inspector Singh asked after I'd been shown to his office. "Have you found Krishna?"

I grinned at his humour. "Why are you working on a Sunday?"

"Crime doesn't stop on Sundays, Ash. You know that."

"If only."

His face became serious. "I heard about what happened in JB. You're lucky to be alive."

I nodded. "Maybe that's why I'm smiling, Ishaan. Happy to be alive, I suppose."

He nodded and smiled. "How can I help you today?"

"Any progress on the murder of Patrice?"

He looked uncomfortable. "I'm afraid there is no more work on it. Not closed, but filed."

"And Saburo?"

"Released."

"What about his boss, Mr Zhao? I asked you to find out why he'd stopped paying rent."

Again the guilty expression. "The chief... sorry, Ash. You know I can't allocate resources I don't have."

I thanked him and said I'd question the man myself.

After letting Madam Chau know where I was going, I walked to Canal Road and the property where Patrice had lived with Saburo.

Zhao was there and in a bad mood. "Where is he?"

"Saburo?" I said. "I have no idea except that the police released him."

"He owes me, and if you are hiding him, I'll—"

"You'll do what?" I said, glaring. Dealing with these types was as much about bluffing confidence as it was anything more substantial. "Anything happens to me and the police will lock you up and throw away the key."

His posture relaxed. "Do you know where he is?"

"No, but if he's got away then I wish him well."

"We'll find him."

"And if he ends up dead then the police will know where to look—and they'll charge you with Patrice's murder as well."

He shook his head. "I told you before that he was far too valuable."

"You never said that."

"I can't remember who I said it to. Probably the police, if you weren't there. Anyway, I assure you that I don't throw away my biggest assets."

"And yet your earnings were declining."

Zhao said nothing.

I said, "All right, tell me why your outgoings went down at the same time."

Again he stayed silent.

"Who do you pay rent to? Who owns this property?"

He shook his head. "I operate within the law. You may not like what I do, but legally..." He shook his head again. "If you continue to harass me... I know people... people in authority."

Now it was my turn to shake my head. "You can't threaten me with that. Who do you think I am?"

"I'm just saying," he said with eyebrows raised, as though he knew something I didn't.

And then I got it. "Your employee's clients," I said. "Or someone in particular."

He said nothing, but I could see that I was right.

"Give me his name."

"Get out of my house."

I tried a few more times before giving up. "It's not over," I said, walking away from the little man. "I'm going to find Patrice's killer and then I'm coming after you."

I thought about going into the office and catching up on the post and going over the list from the Planning and

Development department. However, I got halfway there before changing my mind.

I was in a funny mood. I was angry with Zhao but I realized I was also on edge because of Su Ling.

So rather than go to the office, I went to the boxing gym and worked out my frustration. I kept reminding myself that all was fine. I would be seeing Su Ling tonight. However, I have this innate need for justice, and Patrice's murder bothered me more than I could rationalize. Perhaps it was because of the hardship he'd faced, tricked by the people who'd brought him to Singapore. Perhaps it was because we'd had a connection, albeit for stealing my money clip. Perhaps because he was treated as a second-class citizen because of his sexual status.

No one deserved to be murdered and everyone deserved to have their crime properly investigated.

After two hours of training, I was too exhausted to think as I lay on my bed at home.

Although it was still early evening, I fell into a deep sleep and then woke with a jolt. Someone was on my balcony.

Shaking the sleep from my brain, I rushed to the doors to let Su Ling in. Only it wasn't my girlfriend who walked into the room.

# FIFTY-FOUR

*Monday 15th February*

Jinjing hustled inside, wearing the same dark disguise as before.

I shut the doors behind her. "I'd hoped... I thought it'd be Su Ling."

"She's still recovering," Jinjing said. "But she asked me to see you and thank you for finding her."

"And she is all right, truly?"

"Everything is fine except that she wants to be with you."

"I'll get her away."

"As soon as possible." I must have looked surprised because she added, "Really! I mean it. If it can be tomorrow, she will be there."

"I'll do my best," I said. "First thing, I'll see Arthur Pope and find out when he can get her to the Philippines."

"Any destination, Captain Carter. She's desperate. Just get her away from Singapore—and Mr Yipp."

"Even Hong Kong or Shanghai?"

"Preferably not. She mentioned the Philippines or possibly Japan, but if it has to be somewhere else, then she'll take it."

"First thing in the morning," I said, understanding. "I'll speak to him then get a message to you. It'll just be a string of numbers. They'll be the days in February when he sets sail and the time." A quick check of my watch told me it was just after midnight. "If it's Tuesday at this time, the numbers would be 16-00."

"So that's the sixteenth at midnight."

"Although she'll need to be there two hours before."

"Understood. Could you also add a letter as the destination?

"How about P for the Philippines, J for Japan, C if it's China and O for other?"

She confirmed that she understood and I double-checked that Su Ling could get away tomorrow night if necessary.

I said, "Tell her I love her and I'll follow as soon as I can. Tell her when she arrives to wait and watch the flights coming in."

"I will," she said, and then slipped out and into the darkness.

★

I could hardly sleep and was up before dawn. Arthur Pope left his house in Tanglin early each morning, going to the Singapore Club.

He was surprised to see me waiting on the street.

"What's wrong, Ash?" he asked with genuine concern.

After apologizing for intercepting him there, I explained the urgency.

"Let me check at the office," he said and dismissed his driver who'd been waiting close by. On the way to his office, I told Pope about confronting the gang in Johor Bahru. It put him in a good mood, especially after the detail of me killing the gangsters in the brothel.

Once we were inside the Kelly and Pope Building in Commercial Square, he pulled a ledger from his desk and flicked through to the relevant page.

"I have a boat going to Hong Kong in two days. Or there's Japan in five."

"Could the Hong Kong boat go somewhere else en route?"

"Divert like our previous plan, you mean?"

"Yes, is it possible?"

"Always possible, dear chap, providing we know there's definitely someone inside. You know what happened last time."

"There will be a second X on the box," I said. "Then you'll know for certain."

"In that case, we'll have problems and divert to the Philippines. When can you let me know?"

"Hopefully today," I said, and wrote down the departure times for both boats.

We were about to leave when young Jihan appeared, all bouncy and agitated.

"Sir?"

"What do you want, boy?" Pope snapped.

"Sir, could I speak to the captain?"

Pope looked at me.

"What is it, Jihan?" I asked.

"Sir, my cousin would like to speak to you. He says he has information from his friend in Kuala Lumpur."

★

I wanted to find out what police constable Peter Jihan knew, but it had to wait. My first job was to get a message to Jinjing about the boats.

The note I gave to my messenger was: H17-02 J20-05

He came back within ten minutes.

"I didn't manage to see the lady, *tuan*, and I was given the note back."

Disappointed, I looked at the piece of paper. J20-05 had been struck out. My heart raced. Tomorrow night. Su Ling was confirming the Hong Kong boat tomorrow. I was so relieved that I gave the boy the five shillings he'd asked for previously.

He cried with joy and shook my hand before rushing off, presumably to hand the money to his family. I headed in the other direction, walked to Fullerton Square and up to the Singapore Club.

Arthur Pope was eating breakfast, so I just passed on a message saying, "Seventeenth". Then I strode to my office.

"You look better today, Master Carter." Madam Chau said as she started to prepare tea.

"It's a good day," I said.

She looked out at the overcast sky and then back at me. "Ah, then I'm happy for you."

"I haven't got time for tea or the post," I said.

"Your young lady?"

I shook my head. "Work. I'm going over to the police station on Bukit Timah Road."

"What shall I say to the reporter—Miss Wu?"

I gave her a questioning glance.

"She was trying to get an appointment yesterday, but you didn't come back." Her voice admonished me. She probably waited late for me to return while I was punching bags in the boxing gym.

"Tell her after lunch."

"Today?"

I smiled, although Madam Chau's tone didn't betray whether she was being sarcastic.

"Today," I confirmed.

"And all the other things? The mundane things I need to go through?"

"If I have time, before I see Miss Wu, otherwise afterwards."

Constable Peter Jihan wasn't at the station on Bukit Timah Road. He'd been sent off to Orchard Road and was dealing with an incident.

I found him a short time later, cordoning off a doorway around the corner from Orchard Road Market.

"Keep back," he said before recognizing me. "Captain Carter!"

"I saw your cousin this morning. He said you had information for me."

Constable Jihan looked around. We weren't alone, but I figured most of the people within earshot couldn't speak much English. However, he motioned for me to walk with him and we went down the street away from the market.

When he felt comfortable, he said, "It's about that case."

"Right?"

Unnecessarily, he then said, "About the Chinese gold and murdered men."

"Yes."

"I don't know any detail, only what my friend has told me."

That would be Mr Srivats from Kuala Lumpur, the husband of missing Anu Srivats.

We kept walking and Jihan kept looking around. He said, "You got a message about the reports, did you find anything?"

"No. I got the files, but they didn't help. How is Mrs Srivats? Did she turn up?"

"Dead," he said, his eyes full of fear.

"What happened?"

"Run over by a car."

I shook my head. "I'm sorry. Please pass on my condolences to your friend."

Constable Jihan gripped my arm and then let go, apologizing. "Sorry, I shouldn't have done that."

"It's all right. What do you know about the reports?"

He said, "You should have checked the records—the manageress's records. She logs everything in and out."

And then he told me what I'd missed.

# FIFTY-FIVE

*Tuesday 16th February*

Peter Jihan told me that the second body in the Batu Caves had been found in October, which was too late to have been linked to BlackJack. Which made a lot of sense. Very little about the murder had the hallmarks of BlackJack.

Jihan also told me something else. He told me that his friend had the evidence and I should get it.

Before I left, I assured the constable that no one would know he'd given me the information. Then I raced back to the office and decided to make three phone calls.

My first was to the coroner in Kuala Lumpur. Madam Chau made the connection and handed me the phone.

"The second body in Batu Caves," I said after polite introductions.

"Still looking into that?" he asked wearily.

"When I asked you about it before, you said October. Was that a mistake?"

"I don't"—he sounded flustered—"I'm very busy, so it's possible. Hold on a minute and I'll check."

I listened to the electronic whistles and clicks for more than a minute before he came back on the line.

"I examined the body on the ninth of October last year," he said confidently. "I was right."

"The record shows he was found on the eighteenth of September."

"No," he said. "The body was found on the eighth of October and I examined him a day later. I have it right here in my own handwriting—best record I can have."

My second call was to my friend, Chief Inspector McNaughton.

"George," I said, "I need to see you urgently."

"What's it about?"

"We need to talk about that missing typist and the possible editing of records."

"What? My goodness, do we have a problem?"

"Potentially," I said. "I need to get evidence for you. When can we meet? Tonight?"

"I've got committee meetings this afternoon and then dinner with the high commissioner. Can it wait until tomorrow?"

"Yes."

"I'll have my assistant call your secretary and we'll find a free slot."

My third call was to Lieutenant Colonel Ambrose at Gillman Barracks. Of course, he knew all about the Chinese gold case and the hunt for someone else— someone probably in the army.

I said, "I think I've got it."

"My God, man! Who?"

I told him about the ex-soldier murdered and found in the Batu Caves. "It now looks like he was killed afterwards—too late to be BlackJack. More likely someone cleaning shop. Someone getting rid of a contact, a risk."

"Someone senior in the army."

"Or ex-army," I said and told him what I needed.

★

When Linda Wu arrived, I was going through the large pile of post with Madam Chau. Before that, I'd looked through the list of properties on Major Lamb's list of re-appropriated properties. There was one on Canal Street and another behind, but not the one where Mr Zhao operated.

Linda wanted to discuss the money-counterfeiting case she was investigating. So much had happened with rescuing Su Ling from the old school and her planned escape tomorrow night, then the Chinese gold case re-surfacing, that it took me a while to get my mind on the subject.

"I've not been idle," she said, seeming much more like the hardened reporter that I knew. "The fake five-dollar notes are reasonably easy to spot if you know what you're looking for. Obviously, the paper gets discoloured over time, with use, but the fake ones are impregnated with a faint red dye. It's from the original ten-dollar notes that aren't totally cleaned when they're bleached."

She handed me a five-dollar note and I studied it, unable to see anything obvious. Then she handed me a magnifying glass and I saw pink dots embedded in the paper.

"Interesting," I said. "More proof of counterfeiting if we needed it."

"But we still don't know where the printing press has moved to."

"Or got concrete evidence against Yipp."

"Don't worry"—she laughed and held up the dodgy note—"we'll catch him *red*-handed."

We went over the map like we'd done briefly in Johor Bahru, marking properties that might be interesting.

"How big is this thing—the printing press?" I asked her.

"I don't know. You've seen our printing works, but then we have typesetting machines, and this isn't about laying down type."

"Best guess?" I said.

"Not big. Does that help?"

"Why not big?"

"Well, as I see it, there may be the bleaching process, then drying, then the printing. And the printing is simple since it's just one colour."

I nodded.

She said, "And the preparation might be somewhere else entirely."

I thought about the size of the Malayan Publishing House on Stamford Road—a vast building, but then only occupied for printing money during the war. Then I thought about the old factory off Selegie Road. The clean middle room was also large.

I said, "This isn't just about printing, it's about storage too."

"Storing what?"

"Notes. Ones printed, ones awaiting printing. Ones in use and ones held just in case—for future counterfeits."

I took the five-dollar note from her and looked at its thickness. Hard to judge, but I'd seen bundles of thirty notes left in the box at Pope's warehouse. I guessed they were about half an inch thick. Pristine new notes could be tighter, but used ones would produce bigger bundles and counterfeit notes had to look old.

I said, "We know Yipp's company handled many millions of dollars. Let's say there was just a million dollars' worth of five-dollar notes. That's two hundred thousand notes. Let's round it up, let's say a bundle of one hundred notes are an inch thick."

"Then we have two thousand bundles. Two thousand inches. What's that in feet?"

"One hundred and sixty-six," I said, and roughly measured the note's sides. "If they are stacked five feet high, that's roughly thirty-three stacks…"

Linda looked like she was checking the calculation. She nodded, but I then shook my head.

"Not a huge volume."

"But that's just one million," she said. "What if it's five or ten million? At that point, your office would be full of notes."

I tried to imagine the piles.

"As you said, storage for future use," she added. "And what if it's not just the five dollars?"

I flashed back to Pope's warehouse. The bundles were various denominations. Could it be? Could they have been fake? Had I paid the police with Yipp's counterfeit money?

I said, "There are different sizes."

She raised her eyebrows. "Easy to cut paper to size. That's where the Japanese dollars might come in. Not big enough for the Malayan five-dollar note, but one dollar and the squarer fifty cents. I'm no expert, but what if they can combine the paper and resize it. You know, like redoing the paper-making process."

I nodded, although I had no idea either. However, I could ask the police to test the money I'd paid with. I didn't fancy explaining why I was passing it off as genuine. Singh would be fine, but I suspected the chief superintendent would be less understanding, and I didn't have much time.

I said, "So we don't know. We might be looking for somewhere the size of this room or as big as the old abandoned factory."

"Then we're no closer to eliminating some of these properties. I calculate eighty-three possibilities."

"What does your inner voice say?"

"Unlike you, I don't have a Neanderthal voice," she joked, then got serious. "Big. My sense is it that it'll be big."

I nodded. "So start with the largest and work down from there."

She looked at me askance. "It sounds like you aren't coming. I thought you wanted to catch Yipp."

Of course I did, but on the other hand, I couldn't risk anything with him now. Not with only another day before Su Ling escaped.

I said, "I've other priorities today and tomorrow."

"I'm not waiting that long." She got up, a look of disappointment on her face.

"Take this," I said, picking up the list of properties that Major Lamb had sent over. "It just struck me that these will be empty. They're residential re-appropriations, but there might be one or two that are large enough for the printing and storage."

She nodded.

"Promise me you won't do anything foolish," I said. "Don't take any risks, Linda. You've seen how ruthless these people can be."

She looked like she was considering it.

I said, "If you find somewhere suspicious, then tell the police."

"I can't trust the police, you know that—not all of them, but generally."

"All right then, make sure I know. Call Madam Chau, and if I'm available, I'll join you straight away. If I'm not available, I'll get to you as soon as possible—just don't go charging in. Leave the stupid moves to me."

Linda smiled. "Agreed."

I looked at Madam Chau for her agreement too. She was frowning, the corners of her mouth turned down even more than usual, but then she nodded.

After Linda Wu left, I got back to the mundane tasks with my receptionist and her demeanour improved. Then I finished work early and went to the boxing gym then bought dinner at the Satay Club and watched the sun go down sitting on the sea wall.

I planned an early night and an early start, driving to Kuala Lumpur in the morning. What I hadn't expected was the man who stepped out of the shadows as I walked home.

# FIFTY-SIX

I hardly recognized Saburo. He looked like he hadn't eaten or washed since I'd last seen him in prison.

"Please help," he croaked through dry and cracked lips. "I have nothing and no one to turn to."

"Come with me," I said, and took him home. Once there, I told him to clean up in my bathroom, and then I went back to the Satay Club and fetched him some food.

After he'd eaten he sat on my sofa, his back stiff, with eyes as wide as saucers. Scared. He said he'd been sleeping rough and hiding. He gabbled, but the gist of it was: "I'm afraid of Mr Zhao and the others. And I can't trust the police. I can't stay in Singapore, but I have no money to travel and am too afraid to show my face in public."

"I'm going to Kuala Lumpur tomorrow. I can take you there or somewhere in between—if that would help."

He let out a huge breath of air like he could relax for the first time. "Kuala Lumpur? Would you really take me?"

"Yes."

"I haven't got anything except for this." From his pocket he fished out a pair of pearl earrings.

Taking them, I studied their unusual design.

"Where did you get these?"

"I didn't steal them."

"Then where?" I asked again.

"They were Patrice's. I managed to sneak back to the house on Canal Road and get them while Mr Zhao was out."

"Did Patrice steal them? He stole my money clip…"

"No, they were a gift from—" He clammed up.

"Saburo, you're afraid of this person in authority?"

"Yes."

"He was Patrice's special client?"

"Yes."

"Do you think he killed your friend?"

"Yes. But I—"

"You don't have evidence?"

"No."

I leaned forward. "Saburo, you need to tell me his name."

"I can't. I don't know it. I really don't."

"White and British?"

"Yes."

"Why do you think he killed Patrice."

"His plan… Patrice was going to blackmail the man—threaten to tell the police he was a…"

"Homosexual?" I asked. "It's all right, you can tell me."

Saburo rubbed his eyes and cleared his throat. "The man is married. He pretends to like women but he likes men. It would ruin him, but Patrice wasn't honestly going to do it. Who could he tell? If he told the police, then they would arrest him for being homosexual himself. Patrice just wanted to scare the man—get him to pay so we could leave this place."

★

We got up in the dark and drove to Woodlands Crossing, reaching it an hour before the causeway opened. However, I'd told Ambrose that I'd be there and the MPs were ready. I flashed my lights and they waved me through.

Apart from the need to resolve the Chinese gold case, spending the day occupied and away from Singapore would stop me being obsessed with Su Ling's escape tonight. I needed to see Karthik Srivats followed by McNaughton at three, which would mean a late return, but I'd cleared that with Colonel Ambrose as well. I'd come back after the causeway closed for the night, be let across and be in Singapore with plenty of time before Su Ling's boat sailed at 2 am.

Saburo relaxed once we were in Malaya and he began talking about Vietnam. His early life had been comfortable until his French-born father had died of cholera. Then his mother had struggled to feed her four children. Saburo had been the second youngest. She'd taken up with another man who mistreated them. His youngest brother had died of an undiagnosed illness, and after the new man was killed in a bar fight, they'd struggled even more. Saburo had been to school until six. After his father died, they all had to work to survive—although being a poor half-caste meant the opportunities were limited. Even the poorest peasants looked down on them.

They lived in a hut on stilts. When it rained, everywhere flooded, but at least they had fish to eat. When the rivers dried up, they had nothing.

"Sometimes we ate the mud to fill our stomachs," he said. "It was awful. For months on end, it was a nightmare. My best opportunity was my looks. I left home at thirteen and went to the city. That's where I met Patrice."

I let him talk and talk because it seemed to help. I could barely listen to his stories of hardship, in Vietnam, on the journey to Singapore, and then the mistreatment there.

Only six days ago, I'd done this same journey to Kuala Lumpur with Linda Wu. She'd talked about female emasculation specifically, but it was really about the changing world. As I listened to Saburo's stories, I wondered if this new world would be better. Communism had been fuelled by inequalities and hardships, so if we truly wanted to defeat communism, we needed to change. Protecting our way of life—the privileged minority—would have to end.

"Égalité." I must have said it out loud because he agreed.

I don't know if Saburo was truly interested, but I found myself telling him what I knew about the politics of Singapore and the probable electoral changes. Then I told him what Linda believed.

"She expects women to lead the world," I said. "One day, she says, there'll be a woman US president."

He liked that. "And one day there might even be a homosexual one."

It was midday when we finally arrived at Karthik Srivats' shophouse in Brickfields. Saburo waited in the jeep while I went inside.

"My goodness!" Srivats exclaimed. "You came back." He stopped stacking cans and approached me with a smile. However his face was thinner than I remembered and his eyes were set in pools of darker skin.

"Your friend told me some disturbing news," I said. "But first of all, I'm terribly sorry about your wife."

"To say that I am devastated would be an understatement," he said, and I heard the quaver in his voice. "But I must be strong. Anu wouldn't have wanted me to give up. I will work harder and pray for her and she will be proud of my achievements."

I shook his hand. "That's an amazing attitude."

"We always talked about opening a clothing shop. I want to do that for Anu—and keep this general store going. It's just a dream really. What I want is justice, Captain Carter—for Anu. Can you give me that?"

"Possibly…" I said, but I paused and convinced myself. "No, I mean I expect so. I'll do my best. I'll assure you of that. Now, tell me what you know."

"You were sent a telegram that told you to look at the records? That came from Anu's colleague."

I nodded. It had been from A New Friend. Maybe it had been a post office worker's mistake. Maybe it had been deliberate. A New instead of Anu.

He said, "She was too afraid to say anything publicly because she said that Anu had questioned something and that may be why she was killed."

I said, "And I looked at the police reports but found nothing."

"Because there was nothing to see," he said. "Not unless you knew what you were looking for. Not unless you knew the date had been edited. Anu told her friend that Detective Munsi was suspicious about the body found in Batu Caves."

I said, "The second body. The date of the man's discovery was changed from the eighth of October to the eighteenth of September."

"That's what she told me."

"How can you prove that unless you have the original document?"

He shook his head. "The typing pool manageress would have had the original. She keeps a copy of everything, but she hasn't got it anymore."

I waited as he reached behind a counter and came back holding a buff-coloured sheet. It had rows of lines with reference numbers and dates and times and initials.

He said, "That shows requests coming in and going out. It shows who the job was assigned to and who requested the work."

Pointing to a line he said, "This is that first report, dated tenth October. Here are my wife's initials, because she typed it, and here are the initials of Munsi because it was his report. Anu's friend told me that the detective didn't believe something about the killer."

"Yes," I said, my heart thudding as my eyes scanned the other rows. Then Mr Srivats turned the paper over and pointed to a line dated four weeks ago.

"That's the report coming back. After the detective had been murdered. It went to my wife again." He tapped the paper, hard. "That was their mistake. And those are the initials of the man requesting the change—the change in the date that covered up the Batu Caves murder."

# FIFTY-SEVEN

Srivats was excited and wanted to celebrate, so I let him make me a cup of tea. I thought about what he'd said earlier, and when he returned I asked, "What's holding you back from opening your clothing store?"

"Anu was going to give up the police typing and work in the shop. I can't afford to pay anyone. Not until the money comes in." He looked down. "So I suppose it will remain a dream."

That was when I told him about the young man waiting in my jeep. "Treat him fair and he'll work hard."

"But I can't—"

"How long will it take to establish the new business?"

He shrugged, thought hard. "Two months, perhaps."

"I'll give you enough to pay him for three months. Is that acceptable?"

We agreed on a figure, and leaving Saburo to introduce himself, I raced off to the post office, withdrew the money and returned to find Saburo already serving a customer.

If only everything in life had such a happy ending.

★

I was outside George McNaughton's office early, but he was twenty minutes late.

"So sorry, Ash," he said. "Committee meetings are the bane of my life. Now then"—he waved me towards a chair but I remained standing—"what is it?"

And so I told him the story. The second ex-soldier found dead in the Batu Caves hadn't been murdered by BlackJack. The technique was too crude, too amateur to have been the same man.

I said, "I think Detective Munsi realized this—maybe also that the throat had been slit right-handed. He probably questioned it. Maybe he told the wrong person because he ended up getting killed. Conveniently, his murder looked like a gang killing, and yet he was out on his own in a known rough spot."

McNaughton shook his head. "Ash, you surprise me. This is supposition, not detective work. You can't—"

"The dates didn't work though. The body was found after SIB had stopped investigating, so someone had to change the report—to rewrite it with an earlier date. You can confirm that with the coroner. His notes don't match the official report filed by Munsi. Only Munsi didn't file it because of the change. He was already dead when it was edited. The manageress of the typing pool has duplicates."

"Of course, and we obtained those but found no discrepancies, no re-types as you claim. If this all hinges on the coroner's word, then he's wrong. We can't trust his handwritten notes. That's why we have official typed records."

I nodded. "Where are those duplicate reports now?"

He frowned. "Good God, man, I don't know. They've been investigated and we found nothing."

"And we conveniently have no evidence."

"Conveniently?" He sounded annoyed now. "Look, Ash, I'm a busy—"

"There's other evidence," I said over him.

"What?"

"Summary records for management purposes."

"What evidence?" he said again.

I put the buff-coloured report in front of him and pointed to the appropriate line. "The crime report was rewritten four weeks ago. The date was changed then. And, George, these are your initials."

"I'm sure there are plenty—"

"Don't bother," I said. "When I was working the BlackJack case you wanted updates. In fact, each time I've spoken to you, you've wanted to know what I was investigating. But it's more than that. We were looking for someone high up in the army, but we should have looked ex-army and someone with the connections. You were here before the war. A captain in the 18th. You knew people. And I should have listened to Chief Inspector Stanford-Jones in JB. He said it's who you knew. I thought you'd been promoted because of helping on my case, but it wasn't, was it?"

He was silent now. I could see his mind running through options. I had a gun at my waist in case he made any stupid moves.

I said, "You were brought to KL, promoted highly and live the life of a wealthy man. Maybe if I'd questioned your membership to the Jockey Club, I'd have realized sooner."

He swallowed. "It's not about me."

"Of course it's not. You work for someone else. Did you kill the man found in the caves?"

"No!"

"Detective Munsi? Did you kill him?"

"No!"

"Mrs Srivats, the typing pool lady?"

"It was an accident. I just wanted to talk to her." He took a breath and "Ash, you know me! I'm a good man."

"I thought I knew you, George. I liked you and that was my grave mistake."

He shook his head. "Look, old chap, you have to understand. There are bigger things at work here."

"Money—or more specifically, Chinese gold," I said scornfully.

He shook his head again. "Seriously, what are you going to do about it? This is bigger than me. What are you going to do, report me to the chief superintendent or the police commissioner? This is a police issue and—"

"No," I said, "it's a military issue. It's not just about corruption, George. Chinese gold, for God's sake! This is profiteering by colluding with the enemy."

I opened his office door. Outside, McNaughton's personal assistant was in a flap.

"Sir, I—" he stammered, maybe trying to explain why there were two military policemen by his desk. Colonel Ambrose had sent a lieutenant and a sergeant. There was probably a third, a driver, downstairs.

I said, "Chief Inspector McNaughton will be helping the military with their investigation."

McNaughton stood and walked woodenly towards the door. I stepped out of his way.

He said, "There are five others, as far as I know."

"Then make sure you provide their names. The army will get to the bottom of it, with or without your help. Expect to be found guilty, George, but if you do help, it's likely to work in your favour."

He nodded, and I watched as the man I'd considered a friend for almost a year and a half was escorted from the building.

★

The grey skies seemed to be pressing down on me as I drove from the centre of Kuala Lumpur. I didn't relish the thought of the long drive south, and was distracted as I almost crashed into the car in front. Ahead were three vehicles and flames.

I jumped out and ran towards a burning car that had swerved avoiding a truck coming the other way. Its load of timber blocked the road and had caused the rapid pile-up. The crashed car had driven into a wall, flipped over and caught fire.

Everyone else seemed frozen in time, watching, maybe wondering what to do.

There was a man inside the burning car. I saw him move but he stayed inside.

"Get out!" I shouted as I ran up to them. He turned his head my way and I saw blood on his dazed face.

I got the handle, yanked the door open and he tumbled out. Seconds after I dragged him away, the petrol tank exploded and then some of the timber caught. Within a few seconds more, the whole area seemed ablaze. The police arrived and then the fire service, but no ambulance for the injured driver. He had a gash on his forehead, which I bandaged, but he was also concussed, and I thought he'd dislocated an elbow, or maybe it was broken.

As soon as I could move the jeep, I got out of there and took the injured man to the main hospital.

By the time I left him, it had gone five in the afternoon, and I drove like a madman down Route One. The darkness descended two hours later and I pressed on, taking foolish risks.

I needed to get back to Singapore, and time was ticking.

★

One of the other things I'd asked Colonel Ambrose to arrange was for me to get across the causeway after it shut. But when I finally got there almost five hours after I'd left the hospital, I was confronted by an obdurate Customs man.

"I told you, it's closed for the night," he said.

"I have army clearance," I said again. "Call Colonel Ambrose at Gillman Barracks."

He laughed mirthlessly. "What, and get in trouble for waking the man? No, sir, we have strict orders because of all the cigarette smuggling activity recently."

"Colonel Ambrose will have arranged it."

"When?"

"I don't know—earlier today."

He went into the office and I considered raising the barrier myself, but then these guys were armed and wouldn't hesitate to shoot. If they had orders that no one was to pass then they needed new orders.

He came back out with two other Customs men. As I suspected, they were all armed.

"We came on shift two hours ago and no one mentioned anything about a message from some colonel."

I said, "If you had clearance from Chief Inspector Stanford-Jones, would that do?"

The man smiled at the proposed solution to our showdown. "That would be acceptable, sir."

I jumped back in my jeep and drove the short distance to the police headquarters. But Stanford-Jones had retired for the evening and no one else knew me. However, I persuaded the desk sergeant to let me use the telephone when I asked for the Singapore police HQ.

Inspector Singh was still working.

"Thank God!" I said, and explained what I needed. He said things were crazy there but promised to do what he could, and I hurried back to the causeway.

This time, the Customs man was apologetic. "You understand," he said, "I was just following orders."

I didn't bother speaking. Su Ling's boat would be sailing in under four hours and that's all I could think about.

The thousand yards across that bumpy strip of rubble never felt so far. My lights picked out the boom barrier on the Singapore side and then armed men.

Did they expect me? Possibly not. Not after my experience with Customs behind me.

Two flashlights came on and I slowed.

"Captain Ash Carter," I shouted, and the lights swept across me."

"Sir!" a man shouted back louder than necessary, but the barrier didn't rise.

I rolled the jeep forward.

A sergeant met me, his rifle at port arms.

"Sir," he said again. "We've been expecting you, sir."

"Thanks," I said, noting the barrier was still down. "What's wrong, Sergeant?"

"I have a message, sir," he said. "From Gillman, but originally from your secretary, I believe."

"Madam Chau," I said, but he didn't show recognition.

"The message is about someone called Miss Wu."

"Yes?"

He gave me the address of a property to the north of the city then waved for the barrier to be raised.

"Yes?" I prompted again.

"Sir, the message is a bit confused. I think it is that she's found it and can't wait for you."

# FIFTY-EIGHT

The address was on McNair Road, close to the junction with Towner Road. A remote spot for warehouses, it had a radio mast and a tributary that fed the Kallang River.

Long ago, logging had taken place in Singapore and come downriver. This section used to have sawmills and storage sheds, but they'd fallen into disuse. Logging and preparation of timber all happened in Malaya these days and was transported by trucks to Singapore rather than the rivers.

I could see light coming through the cracks in the old building along where the roof was attached and in vertical places where sections must have moved over time.

After the MPs at Woodlands had given me the message, I'd called Inspector Singh again. Ideally, I'd have rung for army backup, but this wasn't a military issue. Maybe Colonel Ambrose would have sent men, but I already knew he wasn't available, and disturbing him over a police matter wouldn't have been seemly. So I'd called Singh.

I'd told him that I thought we'd found the money-printing operation and to meet me there with men.

"We've got a problem," he said. "I told you things were crazy tonight. We've got most men out dealing with fires in the slums. I'll get there as soon as I can."

"With men," I prompted.

"No promises," he said.

I saw no sign of the police as I walked around the shed. There were big doors that opened towards McNair Road and dim light coming from their edges.

On the right of the shed was a section connecting it to the next building. I thought the other building was probably a sawmill and the shed used for storage. The lack of light from the other buildings suggested they weren't being used.

I circled the other way and found steps at the back rising up to a door. Maybe it was a fire escape or simply a rear entrance. More light came from the door's window and I started climbing. It turned out to be more of a ladder than stairs—wooden, old and creaky. This location was on the edge of the city, and the sound of me going up those steps was loud in the night.

At the top, I peered through dusty glass. I could see a platform with what looked like offices on the left. Ahead, the platform ended with a railing and I figured steps went down into the expanse below. That's where the light came from the ground rather than from the ceiling. I could also hear the drone of an engine. When I listened hard, I thought I could also hear the occasional voice.

There were people inside but I saw no one.

I tested the door handle. Locked. For a brief second, I considered trying to force it, but decided against the move. The noise might attract attention, and I had no idea what I was dealing with here. More concerning, I had no idea where Linda Wu might be.

At the bottom of the wooden stairs, I continued around the building and came to the other side of the connecting section. The darkness was absolute, so I ran my hand along the wall, hoping to find a door or window. I found a door. And it was unlocked.

It opened stiffly with a groan, and I held my breath listening. The engine I'd heard earlier was loud now. A diesel generator, I thought. Maybe there was a low buzz of conversation as well, but I couldn't be sure.

The room smelled of old wood and damp. To my left, I saw a cavernous space with giant shapes that I guessed were machinery, maybe old saws and equipment needed to move logs and sawn timber. Running the length of the connecting room was a raised section. I figured this was the equivalent of a conveyor belt: wooden rollers to transfer heavy items from left to right, from the sawmill to a storage shed.

I went right, towards the shed, towards where I could see strips of light, towards the sounds.

After five paces I realized I was at the end of the conveyor, looking at a hole in the wall with a sort of curtain of rubber strips hanging down. The shed was on the other side of this hole.

I eased myself onto the rollers and parted the rubber strips slightly.

To my left I could see the doors that went out to McNair Road. In front of the doors was a truck. I couldn't see it well enough but guessed it wasn't an ancient relic left here to rot. This was for transport. Tonight.

I couldn't see very far to the right so I shifted my position carefully.

At first, I had registered a dark space on my right, maybe shadow, now I realized I was looking at a big black machine. I could see the words De La Rue embossed on it. I remembered hearing once that it was the name of a money-printing company. The generator and source of light were too far away or behind the printing machine.

Beyond that, I could see people, but they weren't operating the machine, they were sitting on matting. Eight of them in a circle. Eight women.

Behind them, I could see stacked tea chests.

It made sense. Linda Wu had said she could smell tea in the old factory. But these chests didn't contain tea, because, as I watched, a man carrying a chest tipped it over in the middle of the circle of woman. Loose notes tumbled out like a strange viscous liquid, forming a ragged pile on the mat. The women scooped up armfuls, returned to their position and began sorting, perhaps separating the notes into different denominations or splitting Japanese from old Malayan dollars.

I saw another man walk across my field of vision and then I saw Linda Wu. She was standing in the shadows, her arms raised like she was in some kind of diving pose. When she tried to move I realized her hands and feet were tied.

After watching for another minute, I slipped back away from the hole and off the wooden conveyor.

I went outside and circled the building to the front.

There was another car parked behind my Land Rover: a police car with Inspector Singh watching me as I jogged towards him.

"What's going on, Ash?" he asked.

"Thanks for coming. Where are your men?"

Singh beckoned and two men got out of the car, a sergeant and a corporal. They both carried rifles.

"Is that it?" I said dismayed.

"All I could get. I told you there's trouble. There have been a couple of fires down off Havelock Road again and a disturbance—a bit of a riot. The complaint seems to be that someone deliberately started the fires."

I said, "All right, three of you is better than none."

"So, what's going on?"

"Yipp's money-printing operation is inside. It's been moved here from the old factory on Selegie Road. He seems to have women sorting the cash, though I have no idea why. I saw two men and eight women. I saw no arms, but they are bound to have weapons. And the reporter

Linda Wu is in there tied up. She found the place and let me know."

He blew out air. "Is Yipp in there?"

"I don't know."

"So what's the plan? Wait until they come out?"

"I'd be fine with that if it weren't for Miss Wu," I said. "My plan is that we get her out."

"What about a fire?" he asked. "We could start something small and flush them out, catch them unaware."

"They have millions of dollars in there. A fire may make them panic, not just for their lives but for the goods. Plus there are innocent women in there as well as Miss Wu. No, fire is too unpredictable."

"What then?"

"I go in and get Miss Wu out first. I need you to cause a diversion. I'll go around the other side and into the building. Send a man up the fire escape at the back. Have him make a noise—bang on the door—and then run. Hopefully that'll draw the men up there so that I can make a move. Give me five minutes and then make a noise."

"What if you can't get her?"

"I'll get her. If I start shooting then come charging in through the garage doors. But if you don't hear shooting, just wait for me." Then I gave him the layout in detail and he repeated the plan.

"You've got five minutes," he said looking at his watch. "Starting now."

I hurried back the way I'd just come, went into the connecting section and crawled along the rollers to the curtain of rubber strips.

Like before, I eased the strips apart and my breath immediately caught. Not ten yards away was the wiry man I'd seen at Christian Chen's place, the man who reminded me of a junkyard dog. What was he doing here?

Was he also working for Yipp? Had he taken the vacancy left by Wang? Was the junkyard dog Yipp's new henchman?

I looked at my watch. Two minutes to go.

But I didn't have two minutes, because before the second hand had moved through a quarter turn, the plan changed.

# FIFTY-NINE

I expected a bang on the upstairs door. But the next sound I heard was gunfire. Three shots.

Through the gap, I saw Junkyard-dog pull out a pistol and run to the right. I heard shouting, and then the plan went totally wrong.

The garage doors burst open and Singh came in, the sergeant by his side, shouting, "Police!"

Immediately, the room filled with gunfire and women's screams.

I crawled through the rubber strips with my gun drawn. The police had reached the truck for cover and were returning fire.

A Chinese man swivelled from shooting towards them and aimed his rifle at me. I shot him. Then I dived for the protection of the printing machine.

I would have expected the women to rush to the rear. There were three exits: the garage doors, the space I'd come through and the rear fire escape. We were at two of them, so they had one logical choice. But they didn't head for the fire escape. Instead, they dived behind the tea chests.

My back brain processed two things: firstly, there weren't many tea chests. I guessed between twenty-five and thirty boxes were in that shed, nothing like the volume of money I'd predicted. Secondly, the women were afraid of the rear exit.

So far, I'd only fired two bullets, and with the exception of the man I'd killed, Yipp's men didn't seem to realize I was there. Singh and the sergeant fired more in defence than taking serious aim, as they drew a barrage of shots.

A quick shift of position gave me a better view of the rear. I saw armed Chinese, six of them moving fast in the direction of the truck, and I saw steps ascending to the platform and offices I'd seen from the rear door window.

And I saw something that threw my mind into a tailspin. Junkyard-dog's pal, Large, was coming down the stairs, shooting. Behind him was Christian Chen in his white suit and trilby.

Not Yipp's operation after all, but Chen's. Did that make sense?

I looked over towards Linda. She'd spotted me and I briefly considered rushing to her, but it was a crazy idea. Large and Chen were on my right, the other shooters were on my left, and I'd be crossing between them, in the open, an easy target.

So instead I just showed her my palm—like I was saying "wait"—and hoped she felt some reassurance. I'd get to her but needed to deal with the gunmen first.

Large was now at the foot of the stairs, Chen right behind, using him for protection. I shot Large, making him stagger, but he didn't go down. His gun swung my way and a burst of bullets ricocheted off the metal printer. I ducked, moved, and then I hit him with two more shots.

When Large finally dropped, I could no longer see Chen.

Now I'd drawn gunfire from the men on my left. I came around the printer, aiming at the gang members while checking for Chen.

In addition to the one I'd shot earlier, another goon was down. There were five left and two were shooting my way.

I used seven bullets and took out the three shooters who weren't aiming at me. The police were still behind the truck but their shots came more sporadically, and I figured they were either conserving bullets or one of them was unable to fire.

The two surviving gang members split, one after me, one aiming at the truck. I had only two bullets left and halved that when I took down one of the gang. I doubted he was dead, but he looked incapacitated.

With only one bullet remaining, my thinking was to go for a fallen rifle and then get Linda.

I rolled away from the printing machine then sprinted for the nearest rifle. I snatched it up and then dived for the tea chests as bullets whizzed past.

Women were cowering by the boxes and scuttled out of my way, but I wasn't staying. I got up and spun towards Linda and stopped mid-step. Chen was there, twenty yards away, and he now had Linda.

I raised my gun.

"Drop it, Carter!" he shouted, using Linda as a shield.

Time seemed to freeze and I no longer heard the gunfire. And then it started again and I realized someone had come up behind me. I heard them repositioning so that Chen wasn't directly opposite.

There was one bullet left in my Beretta and I shot Chen through the forehead, then rolled and swung up the stolen rifle.

Before me stood Junkyard-dog, his yellow teeth showing through a crazed grin.

He hadn't been one of the five shooting at the police and I'd forgotten about him.

"Drop the gun," he snarled.

But I didn't. I rolled and shot without particular aim, just hoping to give me time. The trigger moved, but nothing happened. I tried again. Nothing.

My Beretta was empty and the rifle was empty.

Junkyard-dog grunted a kind of laugh.

"Just you and me," he said, but instead of shooting me, he stuck the gun in his pocket. I was scanning the floor for the nearest weapon when he started running towards me.

Glinting in each hand was a knife.

I held the barrel of the rifle like a club and prepared as he rapidly closed the gap. The blades moved in his hands, a twisting flash that made focus impossible.

He slashed and I swung.

My jacket ripped as a blade sliced through it.

All I could do was back away and jab with the gun, trying to find a fallen rifle.

The shed was strangely still. Even the women had stopped screaming. I was aware of low groans of wounded men, and the generator, but apart from that background noise, there was nothing.

A blade clattered against the rifle stock and I saw a fine line of scarlet appear on my left hand as the other knife caught me.

And then he took me by surprise with a roundhouse kick that sent me sprawling. The rifle spun away, and as I started to spring up, Junkyard-dog was there, right over me.

He let out his grunting laugh again and slashed my leg. Then he stepped back and I read his intention. He was going to cut me and cut me again. This was a game. He'd bleed me until I died.

I rolled and jumped up, but he was right there, ready to slash again. The blade flashed, and at the same moment, a burst of gunfire broke the weird stillness.

Junkyard-dog looked down at the blooming patches of red on his chest and then sank to his knees, before dropping, face first, onto the ground.

Linda Wu was holding a rifle and pulled me to my feet.

"I'm supposed to be saving *you*," I said.

"It's a new world," she said and started to attend to my bleeding hand.

I waved her away and jogged over to the truck. Singh was there, sitting behind a wheel, panting. He'd taken a shot to the shoulder, but I assessed he'd live. The sergeant, however, had taken a bullet to the head and wouldn't be getting up.

Linda rounded up the women and we let them stagger through the garage doors into the night. Three of the gang weren't dead and I trussed them up.

Only then did I let Linda tie a cloth over my wounded hand and leg. I helped Singh into the Land Rover and went around the back of the shed where I found the corporal crumpled from a fall. He'd been shot, and I figured he'd reached the door before being confronted by Large, who'd shot him. The kid had never even drawn his weapon.

★

It was after midnight when I left Singh at the Singapore General Hospital and insisted that my injuries were superficial. Then I dropped Linda off outside her house. Her mother was waiting for her, and when the two embraced I wondered how much the old lady knew. But I didn't consider it for long because I tore away, driving fast towards the centre.

Su Ling had less than an hour before the boxes would be taken from Pope's warehouse, two before sailing. As I drove there, I realized how tangled my stomach felt. She didn't need me to check on her, but I needed to know. Was she there? Would she escape tonight?

As I got onto Ord Bridge, I could see fires. This was the trouble that Singh had mentioned. As before, they looked like they were on the quay, but I didn't panic this time. Not until I got closer anyway. One fire was further upstream in Kampong Bintang, but there was another, closer blaze, on Havelock Road right behind the quay. I could see the sparks spiral high in the night sky.

I got onto Magazine Road and then Havelock. The fire mainly burned on the left but I could see warehouses on the right had caught. I stopped because the road was blocked with firefighters. They were focused on the right, protecting goods and the warehouses rather than residential properties on the other side.

With my heart beating in my throat, I ran to Alkaff Quay and Pope's warehouse. The doors were open and the wharf alive with men, carrying boxes to waiting boats.

I looked inside Pope's warehouse and saw most of the stored items had been moved.

"Captain Carter!" I turned to see the boy, Jihan, jogging towards me from the quayside.

"The box," I said as he neared. "Where is the box—the one marked with an X?"

"Gone, sir."

"Gone?"

"Because of the fire, Mr Kelly ordered that the goods be loaded early."

Kelly, Arthur Pope's partner, my mind processed. He wouldn't know about the plans. "So they're already on board?"

"Yes, sir."

"To Empire Dock?"

"No, sir. No time. The boat is in the harbour."

I stood on the quay for a while, staring along the river. Normally, the tongkangs and bumboats would be tied up at night, but this section was alive with activity. I saw other boats heading downstream with cargo and I thought of Su Ling. Had she got here in time? Was she in a box or had it been loaded before she arrived?

Only tomorrow would reveal the truth.

# SIXTY

*Wednesday 17th February*

After hearing repeated banging on my door, I opened it. My watch said it was just before 6 am.

A police constable, looking as tired as I felt, stood on my doorstep.

"Sir, please, you are to come with me?" He said it as a question, but he was awkward and nervous.

"What's it about, constable?"

"I don't know, sir. The police commissioner has asked for you."

I told the young man I'd be a few minutes and quickly got dressed, with the service revolver in a Sam Browne under my jacket.

When I opened the door again, the constable turned and started to walk quickly towards a parked car. "We must hurry, sir."

He was already in the driver's seat when I reached him.

"Why does the police commissioner want me?"

"I don't know sir," he said. "I'm just the driver."

I got in the back and assumed he would take me the short distance to a government building or Hill Street Station. Instead, we went away from the centre, over the Rochor River and onto Kallang Road.

I wondered if we were going to Christian Chen's office. Maybe the police commissioner had been informed of the news. Maybe he wanted me to deal with something before sunrise.

We drove straight past Chen's office. Then we went over the Kallang River.

"Where the hell are we going?" I snapped at the driver, now wishing I'd checked his ID before getting into the car. I drew my gun and pulled back the hammer so that he'd hear it.

"Almost there, sir," he said.

"Where, man?"

"The civil airport."

He turned right and the airport buildings were directly in front of us, the terminal with a hangar either side. On the right was the massive Firestone Tyre Company factory. We went past it and came to a series of buildings including a medical centre.

The sky was getting lighter in the east, now a thin line of pale pinkish-blue. I looked left and right. We weren't going to the airport. The river was left, the airfield was right and ahead was a marine depot then the sea.

"We're here, sir," he said and stopped under a lamp post. That's when I spotted another car and a man beside it.

"Put the damn gun away, Carter!" a voice boomed as I got out into a pool of light. Despite being unable to see his face in the dim light, I recognized Secretary Norris's shape and voice.

"What's going on?" I asked.

"We're waiting for the police commissioner." He pointed to my left hand. I'd cleaned it and my leg before freshly bandaging the wounds last night. "What happened?"

"Just a cut. I'll live."

"Glad to hear it."

I said, "You didn't explain why we're meeting the commissioner."

"To take a little trip." He pointed into the darkness. "Ever been in a flying boat?"

Of course! This was where the flying boat docked—if that was the right terminology. I'd seen the impressive seaplane come in and fly off. A BOAC Short Sandringham that was part of the Kangaroo Route from London to Sydney. Just a couple of dozen passengers travelling in luxury, the next stop Darwin.

I was looking for the big plane and heard the sound of rotors when another car joined us and two men got out: the police commissioner and another man.

The senior policeman shook hands with Norris and nodded to me. The other man hung back, awkward, and I wondered who he was.

Norris said, "It's just coming."

We walked out onto a curved jetty, and for the first time, I saw lights on the water coming towards us. My back brain told me it was smaller than expected before I registered that the engine sound was not the drone of a Short. Twin spotlights swung out over the choppy water and picked out a biplane approaching us. It rumbled to a halt and a man climbed out and tied it up to the jetty.

Norris, followed by the police commissioner and then the third man, ran forward, up some steps and into the body of the plane. I was last inside and the door clanged shut, locking behind me.

We were moving before I took my seat. This was no commercial flying boat, but a pre-war air force plane that had been converted for passengers. It smelled of must and old leather beneath the whiff of aircraft fuel. I could see the pilot with his array of little lights, but the cabin had no illumination of any kind. There was one other crew member, the one who had tied up and locked our door. He now handed out ear defenders.

I was going to speak, but no one was making eye contact, and the noise became deafening as we bounced over the waves.

My seat was at the back with no window. The police commissioner and Norris had small portholes and looked out in opposite directions. We bounced and shook and finally we cleared the water, rising and banking east.

The fourth man glanced at me, possibly wondering who I was. I didn't know him and he didn't know me.

"Ash Carter," I said, although I'm sure he couldn't hear me or read my lips in the grey light.

I sat back and tried to relax, but we were only in the air a minute before the crew member looked like he gave a signal to the commissioner and then pointed. Immediately we turned slightly north and started to descend.

I learned later that landing out at sea wasn't advisable since the seaplane couldn't cope with serious waves. Despite an uncomfortable landing that felt like it would never end, when we came to rest, the little plane just bobbed up and down on a swell and gentle waves.

With the ear defenders off, we filed towards the exit and found an inflatable boat tied up to our steps. A police boat.

The horizon was now streaked pale lemon, with sunrise half an hour away. In the opposite direction, indigo still clung on, the last vestiges of night. And then I saw it: a *sengoku-bune*, a Japanese junk with red sails. And in the water were another three police dinghies.

As I dropped into the one by the plane, I could taste bile in my mouth.

"What are you doing?" I said, sitting next to Norris.

He grinned. "Hold on, Carter."

The dinghy's outboard kicked in and we jolted away from the plane. I held on and sea spray stung my eyes as we raced to the boat.

I shook my head at the secretary and he kept grinning.

"Information," he shouted above the thundering noise, tapping his nose.

I shook my head again. What was he playing at?

We came alongside, and with resignation, I followed him out of the dinghy onto the junk.

"This way," a policeman said, and the other three moved. I stayed by the railing and looked towards where the sun would appear. I looked the other way into the dark seas and I looked at the old biplane. Now I saw that it had *Customs* written on the side.

Was this a smuggling issue? Was I mistaken about why we were here?

Finally, I went to where the others stood, looking into the hold. My stomach clenched. Down below, I saw a crate with XX drawn on the side. A crane contraption raised it and swung the box onto the deck.

"Secretary Norris," I said, my voice suddenly sounding louder than I intended.

"Wait!" Norris barked at me. Then he grinned again, and this time I thought he wasn't mocking me but perhaps expecting me to join in the fun.

The crate came over the side and two policemen immediately crowbarred the top off. I held my breath. They reached inside and pulled out blocks. No, not blocks—bundles of cash.

The fourth man stepped forward and took a bundle. He pulled a torch from his pocket and popped a loupe in his eye. He scanned one, then another, then a third note before nodding.

"Forgeries," he said.

Norris thumped me on the back and shook the commissioner's hand. I read relief on the commissioner's face. This had all been Norris's operation and the police had just carried it out. Now they had their justification, their evidence.

"Get the other box up here," he said, and a second crate had bands looped over it.

"Heavy," one of the men down below shouted.

The same-sized box appeared and I spotted another XX on the side.

Two boxes!

I stepped forward. "Sir—"

Norris glared at me. "Carter, I brought you along as a favour. I thought you'd appreciate this after all your hard work." He turned to the men with the crowbars and shouted, "Get this bloody box open!"

My chest constricted and I stepped back to hold the railing again. The metal bars went in, wood splintered and then the top popped off the base.

"Another box inside," someone said.

I saw them work at a second lid, although this one seemed fixed down. Eventually, it was levered free and I heard a gasp, but I couldn't see between the bodies as they crowded around. Then I saw movement. A figure sat up from the box. The senior men moved back and the two police constables closed in.

I heard a voice.

"Where am I?"

A man's voice. Not Su Ling.

"Where the hell am I? What's going on? Take your hands off me!"

The constables pulled him upright, and I saw handcuff's flash and heard them click. The man was pulled from the box. He looked angry and disorientated.

He glared at me, and I stared back at the face of Andrew Yipp.

# SIXTY-ONE

The revolving doors of the Cathay Building were still locked for the night, but I was at the side entrance where staff came and went.

I was no longer concerned about being seen here. Wang, the henchman, was dead. Yipp was in custody, probably destined for the notorious Outram Prison where Chen Guan Xi had been held and died.

Yipp had been charged with counterfeiting money. He was also charged with trying to flee the country. Without the fake money, Secretary Norris would have been happy to refuse Yipp re-entry, branding him as an undesirable and a state security issue. However, we knew that exiles managed to come and go. Chen Guan Xi had done so with ease, and I'm sure Yipp would have continued to run his empire and influence the politics of Singapore whether remote or not.

No, I wasn't worried about any of that. I was concerned about Su Ling.

I'd been outside for fifteen minutes before Jinjing appeared at the door and hurried over.

"Su Ling wasn't on the boat," I said. "Please tell me she's all right."

Jinjing nodded. "She's fine, Captain."

"Can I see her?"

"Of course, but not for—not until ten o'clock. Come back then."

"She'll be here?"

"Yes."

There was something in Jinjing's eyes that I couldn't read. Maybe it was tiredness. Maybe it was sadness.

"What's going on, Jinjing?" I asked.

She forced an unconvincing smile. "Su Ling will explain. Come back in ninety minutes. In the meantime, I have something for you."

Now I noticed that she was holding a folder. She handed it to me and a glance inside confirmed it was the information from Major Lamb—the re-appropriated properties.

"What are you doing with this?" I asked. I'd given it to Linda Wu two days ago.

"The factory on McNair," she said, ignoring my question, "it's not included on the list."

"No," I said, pretty sure I would have remembered it otherwise.

"But it should have been."

★

I went home and looked at the report. I thought about what had happened. I'd given the list to Linda two days ago. She'd found the shed on McNair Road. We'd been looking for the printing machinery and a huge amount of money. We thought Yipp was controlling it.

But Chen and his gang were there and the amount of money was much less than I'd anticipated. Maybe thirty tea chests when I'd expected many times that number.

Linda had found the property and yet it hadn't been on the list—the list that Jinjing had given me. How did she get it? What was she doing with it and how did she know that the shed should have been on the list?

That thinking led me to thinking about Chen and then Wang. Which led me back to Su Ling's kidnap. Who had been holding her? Did that make sense?

Who had been following in that other car I'd heard?

And what was Yipp doing on the boat?

No way had he expected to be there. So someone had put him there and someone had told Secretary Norris.

As I worked it out, I put my head in my hands and wondered how I could have missed it. Perhaps because it was hard to accept. Like being told your old favourite shoes never belonged to you. Like learning that the earth spins the opposite way. Maybe like discovering that black is white. Unsettling. It doesn't make sense, so you suppress the obvious.

But as I sat there I felt anger surge, and I knew where to direct that anger. First I needed the evidence.

I still had over half an hour before I could see Su Ling, and so I hurried to the government offices, where I located the typing pool. It was about twice the size of the one in the Kuala Lumpur police headquarters. The manager had a desk just like the manageress in Kuala Lumpur. Three trays: In, Out, and an unlabelled third. After introducing myself to the man, I presented him with the folder.

"Do you keep duplicates of what's typed?"

"Of course, sir."

"You have a copy of this one?"

He pulled a sheaf of papers from his desk drawer: a log of movements, dates and references and initials.

"These documents were typed up four days ago," he said.

"And the last time they were produced?"

"The same documents?" He frowned, then went through his papers. "Ah yes, it's been updated a few times."

"The last time?"

"Eleven days ago."

"And you have a copy of that one? Please may I see it?"

"Of course," he said. He shuffled off to a filing cabinet and returned in seconds with a few sheets of paper. The typing was less crisp since this was a carbon copy, but I saw at once that it looked almost identical.

He made me sign for it and I spent a minute comparing the two sets of paper. Both lists of re-appropriated properties. The one I'd been sent by Major Lamb, subsequent to the one typed up eleven days ago.

I had my evidence, but first I needed to see Su Ling.

# SIXTY-TWO

Jinjing met me in the foyer of the Cathay Building, bowing as I approached.

I took air-conditioned breaths and felt the heat of the morning evaporating from me.

She pointed to the elevator.

"Before we go up," I said, not immediately following her. When she turned back, I continued: "Who kidnapped Su Ling?"

Jinjing shrugged and said nothing, but I could see she knew.

"It wasn't Wang or Yipp's men was it?"

Her eyes said no.

"And it wasn't Christian Chen's gang."

"I should take you up now," she said.

We got into the elevator and the doors closed.

I said, "You aren't going to tell me anything, are you?"

"It's not my place."

We began to rise towards the twelfth floor.

"Who am I meeting? Are you taking me to Su Ling?"

She looked down and away. No eye contact, so I examined my reflection in the side mirror. I'd been such a fool. I'd been played expertly. I was pretty sure I now understood, so waiting a few more minutes didn't matter. At least it would be confirmed and I could move on.

We came out onto Yipp's floor and I was led towards Yipp's office. I looked around. I saw normal office activity, although in the past I would have seen Wang looking threateningly at me. Now I saw no one who looked like a thug. No henchman. However, I did see something I didn't expect. In a distant room, I saw an elderly woman with her hand on a boy's shoulder.

"Who's that?" I asked Jinjing. I didn't expect an answer, but she surprised me.

"Mrs Yipp."

"Andrew Yipp's wife?"

"Yes."

We were at a door. The door that led to Yipp's office. Was there some kind of insane twist? Had something happened this morning? Had Yipp been released?

Jinjing knocked, entered, and left me outside. A moment later, she came out and held the door open for me to enter.

I stepped into the room and heard the door click shut behind me. And my heart stopped beating.

Standing with her back to the expansive window was Su Ling.

She wore a scarlet dress, stunning and yet business-like at the same time. She'd cut her long hair into a modern American style that suited her pretty face.

This was the painful truth that I'd tried to deny.

Su Ling was the new boss.

"Congratulations," I said with irony.

She forced a smile.

Neither of us spoke for three beats before she said, "I want to explain."

"Let me," I said. "This has all been a game."

She took a breath but said nothing.

I continued: "Last night, you got rid of Andrew Yipp. You somehow got him into that crate against his will or by deception. You got off the island with counterfeit money and informed Secretary Norris. You had him incapacitated so that you could take over without being seen to betray him."

"No," she said quietly.

I said, "You arranged for me to capture your biggest rival, Christian Chen. You got me to charge into the old building on McNair Road thinking I was saving Linda Wu, but she was working for you all along. I know this because she gave the property list to Jinjing. In fact, you probably chose that property deliberately to incriminate Major Lamb."

She started to speak, but I spoke over her.

"And realizing that Linda Wu was working for you made me realize that she was the one who led me to Rafflesia School. My God! I thought it was a coincidence. Leading me back to somewhere I could easily find. And she was the one who told me what the girl said. I bet that poor prostitute didn't know anything. The whole thing with Wang's brother's gang in JB was a charade."

"It was, but not—"

"You did it to remove Wang. My theory is that you couldn't risk taking charge with Wang around. He was actually really loyal to Andrew Yipp, wasn't he?"

"Let me talk," she said.

"One other thing,"—I was on a roll now—"the money. You sacrificed the counterfeiting because it's finished, hasn't it?"

"Yes. Most of what was left was useless. The main printing happened years ago. But, Ash, what you need to—"

"Did you ever intend to run away with me?"

"I wanted to."

"But you didn't. Did the opportunity to take over the empire outweigh our love—if you did ever love me?"

"I have a son."

I didn't expect that. It took a few seconds to sink in, then I remembered what I'd seen. "The boy outside with Mrs Yipp—he's your son?"

"His name is Cooper. I couldn't leave him."

"Is he Andrew Yipp's?"

"Yes."

"You should have told me."

"It would have made a difference?"

"Maybe, maybe not."

"Yes, it would have, Ash. I thought I'd take him with me. Two boxes, one each."

I said, "You never really intended to escape."

"In a way I have."

I nodded.

"It was coming to an end. Andrew's whole approach was coming to an end. The counterfeit money was running out and a new era is coming. A new approach is needed and a woman can be a leader."

There was a catch in her voice. It was as though she was trying to convince herself, as though there was more to it.

"You used me," I said. Despite trying to suppress my feelings, I couldn't help myself.

"I loved you. I still love you. But—"

"Different sides of the track," I managed to say, despite a lump in my throat. I forced a smile then nodded and left her standing by that window.

★

I went via my home, and ten minutes later I walked into Major Rupert Lamb's office.

He smiled, "Captain Carter, for what do I owe the pleasure?"

"I want the truth," I said.

"I believe congratulations are in order. Am I right, you've got Yipp under lock and key?"

I repeated: "I want the truth, Rupert."

"I told you the truth. I wanted people to think I'd spent the night with the beautiful Su Ling. Just foolish vanity, dear chap."

"I want the truth about the sawmill and shed on McNair Road."

He swallowed.

"The list you sent me was incomplete." I pulled the list from my breast pocket and placed it on the desk in front of him.

He stared at the paper and I put its almost identical twin beside it.

"The property on McNair Road was re-appropriated for demolition and development three weeks ago. It was on a list eleven days ago"—I pointed to the line on the relevant paper—"but was dropped from the list you sent me."

"A mistake," he said, unconvincingly. "It must have been a typing oversight."

"It was being used for holding and printing counterfeit money."

"What?" He looked surprised, and I figured that was a genuine reaction.

I said, "You let Andrew Yipp use it. You are complicit in his money-counterfeiting operation."

His jaw tensed. "That's an outrageous accusation that you'll have to back up."

I said nothing. Just waited.

He said, "Honestly, I had no idea. I helped Su Ling. My reward was dinner with her. I honestly had no idea what they would use it for."

I said, "Now tell me about Patrice Dang."

"Who?"

I shook my head and pulled something from my pocket: two pearl earrings, identical to the ones in the painting of Lamb's wife. The ones that Saburo had given me.

"Ah," he said. "Thank goodness they've been found. I wondered who'd stolen them. Someone called Dong, you say?"

"Patrice Dang." I shook my head at his pretence. "You're well known for entertaining beautiful women. And yet you are married."

His eyes narrowed, his jaw tensed.

I said, "Patrice didn't steal them, did he?"

Lamb said nothing.

"That's your cover story. You gave them to him. Don't deny it. I can see it in your eyes."

Lamb took a deep breath. "He was going to blackmail me. Me, a respectable member of society! Who the hell did he think he was? I treated him very well—"

"You saw him regularly. Dated him."

"Her—I thought he was a woman. Did you ever see him? He was very pretty. As you said, I like being seen with pretty girls. Only Patrice was a boy. I didn't know."

"I think you did."

Lamb said nothing.

"I think you prefer boys."

He shook his head. "He tried to blackmail me. He said he'd claim I was homosexual."

I said, "Patrice was trapped, working for a man called Zhao. He needed to escape—him and his friend—that's why he needed money. That's why he tried to blackmail you. Did you know that?"

Lamb said, "I'm a respectable member of society."

I said, "When you dated beautiful women like Su Ling, it was a cover. You didn't have sex with them, because you preferred the boys."

"He was going to blackmail me."

I said, "And you killed him."

"Rubbish! Anyway, he was scum!"

I stepped around his desk and stood over him, my anger barely restrained.

He looked up at me. "I'm a respectable member of society," he said again, stroking his moustache. "Patrice was a nobody."

I punched his fat nose. His chair went back and he went with it, crashing to the floor. When he stood up, he was shaking. Blood ran between and into his fancy moustache, quickly turning the whole thing red.

I said, "You planned it, didn't you? You wanted to pretend you spent the night with Su Ling but I knew you hadn't. You had a prearranged meeting with Patrice. You left the Hotel de la Paix and met him. You probably drove to a remote spot then strangled him there. Then you drove back, went down Canning Street and dumped his body on North Boat Quay before returning to the hotel and your alibi. But your alibi failed because Su Ling went missing."

He had a handkerchief under his nose, stemming the flow.

"Just supposition," he said, finding his voice, breathing through his mouth. "Your word against mine. He was a nobody. Blackmail is a crime."

"Homosexuality is a crime," I said.

He shook his head and spoke calmly. "You have no proof. Now get out of my office. Just this once I'll put it down to over-exuberance after your success with Yipp, but don't come here making accusations against me again."

I pulled a second pair of pages from my pocket.

"Eleven days ago, a property on Canal Road was included. It wasn't on my list. Why was that?"

Nothing.

"I spoke to Mr Zhao," I said. "You let him use the property. He was paying you rent."

"Is that what he claims?"

"How many other properties were you re-appropriating and renting out?"

His eyes were darting, assessing his options. Then he said, "Ridiculous!"

I said, "You were being paid in kind by Su Ling and also by Mr Zhao. Zhao stopped paying rent when you started seeing his employee Patrice Dang."

Lamb righted his chair and began to sit. Midway, I surprised him with a quick move that spun him around and forced his arm up behind his back. When I lifted the arm, he lurched forward.

"I'd like to get you for Patrice Dang's murder, Lamb. Maybe the police will charge you when they hear about the homosexuality. But even if you get away with that, then it'll be for inappropriate benefits from your position. We'll find that rent in your bank accounts and I'll link you to Andrew Yipp."

I strong-armed him through his door and down the corridor. People stopped and gasped and I kept on driving him forward all the way to the police station.

# SIXTY-THREE

The shipping office next to the post office was always busy, but it didn't take long to be served. There were three queues, of course, because of the different classes of ticket. I walked straight up to the First Class counter and found out which boats were sailing when and where.

I didn't care where they were going. I just knew I needed to get away. The agent liked that. He was less excited when I bought a starboard cabin ticket. Port-side cabins would be cooler and more expensive.

Afterwards, I went into the post office and withdrew money. My next journey was over to Gillman Barracks, where I said goodbye to the men I called friends, Captain Robshaw in particular. When Colonel Ambrose was available, I went into his office and shook his hand as well. He was a good man, much better than the acting CO I'd first met here, two years ago.

"Where are you headed, Ash?" he asked me.

"Hong Kong Island."

"Been there before?"

"No, sir."

"Know anyone there?"

"No one."

He gave me the name of the CO at the barracks in Victoria. Colonel Simon Montgomery. "I'll warn Monty you're coming. Tell him to raise the barricades." He laughed and shook my hand again. "We'll miss you, young man," he said, serious now. "I'll miss you."

After a final farewell wave to the men, I drove to the General Hospital where I found Detective Inspector Singh, persuading the doctors that he should be allowed home.

"I am proud to call you my friend," he said, walking me back to my jeep.

"You too, Ishaan." I handed him a packet of Mint Humbugs.

"Is that all I get for saving your ungrateful life?" he said with mock seriousness.

Holding out my car keys, I said, "I'd like you to have my Land Rover."

"It's a bit shot up. Probably worthless," he said. "I'll tell you what: I'll look after it until you come back."

He gripped my shoulder and we pumped hands. Another good man that I'd miss. As a trishaw took me away, I glanced back and smiled. My last image of the inspector was of him tucking into the Mint Humbugs.

I returned home and packed and arranged for my cases to be collected. Then finally, I paid my most difficult visit.

At my office, I gave Madam Chau her notice. I also handed her a packet that contained enough money to see her right for a year or more. She cried and hugged me and told me I shouldn't leave.

"Perhaps I'll come back," I said, and kissed her on the cheek.

I'd miss this place, this tiny country off the tip of Malaya. I'd miss its vibrancy, its diversity, and most of all, its people.

★

As I boarded the late afternoon steamer leaving Empire Dock, I looked back. Despite trying to avoid it, I'd caught sight of the Cathay Building a few times during the day. It was impossible not to. I didn't want to think of Su Ling, but couldn't help it, and had a sick feeling in the pit of my stomach.

She would be up there now. I'd always remember her framed by the window, looking stunning in that red dress.

The ship's horn blew a final time and the gangplank came up. People on the dock waved handkerchiefs and called their goodbyes.

The sea sparkled like crushed diamonds and the sky was big and perfect.

We set sail.

I faced east and never looked back.

# SIXTY-FOUR

*Tuesday 16th February, the previous day*

Mrs **Chenguang** Yipp stood over the body of her husband. He seemed to be sleeping peacefully. One second they had been looking at the body of her departed cousin in the death house on Sago Lane, the next Andrew Yipp was unconscious, the sedative in his drink working remarkably fast.

Her friend Mrs Xifeng Wu had been praying in another cubicle, hiding her face, waiting for the right moment. Now she stepped out and walked over. Her face was etched with worry and Mrs Yipp didn't know whether her friend was concerned about her daughter or what they were doing.

"She'll be all right. She's a strong girl," Mrs Yipp said.

"Will it work? Will she get Chen killed?"

"Have faith. Carter will go charging in to rescue Linda."

Resigned, Mrs Wu nodded. "Now we have to get the body moved."

Mrs Yipp clapped her hands and an attendant appeared. He was old. His white shirt hung loosely from his skinny frame that was extenuated by baggy black trousers that showed his thin shins and bony feet.

Mrs Wu shook her head. "Is he strong enough?"

"He's stronger than he looks, but we'll have to help."

The attendant pulled a casket from an empty partition and slid it over. Together they lifted Yipp from the floor and into the box. The man shut the lid and began sliding it across the floor.

"He's got a cart waiting at the back," Mrs Yipp said.

"Will he help pull it?"

"No. We'll manage. The fewer people involved the better."

"Where is Shuang?" she asked, referring to Mrs Li, Jinjing's mother.

"She'll meet us there. We'll all meet there."

They helped the death house attendant lift the heavy box onto the cart. He lit candles and checked the ribbons and papers. It looked perfect. It looked just like a coffin being transported, which of course, is what Mrs Yipp wanted—a normal sight that people would notice but think nothing of.

Both women took a bar at the front of the cart and the attendant gave it a push to get them rolling. It took almost ten minutes to reach Havelock Road.

Ahead they could see fires starting to burn. The timing was important. Too early and they'd literally miss the boat.

Mrs Wu made them stop twice before they reached Pulau Saigon Circus. She rubbed her hands and complained of blisters. Mrs Yipp waited patiently, but her friend didn't see the clenched teeth.

"Ready," Mrs Wu said, and they started again, tugging hard and getting back into the rhythm.

From the roundabout, they went onto the quay. The river was quiet now, but Mrs Yipp predicted that within an hour the warehouse owners would panic and start moving the goods.

Rounding the bend in the river, Mrs Li joined them and took over the bar on Mrs Wu's side. The other lady went around to the back and pushed. It helped a little, but Mrs Yipp knew her old friend was tired and weak.

They were on Alkaff Quay with only fifty paces to go. Finally, they came to the warehouse owned by Kelly and Pope.

Another woman waited at the doors.

Mrs Yipp's heart thudded in her chest. Was her friend correct, were there really two boxes in there waiting to be shipped away?

The other woman smiled. She rarely smiled, and Mrs Yipp could have hugged her now.

"Are there two boxes?"

"There was only one with an X. I emptied another box and made sure they both have two Xs." She pulled open the doors and the four women pulled the cart inside.

"The money?" Mrs Yipp asked.

"Already in that box," the woman said, pointing at the furthest. "That's the one I emptied. I had to force the lid, so it's less secure. However this one"—she popped the lid off the second crate—"can be banged shut. It's ideal."

The four women each took a corner of the coffin, manoeuvred it from the cart and staggered to the crate.

When it thudded into the larger box Mrs Wu gasped.

"It's all right, Xifeng, he won't wake up. It's not called the sleep of the dead for nothing." The other woman laughed, and it was the laugh of a relieved woman. So far everything had gone to plan.

The nearby fire would move things ahead. The cargo would be on the river within the hour, she predicted. Kelly and Pope couldn't risk their precious goods being destroyed.

The four women retreated. They crossed the river and found a spot on the opposite quay where they waited. They sat in shadows, watched the fires burn, and listened to desperate shouts. Less than thirty minutes after they had left the warehouse, the first men arrived and threw open the warehouse doors, then they started moving the boxes. More employees came and the boats got loaded.

They watched as the two boxes marked with the Xs were put on a tongkang and launched into the river. The black water was streaked with orange from the flames, and the boats ploughed arrow-shaped furrows as they chugged downriver.

Mrs Yipp stood and stretched.

"Like I always say, ladies, you have to play the long game."

Mrs Li said, "Mah-jong on Wednesday night?"

"Of course. Like always. The wind has changed but the game goes on."

The first three women left in different directions—Mrs Wu hurrying home desperate to learn that Linda was safe and well.

Only the fourth woman remained, watching the activity. She was the one who would call the police and tell them Andrew Yipp was fleeing the country with counterfeit money.

They would catch him and his rule would be over. His mistreatment of her friend Chenguang would be over. No longer could he treat her as a chattel, a stupid woman who could do nothing but keep house and play mah-jong.

Andrew Yipp had underestimated his wife. Chenguang Yipp was so much more than just a wife. She was a master strategist, and she would rule through Su Ling.

The only thing that the fourth woman was uncomfortable about was Su Ling. But then Chenguang could have mistreated her, could have hated her for being the mistress of her husband. But she didn't.

And then there was the matter of Captain Ash Carter. The fourth woman saw him arrive at the quay and check the warehouse. He expected Su Ling to be in that box. He thought he was saving the woman that he loved.

The fourth woman was almost directly opposite Carter when he stood on the quay, probably imaging Su Ling out at sea. Then she realized that she'd deliberately waited for him. She felt an obligation. She felt like she should comfort him and explain it all.

But she couldn't.

That would be a betrayal of her friend.

So Madam Chau stood and walked slowly home, wondering what tomorrow would bring.

## Acknowledgements

This series has been a labour of love, and I was delighted that my father was able to read this final instalment before he passed. However I should say that he held out a hope for a different ending!

As usual, I'm grateful to Richard Sheehan for his excellent editorial services. Thanks again to Pete Tonkin for his edits and comments. Also to the beta readers, especially Richard Lipscombe and Lynne Barnes for their time and support.

The final mention goes to my wife, Kerry, for her continued support and encouragement. I should add that she loved the ending!

Before Singapore there was…

# CYPRUS KISS

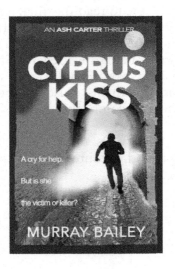

A gang has been operating for years in Cyprus, the only clue, the occassional execution-style killing and the mark XIS.

The police call it the Kiss of Death, but have never made progress on identifying the purpetrators. That is until Lieutenant Ash Carter starts investigating.

*Read on for the first few chapters of this new series.*

# ONE

Johnson looked at the photograph for a long time, although he wasn't really looking, he was thinking.

"So where is Lieutenant Carter?" he eventually asked the investigating officer.

The younger man shook his head. "We can't find him, sir. His office is closed and no one's seen him since Friday evening."

"Since the murder, you mean."

"Yes, sir. He's just disappeared."

This didn't look good for Ash Carter. The man had been an irritant, poking his nose into matters that shouldn't concern him. Personal things. Carter hadn't got his way and had taken matters into his own hands.

"An innocent man doesn't run," Johnson said, more to himself than for the benefit of the investigating officer.

"No, sir."

Johnson looked at the photograph again. A very pretty young woman. A black-and-white photograph, not professionally shot, but good, none the less.

He said, "Tell me about the case again."

"The victim was at the Red Lion. At nineteen fifteen he said he was going outside to meet this girl. According to one witness, the meeting had been pre-arranged the previous week."

"What about outside? Tell me again about the man who saw them together."

"Right. They—the victim and woman—were seen meeting. They walked through to the adjoining road, beside the pub and across the road behind. There's an alley between buildings and they went down there."

"And that's where he was found?"

"Yes, sir, less than fifteen minutes later. Dead. A single, effective stab wound. The attacker must have known what they were doing. It was an assassination, clear and simple. A second witness led me right to the address. There's no doubt about it, sir. We know the killer."

Johnson thought about the younger man's words. He had a tendency to make assumptions. He wasn't a trained investigator, not like Carter. Should he, Johnson, take over or should he influence and guide from the wings?

Johnson cleared his throat. "You haven't dealt with a murder investigation before?"

"No, sir, but—"

This wasn't just a murder. The victim wasn't just anybody.

"But what, man?" Johnson said. Tension pulled across his chest like piano wire, and he knew his Scottish accent would be more pronounced. He paused and breathed. "This is a big responsibility."

"I can handle it, sir. I've attended court-martials before."

Could Johnson risk it? On the other hand, could he risk getting directly involved? Would his own connection be exposed and brought into question? Again Johnson cleared his throat.

"This isn't like a court-martials. This is big. The goddamn murder of one of our own men." Johnson realized he'd raised his voice, but the younger man didn't flinch. Maybe he was up to it.

The junior officer nodded. "Understood, sir."

"This needs to be watertight."

"Yes, sir."

"Good man." Johnson returned the photograph to the investigating officer and dismissed him.

Just before the door clicked shut, another man entered Johnson's office. His cheeks twitched as though he was holding back a smile.

"You've heard," Johnson said, as the other man made himself comfortable in the chair opposite.

"Everyone's talking about it."

"Could it be a problem for me?"

Finally the man released his smile. "You worry too much, Jonny. Ellis was a problem and now it's gone away. If anything, I'd say it's time for a celebration."

Neither spoke for a moment, their eyes searching one another's before the other man stood and poured two fingers of single malt Scotch into crystal-cut tumblers. He handed one to Johnson.

The major knocked back his drink, felt the burn all the way down then sucked in air and enjoyed a second burn. He nodded and held out the empty glass for another shot.

Finally the tightness in his chest was evaporating.

The murder of a military policeman. It looked very bad for Lieutenant Ash Carter. Very bad indeed.

This wasn't going to result in a prison sentence. Oh no. The only reasonable outcome would be the death penalty.

# TWO

*Three weeks earlier*

Only my fifth day in Cyprus and I'd already found trouble.

"You're chicken," the big man said. Beside him were three others, all of whom looked eager. They had the kind of fixed expressions and clenched fists that spoke volumes.

I'm six two and have rarely had men square up to me like this, but the three cronies were all solidly built, all over six foot. And the big guy was probably six five.

I said, "We don't want trouble." The "we" in this case included the girl I'd come out with: Penny Cartwright. She edged behind me and I used my arm to guide her so that we had a wall at our backs.

The big guy said, "We're gonna whip you."

The men took a step closer.

"We?" I said. "Can't take me on your own?"

The man laughed. The three cronies laughed.

"Ash," Penny whispered. "Let's run."

I could hear the fear in her voice. They could too, and it made the big man grin even more.

"Fun's over, lads," I said as calmly as I could. "We'll leave now."

I gave Penny a nudge, and we stepped sideways.

"You're a yellow-bellied chicken," the big guy said. "And your tart is fair game."

"Excuse me?" I said, stopping. I smiled at him. "What did you say?"

"Next time I see her, your little floozy is mine."

I reached for Penny's hand and felt it shaking.

"This is ridiculous." I could hear the strain in my own voice now. Stay calm. Fighting when angry could lead to mistakes. My first boxing coach back home taught me that. He was the toughest man I've ever met—and he had to be. A Liverpudlian living in Manchester. Two towns that hated one another, so whenever a thug from Manchester heard Sammy speak, he would go for him. Sammy taught Queensbury boxing rules in his gym, but he would also give lessons on street fighting.

"Because your opponents might not know the rules," he said. And of course, he was right. The skills had immediately come in handy in Palestine, my first posting as a Royal Military Police, Special Investigations Branch officer.

"We'll take turns," said one of the goons.

"She'll love it," said another.

"Because she's a fair-game slut," the third one said.

How had we got into this crazy situation? Penny had invited me to the cinema in Larnaca. She was a typist assigned to our small SIB unit that had just transferred from Palestine. We hit it off and she was being nice to a new arrival. This wasn't a date. Although I admit she was pretty. Five eight in heels with raven black hair, which she wore tied back. She said that her bright eyes and a dark complexion came from her mother, who was half Indian. She was two years older than my twenty-four and had a confidence that belied her status. At least in my limited experience.

The film we'd seen was called *Down to Earth*, a strange musical comedy that would have been an easy way to spend a Friday night if it hadn't been for the four hooligans who now confronted us.

Everyone in the army is used to catcalls and tomfoolery at a cinema, but this wasn't an army screening. It might not have been *The Rex* but there was a reasonable-sized audience—a mix of locals and military. Each time Rita Hayworth appeared on screen, men wolf-whistled so loudly that no one could hear the dialogue or songs.

The Greek gods in the show were mocked, and the leading man prompted missiles to be thrown at the screen.

It hadn't just been the four thugs who'd been rowdy, but they had been only two rows behind, and when an ice cream tub sailed over Penny's shoulder, she turned and I heard them laugh.

She'd politely asked them to settle down and, in response had received a wet paper ball in the face.

That's when I'd stepped in. I turned, raised a hand and asked them to calm down.

The big guy had nodded, but as soon as I was looking away again, something struck me on the back of the head.

"Enough!" I'd said, glaring at them. "You've had some fun, don't spoil it."

"You challenging me?" the big guy said.

"No."

"Right now," he said, shouting above the latest musical number. "You and me outside now."

"After the film," I said.

"You're chicken!"

"If that's what you want, then yes, I'm chicken."

I turned and sat and heard them laughing. Penny put her arm through mine and smiled. Yes, she had a lovely smile too.

"That was the big-man thing to do," she whispered.

"I'm glad you think so," I said, expecting that the men would forget the challenge when we came out in another half an hour. Or they'd turn their attention to something else—beer, probably.

But no.

Here they were, not only confronting me but insulting Penny—threatening Penny.

"OK," I said.

The big man blinked. "OK what?"

"Let's do this."

# THREE

Penny moved away and the four men stayed focused on me. I had a wall behind me, which might not seem the sensible thing because I couldn't turn and run, but coach Sammy had explained that keeping the opponents in front of you was more important than having an exit strategy.

When faced off, the Englishman's natural response is to fight one-on-one. "It's basic cowardice," Sammy said. "Men attack in packs when they know they can win. The others join in when you are down or have your back turned. So guess what? Don't show them your back and don't go down."

Good advice.

So, facing four men, I expected the big one to make the first move, and he did. He had one man on his right and two on the left. I prompted his attack by deliberately looking at the man furthest on the left.

Give him a target.

The big man stepped in and swung a right-handed roundhouse. More exaggerated than a right cross; too much power and stupid.

A roundhouse isn't a wise first punch. Not against a trained boxer. It's slow and telegraphed. But I'd done nothing to warn him that I could box. He went for a show-boating punch when he should have jabbed.

At the last second, I inched out of range, let him continue with the momentum, and then stepped inside what should have been a defence. He had none and was now an easy target.

When you're in the ring, staying calm means you can think, and most good boxers feel like time slows down. You see, you predict the moves, you see your target and you pick your counter.

Without gloves, the wise man chooses a soft target like the throat. One punch there and he'd be down and gasping. However, I could do serious damage and he'd be hospitalized, maybe never breathe easily again.

Maybe he deserved it. Maybe he didn't.

I used my stronger, faster left hand and drove it into his neck, just below his right ear. Enough muscle to save him, not enough to stop the jarring shock.

The big man hadn't finished his flailing first punch when I made satisfying contact. His rotation continued, he lost balance, and he went down like a Messerschmitt in a tailspin.

I wish I'd had a camera to capture the faces of the other men. They'd clearly never seen their leader dispensed with so easily. Three open mouths, three pairs of bulging eyes and uncertainty. Hands unclenched, half clenched, and Adam's apples bobbed as they swallowed.

"Next?" I said.

No one moved except the big guy on the floor.

"I thought not," I said. "Now apologize to the lady."

Penny got three apologies. The big man levered himself to his feet, shook his head to relieve the ache in his neck, and dusted his trousers.

He didn't apologize, but his humiliation was enough.

"OK, you can clear off. And don't try it again. If you give anyone any more trouble, I won't pull my punch next time—and I won't stop at one. Got it?"

They got it.

Three relieved men turned and tried to saunter away as though it was their choice. The big man looked at me hard, shook his head, and then a second later joined his buddies.

Penny put her arms around me. I could suddenly feel the tingle of adrenaline in my hands and the tremble in my chest, but if she noticed, she didn't say.

We'd only planned for the cinema, but it didn't seem right to take her home just yet and she must have felt the same.

"Let's go for a drive," she said.

It had been a scorching day and the sun was now leaving purple and orange streaks across the sky. At eighty degrees Fahrenheit, the temperature was now comfortable and getting better.

I collected my Land Rover from outside the SIB office on Pine Street, and we drove, roof off, along the long, sweeping coast.

With the wind in her hair, Penny relaxed, and I smiled over at her in the rapidly fading light.

"You all right?"

She smiled back. "Stop just up here."

I pulled off the road onto a promontory overlooking the sea.

"I love this spot."

I switched off the engine and enjoyed the dying light and hum of cicadas.

"I didn't know you could fight," she said. "I wouldn't have been so worried if I'd known. Are all SIB men like that? Can Captain Wolfe, box as well?"

"No," I said. "But he can take care of himself. You learn how to do that pretty quickly in Palestine."

"But the Emergency is over now, right?"

"The British Army's left, if that's what you mean. But I sense there'll be trouble for a long time yet."

"What's it like? How does Cyprus compare?"

"Totally different. Mandatory Palestine was a war zone. A war between the Palestinians and Jews, for taking their land, for arriving in their droves—thousands a week. And a war with the British, who both sides hated."

"And Cyprus?"

"Too early to say."

"But we don't have a war here."

I smiled and stretched my legs out, hands behind my head. "No, you don't. So far, it's been the first break I've had in two years."

"Two years in Palestine? Before that, where were you?"

"Officer training in Sandhurst and then specific SIB training in Mytchett Hutments. First posting, straight into the thick of it."

"So, Lieutenant Ash Carter, what is the Special Investigations Branch doing in Cyprus?"

I was surprised by the direct question. She knew we couldn't talk about it. As a secretary, she had been privy to some communications, but our orders were secret.

Then she laughed at me. "I was joking! I know you can't tell a civilian."

"I can't tell anyone," I said. "Except that we have our new posting in Larnaca."

The embers of the dying sun had vanished, and the clear skies were lit by more stars than a man could count.

"The sky is so clear here," I said, changing the subject.

"I love it—most of the time," she said.

"Best and worst?" I asked.

"Well, you saw the worst, back there. Young white men."

"Army," I said, recognizing the type despite their civilian clothes.

"Undoubtedly. They can be quite racist."

I didn't know Penny's heritage. Her brown skin suggested an Asian influence despite her very English name.

"What about the best?" I asked.

"The views, the weather—when it's not too hot—and the food."

"The food?" I asked, suddenly feeling hungry despite an early dinner. Perhaps the adrenaline from the fight had stirred my appetite.

"Come on," she said. "Let me direct you to a quaint tavern I know. It's in the middle of nowhere, and patronized by locals, but—come to think of it, perhaps that's why I like it so much. We'll be the only Brits."

Fifteen minutes later, driving across dusty roads that seemed more suited for animals than cars, we arrived at a village and a tavern with eight tables arranged outside.

Fortunately the staff spoke English, and we soon had plates of food that we shared. It was far better than what I'd eaten in the Middle East.

I don't drink alcohol, and I was surprised to find that Penny didn't either. Mine was mainly for health reasons, hers because of family history. I could tell she didn't want to talk about it, so I didn't press her.

The journey back made me regret eating so much. Each jolt threatened to reveal the contents of my stomach. So at a junction, I stopped for a moment and turned off the lights.

Warm dry air filled my lungs, and we enjoyed the panoply of stars for a while until my stomach settled.

"I love the song of the cicadas," she said quietly. "Most people either tune them out or hate them, but for me, they're beautiful."

I didn't feel so strongly, and wondered if that would change over time. Naturally, I'd heard them in Palestine, but I'd spent most of my time in built-up areas and just thought of them as the sound of the countryside. Here in Cyprus, their clicking never ceased.

"Can you hear their songs, Ash?" she asked as I relaxed and listened.

Then a gunshot shattered the peace.

Close by.

"My God!" Penny said, alarmed.

I switched on the headlights. Could I hear voices?

Starting the engine, I turned right, away from the road home. Then I stopped, switched off and listened. Another engine. A car had started and was driving fast.

What the heck was going on?

I fired up the engine once more and put my foot down. Then I braked hard. Just off the track, the headlights caught a dark shape on the ground.

Grabbing a torch, I jumped out and approached.

I feared the worst, and it was the worst.

The shape was a man. His legs and hands were tied, and he had a bullet hole in the side of his head.

*Cyprus Kiss is available in paperback and on Kindle*

# THE SINGAPORE SERIES

# BLACK CREEK
# WHITE LIES

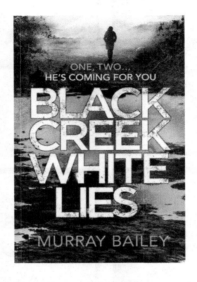

One night, Jade Bridger takes a dead-end path by the creek, and vanishes. Eighteen months after being wrongly accused of her murder, Dan Searle returns to Cornwall to rebuild his life and forget. But others won't let him forget.

He is quickly drawn back into the case and a dark and violent mystery; one that involved another girl years before. As the lies begin to unravel, Dan uncovers startling truths about his family and the past.

With dangerous people trying to keep their secrets safe, he must save those he loves - before time runs out...

# I DARE YOU

Why was Kate's boyfriend snatched off the street?
People said she couldn't trust him. They said he was a
liar. But a year later she discovers a photograph that
makes her question everything she thought she knew.

As she investigates, people start to die and Kate is left
wondering who she can trust.

She follows clues from England to the Czech Republic
and finally to the US. All the while a killer is on her tail.

Kate just wants the truth.
But is the truth worth dying for?

# DARE YOU TWICE

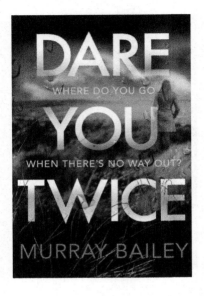

A teenage girl disappears from her locked bedroom. With no way out, and a trace of blood, the police conclude the worst. As Kate investigates the strange case, she finds her own life threatened.

She goes into hiding only to find herself drawn into another mysterious case. On the Dorset coast, a young man has vanished without trace. Except for a cryptic message he seems to have intended for Kate.

Accompanied by her friend and a British Detective, Kate follows the clues that take her to Paris, France. As the puzzle unfolds, Kate questions what she believes and has to work out what is really going on - or die trying.

# MAP OF THE DEAD

Within days of solving a 3,000 year old puzzle, a researcher dies in suspicious circumstances.

With only a few clues and a mysterious object Alex MacLure follows a trail from London to Cairo.

He must crack the code and expose a shocking, inconceivable truth before the secret is buried for ever.

# SIGN OF THE DEAD

**Atlanta, Georgia.** When a body dump is found, FBI Special Agent Charlie Rebb thinks a serial killer has resurfaced. Called the Surgeon by the media, his telltale technique has everyone wondering why. But then the murders seem to stop again.

**Cairo, Egypt.** Alex MacLure is contacted by a student who thinks he's uncovered a conspiracy involving the pyramids. He asks for Alex's help to piece together a message using new discoveries. But the student disappears and Alex is arrested for a murder. Meanwhile, the special agent sees a sign that the Surgeon is now in Egypt.

MacLure links up with Special Agent Reed to track down the killer. As he decrypts an ancient story, MacLure realizes this is a race against time. The Surgeon must be stopped before he completes his terrible and startling mission.

# THE LOST PHARAOH

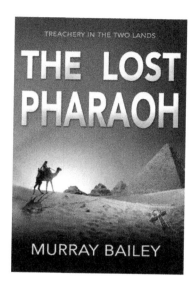

The year is 1318 BCE. Horemheb is pharaoh and Yanhamu is Lord Khety, magistrate of Egypt's ninth nome.

Invited to sit as a judge on a High Court case and it looks like his future is secure. However, when the case is concluded he knows that justice has not been done.

A meeting with the emissary of the High Priest of Amun leads to Yanhamu's arrest for treason. Accused of conspiracy and thrown into prison he must prove his innocence.

The Two Lands are on the brink of civil war. Yanhamu may hold the key, but he must battle his own demons before he can save his country.

murraybaileybooks.com

## IF YOU ENJOYED THIS BOOK

Feedback helps me understand what works, what doesn't and what readers want more of. It also brings a book to life.

Online reviews are also very important in encouraging others to try my books. I don't have the financial clout of a big publisher. I can't take out newspaper ads or run poster campaigns.

But what I do have is an enthusiastic and committed bunch of readers.

Honest reviews are a powerful tool. I'd be very grateful if you could spend a couple of minutes leaving a review, however short, on sites like Amazon and Goodreads.

Thank you
Murray

Printed in Great Britain
by Amazon

39770977R10223